HOP

LIGHTHOUSE SECURITY INVESTIGATIONS WEST COAST

MARYANN JORDAN

Hop (Lighthouse Security Investigation West Coast) Copyright 2022

All rights reserved. No part of this book may be reproduced or transmitted in any form or by any means, electronic or mechanical, including photocopying, recording, or by any information storage and retrieval system without the written permission of the author, except where permitted by law.

If you are reading this book and did not purchase it, then you are reading an illegal pirated copy. If you would be concerned about working for no pay, then please respect the author's work! Make sure that you are only reading a copy that has been officially released by the author.

This book is a work of fiction. Names, characters, places, and incidents are either products of the author's imagination or are used fictitiously. Any resemblance to actual persons, living or dead, events, or locales is entirely coincidental.

Cover: Graphics by Stacy

ISBN ebook: 978-1-956588-19-4

ISBN print: 978-1-956588-20-0

❦ Created with Vellum

Author's Note

Please remember that this is a work of fiction. I have lived in numerous states as well as overseas, but for the last thirty years have called Virginia my home. I often choose to use fictional city names with some geographical accuracies.

These fictionally named cities allow me to use my creativity and not feel constricted by attempting to accurately portray the areas.

It is my hope that my readers will allow me this creative license and understand my fictional world.

I also do quite a bit of research on my books and try to write on subjects with accuracy. There will always be points where creative license will be used in order to create scenes or plots.

1

The dawn was slipping over the horizon, but the dim illumination didn't faze the men and women running up the California mountainside. The Keepers of Lighthouse Security Investigations West Coast enjoyed their downtime training, throwing in good-natured competition along the way.

Frank "Hop" Hopkins darted past two others, swiping the underbrush from his path, his thick legs surprisingly agile as he pounded the dirt underneath his booted feet. He was big... he'd always been big. His mom often said she thought she'd never get him pushed out, and once he took his first breath, he'd squalled loud enough to bring the nurses running. Of course, as her oft-told story continued, she added that he'd been talking ever since.

That thought hit him as he continued up the path, reminding him that he needed to call home later that day. Loose gravel gave way underneath his feet, and he almost lost his balance. Bennett shot past him. "Fucker,"

Hop grumbled, not sure if he referred to himself or his coworker and friend, speeding up as they rounded a curve.

He ran through the forest filled with oaks, redwoods, sycamores, maples, cottonwoods, and other native trees he was still learning about. Much of his youth in Tennessee found him with his grandfather and cousins tramping through the woods, listening as his grandfather taught them all about the surrounding nature. Now, wherever he was, he learned as much as he could, thinking that one day he might be lucky enough to pass on that knowledge to a child of his own. *Yeah, well, I've gotta find a woman first.*

His thoughts were interrupted by the sound of more approaching boot steps hitting the ground. Increasing his speed, he raced past Bennett. Poole and Dolby were on a different trail, but he had no idea how close to the top they were. Same with Abbie and Natalie. With seventy-five acres of undeveloped land consisting of mostly national forests adjoining their main Lighthouse compound, they had plenty of room to train without landing on top of each other. But now, he wished he knew where they were, considering the loser had to buy beer for everyone at the bar tonight.

Another sound caught his ears, and he watched as three adult mule deer and two fawns darted past, probably in hopes of not only seeing who was running through the forest but attempting to stay out of danger's way as well. His attention on the nature around would cost him the win, but finally, skirting around a fallen log, he raced to the flag he spied tied to a tree near an overlook, arriving just as three other Keepers were reaching for it as well.

"Shit, Hop! How the fuck can someone so big run so fast?" Leo groaned, bent over at the waist as he sucked in air, one hand flat against a tree trunk and the other wrapping around the approaching Natalie, who was panting just as much.

Looking over, he grinned at his muscular but leaner friend. "Track and field as well as football and wrestling."

"Yeah, well, shot put doesn't count," Jeb complained.

"Didn't do shot put. My ass was running distance." He grabbed a water bottle from the pack that Teddy had brought earlier and fell to the ground as the rest of the Keepers rounded the bend, racing forward.

"Distance?" Leo didn't hide his incredulity.

"Yeah. The football coach made us. Said it would keep us in shape for the summer practice."

Their boss, Carson, was at the top with his stopwatch, a wide grin on his face. "Best times yet. So that means I'll buy the first round tonight."

They cheered as they sat near the overlook, enjoying the fresh air, surrounding nature, and the privacy their facility offered. Hop reached behind and grabbed the back of his sweaty T-shirt, jerked it over his head, and swiped his dripping brow. Leaning back against a tree trunk, he soaked in the view. And couldn't believe his good fortune.

Carson Dyer, a former Army Special Forces and CIA Operative, opened Lighthouse Security Investigations West Coast after partnering with Mace Hanover, who started the LSI franchise in Maine. They hired former military special operators and others who fit their specific requirements. Called Keepers to honor the old lighthouse keepers guiding others to safety, they worked in an elite environment and offered a specialized service. Hop couldn't imagine a better job.

What he loved most was that every day was different. Some days, they worked on specialized security design, much more intricate than what a typical security company could provide. Others did the installations after LSIWC created the design. They provided security, but not the ballyhooed-hulks-watching-over-the-stars kind of bodyguarding. They operated under government contracts as well as being called in to work with the FBI on cases where the need for circumventing red tape made it worth the capture. And Carson, just like Mace, was keen to take on some cases that included those who couldn't pay for the services, especially if it involved someone the Keepers knew. Not bad for a kid from the mountains of Tennessee who just wanted to be a pilot.

"Earth to Hop!"

He jumped slightly as Poole kicked his foot. "Shit, what?"

Poole laughed and shook his head. "Bennett was saying that we needed zip lines up here."

Eyes wide, he grinned. "Fuck yeah!"

Carson laughed. "I'll have Teddy take a look at what we can do."

Hop offered a chin lift toward Teddy. Theodore Bearski was the former special operator sniper who, in his sixties, didn't want to slow down. He was the equipment and weapons manager for the business and took care of the training facility. Hop had no idea how the man managed to handle everything, but he was fuckin' good at taking care of them.

"You ready to celebrate, Leo?" Bennett asked.

"You know it." Leo grinned, then elbowed the woman at his side. "Natalie would just as soon get married by a justice of the peace tomorrow, but out of *deference* to my mom, she's agreed to the whole engagement and wedding extravaganza. So tonight, we'll celebrate our engagement at the bar just for us." Leo, a former Army Delta, was marrying the newest Keeper, Natalie, who'd served with Leo's Delta team.

"I've known his mom for years." Natalie sighed and rolled her eyes, but we all knew she loved Leo's family. "Damn, I'm not going to piss her off at the beginning of our marriage!"

"Stella's mom is cool," Chris said, "but it's my mom who wants the fancy wedding. We've got her talked down to just something simple." Chris, a former SEAL, was now engaged to the free-spirited artist Stella.

Rick Rankin was another former SEAL and decided to come to California to help Carson get the business off the ground after having started his LSI career with Mace. "With Abbie's brother and my brother working for Mace, we'll have most of the Maine Keepers out here for our wedding in a few months."

Abbie Blake, a former Army captain, grinned up at him. "And both of our moms would kill us if we eloped!"

Carson grinned and shook his head. "Glad to have that behind me and just have Jeannie as my wife."

As everyone climbed to their feet again and started down the mountain, Hop thought of the Keepers who were still single like him. Adam Calvin was a former Ranger. Frederick Poole, a former SEAL. Terrance Bennett, a former Ranger sniper. And Jonathan Dolby, former Army Special Forces like Carson. Jeb, their computer guru, was a former SEAL.

As soon as they arrived back at the Lighthouse compound, they hit the showers, barely making it into the workroom before they were met by their administrative manager. Rachel Moore was a former Naval Intelligence officer, widowed, and didn't want to sit at home and wait for grandchildren during her retirement. No-nonsense, she managed the office as well as all of them.

"New requests have come in," she said to Carson. "They're on your tablet. System analysis, security, and the bureau liaison want a conference sometime today."

Carson nodded, and as the others began working on their various assignments, he reviewed the new requests.

"That's in your neck of the woods, Hop," Adam called out, jerking his head upward.

Hop looked up from his computer and spied Adam inclining his head toward the wide-screen TV on the wall. A weather station reported on the "tremendous rainfall in the Smokies."

His brow furrowed as he listened to the threats of flooding in the area. "Some of my extended family live near the rivers, but my dad, uncles, and cousins are all involved in the local rescue. Damn, I was going to call my mom tonight, but maybe I'd better go ahead and check in on them now."

Carson looked over and nodded. "Do what you gotta do. And if you need to head home to help out, you know you can leave anytime."

Hop lifted his chin in response, grateful for Carson's support when any of the Keepers needed to deal with personal issues. He stared at the TV screen for a moment longer, then pushed his chair back and stood, walking out of the main workroom and through the outer office where Rachel sat. Pulling out his phone, he headed outside to the patio that surrounded the area and overlooked the waves crashing on the rocks below the lighthouse.

Dialing, he only had to wait a few seconds before his mom answered. "Frank! What's got you calling this time of the day? Is everything okay?"

Chuckling, he shook his head. He'd earned the nickname Hop when he was in middle school, always active, always "hopping about," as one of his coaches used to say. He didn't figure it would stick, but when a flight instructor shortened his last name from Hopkins to Hop, the moniker stuck with him into adulthood. Except for his parents. To them, he'd always be Frank. "Mom, I think you answer the phone quicker than anybody I know."

"Well, with a son who works a dangerous job on the other side of the country, grandkids who sometimes need to be picked up from school, and your dad and uncles on emergency calls, I've learned to keep my phone with me at all times. If I don't have a pocket, I stuff it in my bra—"

"Whoa! Too much information, Mom!" He squeezed his eyes shut and shook his head, torn between wanting to laugh and wanting to unhear what he'd just heard.

"Never knew you'd be so squeamish, son." She laughed heartily. That was one thing he'd always been sure of— Jennifer Wilson Hopkins loved hard, laughed often, and said what she thought. "Anyway, are you okay?"

"I think that's my line, Mom. I saw on the news where you guys are getting so much rain that they're talking about flooding in the area."

"Lord have mercy! From the looks of it, I'd say Noah had better get that ark built for all of us!"

This time, the urge to chuckle won out. "So I take it, it's gonna get worse?"

"They're saying parts of Kentucky, West Virginia, east Tennessee, and western Virginia are going to have problems with flooding."

"I figure you all are okay where you are, but I wanted to make sure."

"Roscoe's and Jules' places might be the closest to the river, but we'll take care of them." His mom continued to rattle on about many relatives he hadn't heard about in a while. Considering his dad had five siblings, all married with kids and grandkids of their own, and his mom had four siblings, married with kids and grandkids also, his extended family was huge. Many had left the area, but quite a few of the Hopkins and Wilsons still occupied the beautiful Smoky Mountains.

"Carson gave me leave to come home if I'm needed, so stay in touch, Mom."

"Honey, if we start to float down the river, I'll call," she promised.

With vows of love, he disconnected, hoping his mom's lighthearted view of the impending floods remained in place and that the weather didn't decide to get worse.

By the end of the day, he met the other Keepers at the local watering hole for Leo and Nat's engagement celebration but kept one eye on the television in the corner over the bar. It was set on a sports channel, but the weather news kept popping on during the commercial breaks. So far, the rain was falling, but there was no reported flooding.

"Shit, Hop. Incoming," Dolby said, his voice low and his brows lower.

He turned to see a model-tall, blue-eyed blonde with curves walking toward him. Although, stomping might be a better description. "Fuck," he said with a long exhalation.

"Well, well, if it isn't Hop. Haven't heard from you, so I thought I'd come over to say hello."

He dipped his chin. "Sheila."

She stood with her hands on her hips, tapping her long, tapered nails. She waited, then cocked her head to the side. "That's all? That's all you have to say?"

"I'm not sure what else you're looking for," he replied, knowing it was a lie. He knew exactly what she was looking for... another night like the one that happened weeks ago. But he'd been upfront at the time. Sex only. No spending the night. No repeat performances. He wasn't an asshole, but he knew when a hookup was just that and nothing more. Never wanting to lead a woman on, he made sure they understood the score. And weeks ago, she'd laughed, tossed her hair over her shoulder, and winked while assuring him that she was completely on board with a one-and-done.

Then the last time he'd been in this bar, one of her friends had approached to say that Sheila was pissed he hadn't called her back. And now, in front of him, was evidence that she didn't take him seriously the first time. He sighed, glancing at the sympathetic expressions of his friends.

"What I'm looking for is for you to step up and be a gentleman. You haven't called. You haven't come around."

Keeping his voice low to try to save her embarrassment, he leaned closer. "Sheila, we talked before we left the bar weeks ago. You knew the score, and you agreed. You just thought I was full of shit or that no one could resist you. Either way, we were clear. So I'm not sure where you think this attitude is going. But I assure you it won't lead me back to your bed, which I already realize was a mistake the first time."

"You prick!" she growled, her eyes narrowed. She leaned forward and poked him in the chest. "You walk around like God's gift and then act so entitled."

His hand snapped out and closed around her wrist firmly but in a way that wouldn't hurt. He'd never hurt a woman but wasn't about to take her shit either. Not keeping the growl out of his voice, he said, "Walk away, Sheila. Walk away and find your dignity."

Her chest heaved, but she jerked her hand away. Shaking her head, she sneered. "What was I thinking? Fucking some backwater hillbilly?"

It was on the tip of his tongue to remind her that she hadn't had any complaints fucking him a few weeks ago, but he remained quiet. When she didn't get an argument from him, she turned quickly and stomped away. He let out a long, slow breath, glad to have her gone.

He wished she hadn't ruined his celebrating mood, but between the pissed-off one-nighter and the flood reports coming in on the TV, his heart wasn't into it. Deciding to head home alone to keep an eye on the weather back in Tennessee, he called out his goodbyes to the others. With handshakes, back slaps, and a few cheek kisses to the women, he walked out of the bar, reveling in the quiet night as soon as the door closed behind him. Sucking in the fresh air, he tilted his head back and stared at the stars in the clear sky before dropping his chin and weaving through the crowded parking lot to his SUV.

Driving home, he thought about Sheila and wondered why he wasted his time on women who he knew were never going to be the right one. Sure, he had a healthy sex drive and didn't plan on living like a monk, but he'd known when he met Sheila that she saw herself as a princess. In her mind, she just saw his muscular body and good ole boy attitude and was sure she could bend him to her will. And he'd also known that was the worst kind of woman to take home from a bar. *Entitled, with plans to lead me around by my dick. Jesus, I fucked up.*

He'd been a big teenager, growing taller and more muscular than a lot of his classmates. Being athletic, a decent student, and possessing an easy-going smile, he'd learned early on that getting girls' attention wasn't hard. Only one had really wanted to be his friend.

With long-lasting, loving relationships in his family, he knew love existed. And he knew a one-and-done wasn't the way to start. *What I really want to find is someone who sees beyond the brawn. Someone who can look inside and see the real me.*

2

It was three o'clock in the morning, but it was daybreak on the East Coast. Hop had slept fitfully, and once awake, he'd turned on the TV in his bedroom to see the rising waters and riverbanks overflowing in Tennessee. "Fuckin' hell." He grabbed his phone and dialed, knowing his parents would already be up.

"Figured it'd be you, son," his mom said. "Knew you'd be checking up on us. I can't remember gettin' so much rain in such a short period."

"What's happening, Mom?"

"Your dad, Uncle Matt, and Uncle Mike are getting their boats ready. They've got some idiot campers who are stuck out on Oak Island. Terry and Sam are going with the National Guard to pick up more volunteers. A bunch of the cousins are out already helping those who are stranded."

Matt and Mike were two of his dad's brothers, and Terry and Sam were his mom's brothers. He'd lost count of how many cousins he still had in the area.

"What about BethAnn?"

"Lord, you know your sister. She's at the high school getting it ready to take in evacuees. I'm making sandwiches with your aunts, and Larry said he'd stop by and pick them up to take over there while bringing us more bread at the same time."

"Listen, Mom, I'm getting the plane ready, and I'll fly in. I can be there by midafternoon. Tell Uncle Matt I'll need his bird." His love of flying was born when his uncle, who'd flown helicopters in Desert Storm, had taken him up when he was younger, giving him a bird's-eye view of the mountains. From that moment on, he'd been hooked.

The other end of the line was silent for a few seconds, and he knew she hated for him to come, so he pushed, "You know I can't stay here if I'm needed there."

"Never could tell you to stay put, could I, son?" She chuckled ruefully. "Okay, Frank. Be safe, and we'll see you when you get here."

He disconnected, then called Carson, hating the early hour but knowing he had no choice.

"Hop, what's happening?" Carson answered. "You heading to Tennessee?"

He wasn't surprised by his boss's question. Hop had no doubt that Carson had kept his pulse on the situation and was already anticipating Hop's need to leave. "Yeah, sorry—"

"Never be sorry about being where you need to be. Do you need anything from us?"

"I shouldn't think so. My uncle will have his helicopter ready for me when I get there. My guess is that

I'll only be needed for a couple of days to help rescue anyone who is stranded. Then I'll be back."

"Don't rush on our account. Let us know if you need any assistance from us."

"You've got it, Carson. Thanks." With that, he disconnected and jumped from the bed. Stalking into his bathroom, he showered, glad that he'd updated the room when he'd bought the property. The house was built in 1945, and while the previous owners had completed renovations, the shower needed to be large for a man his size. The house was modest in size but there was room to add on if necessary.

Once dressed, he looked out the bedroom windows that took up one side of the room. The sight never grew old. He'd paid more for the house than he'd initially wanted, but the view was killer. It was nestled in the side of a mountain with the ocean in the distance. Cedar planks now dark with age covered the outside, giving the home a mountain-cabin vibe. This same effect was carried to the inside, where the original wooden kitchen cabinets co-existed with the granite countertops. Downing a cup of coffee and a slice of toast, he headed back into the bedroom.

It didn't take long to pack, and after he'd sent a couple of texts out to a few of the other Keepers, he headed out to his pickup truck. Glad he kept his plane ready, it didn't take long to get to the airport, file the paperwork, and get into the air. The storms had traveled from west to east, so by the time he got there, he hoped the worst would be over. But then, he often found that if things could get fucked up, they would.

He climbed from the cockpit of the helicopter, bending slightly to try to keep the rain from pounding his face. Darting into the emergency compound set up at the local high school, he jerked off his ball cap and swiped his hand over his face, slinging water to the side. Heading straight to the table where volunteers were handing out coffee, water, and sandwiches, he grabbed a to-go cup of coffee and had just taken a sip when his name was called.

"Hop? Is that you?"

He looked up to see his old high school chemistry teacher behind the table, keeping it stocked with food. Grinning, he nodded as he stuck out his hand. "Mr. Fox! Good to see some things never change." Although, in truth, Charles Fox was a bit thicker in the middle and thinner on top, with silver streaking through his formerly dark brown hair. He was wearing a school sweatshirt with the familiar Go Eagles imprinted on the front.

Mr. Fox chuckled and shook his head, shaking Hop's hand. "Well, it certainly looks like you've changed. You're even bigger than you were in high school. I always try to keep up with some of my students, and I heard from your sister that you'd joined the Air Force after college and become a pilot. Are you back here helping us?"

"Yes, sir. I've got my uncle's bird—um, helicopter out there, and I've been trying to bring in as many people who were stuck as possible. I figured the

National Guard could use all the volunteers they can get."

Mr. Fox smiled widely. "You always were a good guy, Hop."

He shrugged with a wry grin on his face. "I figure I got in as much trouble as most of the other teens around here."

"Well, you passed my advanced chemistry class, and that was no easy feat."

"Oh, hell, Mr. Fox. I had a lot of tutoring help to get through your class. But thank God it worked out because I was able to get through basic chemistry in college."

Mr. Fox opened his mouth to say something else, but a new group of bedraggled rescuers came in. Hop moved out of the way so they could get to the food.

He hadn't been inside the high school since he graduated, and while he'd visited his family over the years, he spent most of his time at their houses. It wasn't a tiny school, but it was a place where everyone knew everyone. Now, looking around at the freshly painted walls with the Eagle decorating the entrance, memories flooded back.

Football practice. Learning to drive in the parking lot. Winning the regional championship. Volunteering to collect canned goods for those less fortunate during the holidays. His first kiss behind the stadium. Snorting, he rolled his eyes, remembering the last kiss he'd had behind the stadium and a hell of a lot of kisses in between. *God, I was such a dog... I'll never know how the hell I passed my classes and made it to college...*

Another memory slid over him, and he smiled. Lori Baker. The smart, quiet, studious girl who helped him learn chemistry without ever asking for anything in return. *Funny, she passed through my mind recently.* Spending so much time with her his junior year, they'd forged a friendship that lasted until graduation. He remembered clutching his diploma and finding her in the crowd, giving her a hug while telling her that she'd helped him earn the piece of paper in his hand. And he remembered the smile she'd bestowed on him at the time, her unusual ice-blue eyes sparkling in the spring sunlight.

He'd never shared a kiss with her behind the stadium or anywhere. Not that he didn't think about it a lot back then. Dropping his chin to his chest, he remembered he'd jerked off plenty of times in high school while fantasizing about her pretty face and hot body. But she wasn't like the other girls… those who chased after him, flirted with him, begged to go out with him. Or even like the girls who appeared to hero-worship him from afar. No, Lori didn't fit into any mold like the others. She'd simply been a good friend and patient tutor. Before her, he couldn't imagine just being friends with a girl, but while he sure as hell dreamed about it, he wasn't about to screw up his one chance to pass the class he needed to graduate. And then, he wasn't about to screw up the friendship they'd forged. He respected her way too much to lead her on or take advantage of her.

He stopped and looked around, realizing he was at her old locker—the one he'd wait for her at the end of the day before they'd drive to the library, his house, or her house to study. Placing his palm on the cold metal, his thoughts drifted to the way her face glowed as she smiled up at him. *Christ, how many times did I think about leaning in to kiss her?* His smile faded at the realization of how many years had passed.

They'd all gone out into the world just when social media had become a way to keep up with friends, but he'd never gotten into it, like many others from his high school. Unless they stayed in the hometown and he could occasionally see them when he visited, they fell by the wayside.

Taking a sip of the now-cooling coffee, he rubbed his chin, wondering what had happened to her. Hop's attention was jerked to the present when his dad rushed over.

"Glad I found you, son," Marty Hopkins said, breathing heavily from running. "Your uncle just got a call that there's a pregnant woman ready to have a baby, and she's stuck in her house, cut off from the road that's underwater. Your uncle managed to fly a Red Cross doctor to her, but he couldn't wait because another call came in. Now, the doctor has radioed and said she needs to get the woman to a hospital."

Tossing his barely sipped coffee into the trash, he raced out to his helicopter after obtaining the location from his dad. Time was of the essence as the skies were still dumping water, although at a lesser velocity than earlier in the day. The river hadn't peaked and probably wouldn't for a couple of days after the rain stopped, but it had flooded the banks, cutting off some of the smaller towns. Add in the downed trees and powerlines from the winds and plenty of people needed assistance.

Lifting into the air, he headed toward the destination. The worst of the storm had passed, for which he was grateful, considering he didn't have to wait out against the strong winds. Looking down over the treetops, he could see the swollen river, brown and muddy, as it churned rapidly along, spilling over the banks. He spied sections of roads that were now underwater, as well as places where the water overtook the first floor of some of the houses closest to the river.

Following along the path of destruction, he made it to the location as late afternoon was making the cloudy skies even darker. Grateful there was a place to land at the back of the house, he cut the whirling blades when he spied a man running from the house, his arms waving above his head.

"They're inside! My wife just had the baby! Can you help us?"

Hop jumped down from the cockpit, bending low and sloshing through the sopping wet grass to where the man had entered the back door, trying not to get soaked in the process. The water had risen toward the porch, lapping against the front steps.

"The doctor is getting them ready now!"

Hoping to keep the man calm, he asked, "What did you have?"

"A boy!" The new father looked over his shoulder as he ran into the den, a mixture of anxiety and awe on his face. "I have a son!"

Entering the den, Hop spied the woman stretched

out on the sofa, a bundle in her arms, snuggled against her chest. A blanket had been laid over both her and the baby, and the doctor was still between the woman's knees.

"The helicopter is here to take us to the hospital," the new father said, his voice much softer now that he was in the presence of his baby.

The doctor's raincoat was tossed to the side, and it was evident her jeans and boots were soaked. Hop knew she had to be uncomfortable, but her attention was focused on the new mother and baby. Her hair was plastered against her face where wet tendrils had fallen out of her ponytail. Without looking up, she ordered, "Thomas, get your raincoat on and gather the blankets I told you to get. We're gonna wrap Carrie and your son up in them, and then you're gonna carry her out to the helicopter. I'll follow along with the baby."

Thomas darted to the other side of the room, and Hop watched as the young man gathered the blankets and the emergency waterproof cover he felt sure the doctor had brought.

"How can I help?" Hop asked, trying to stay out of the way and uncertain of what to do.

"She and the baby are stable," the doctor said, her voice confident, "so if you can just get them to the hospital as quickly as possible, you'll be their hero."

Shaking his head, he stared at the top of the doctor's head as she slid thick socks onto the new mother's bare feet.

"I think if anyone is a hero to them, it would be you."

She offered a small snort-laugh which he found

strangely endearing given the extreme circumstances. "Okay, let's get them out of here," she said, standing.

Thomas slid his arms under his wife's knees and back, lifting her easily while Hop pulled the waterproof blanket tighter around the young mother. As he led the way back to the kitchen, he looked toward the front of the house, glad that the water had not begun to seep in. Turning to look behind him, he spied the doctor with the carefully wrapped baby in her arms and a waterproof blanket around her and the child.

Hop kept one hand on Thomas's back as he held a large umbrella over the couple. Once at the bird, he grimaced. Opening the door, he said, "Get your wife inside carefully, and then we need to evaluate how to get everyone there."

Thomas followed Hop's instructions and gently set Carrie into the back seat, and then Hop climbed in to buckle her in safely. He looked over at the doctor who'd approached with the baby in her arms.

"She and the baby will be fine on the trip to the hospital." The doctor climbed in and handed the baby to the eager mom, who was beaming despite the crazy circumstances surrounding her son's birth.

"You can sit back here," Hop said to the doctor, then turned to Thomas. "You can sit up front."

The doctor glanced toward him, blinking the water away from her face, and shook her head. Looking back down at the new mother and baby getting buckled into the back seat, she said, "Don't worry about it. I've got someone to see just down the way, and a boat is coming for me."

Hop glanced toward the rising waters and whipped his head around toward her. "I don't think that's safe."

"You don't have a say," the doctor barked. "We've both got a job to do. Please, get them to the hospital."

Not wanting to argue while the sky became darker, he nonetheless hated leaving the doctor behind. Growling, he argued, "I can take you to your next destination after we drop them off at the hospital."

"I'm needed elsewhere, and you're needed for this! For goodness' sake, go!"

A shout from nearby had them all turned to see a man in a boat motoring where the road used to be. The doctor waved before shouting back at Hop. "There's my ride. Take care of my patient!"

Quicker than he thought possible, she turned and started to dart away. At the last second, he climbed into the cockpit and looked at her again before closing the door. The woman, like the rest of them, was even more of a bedraggled mess with rain dripping down from her hair. She lifted her face toward his fully for the first time, and his heart jumped when he saw ice-blue eyes looking at him. She blinked, then, before he could shout, she turned and ran toward the boat. He gasped, his heart in his throat as she stood in knee-deep water, then raised her arms so the two men could lift her up into the boat along with the huge backpack she wore, probably full of medical supplies.

"Please, can we go now?" Thomas called from the back seat, and the cry of a baby startled Hop.

"Absolutely. Stay buckled, and we'll be there in a few minutes." Lifting off the ground, he peered back down and grimaced at the sight of the boat staying close to the edge of the water as it sped away. He had no idea who the doctor was, but he'd never seen eyes that color except for one other person... the girl who'd tutored him in chemistry. Lori Baker.

3

By the time Hop had flown Thomas, Carrie, and the newborn to the hospital safely, it was dark. He was hungry and ready for some shut-eye but drove back to the high school where the emergency services had set up a command center along with the shelter. *I'd just like to know if the doctor got to her next destination safely.* He snorted as he scrubbed his hand over his face. *Okay, and maybe find out her name.*

The gym was lined with cots, about half of them occupied with those who'd been evacuated from their homes and didn't have someone else to take them in. He slipped around to the volunteers and personnel in the building, frustration growing as person after person looked at him with blank eyes and shrugged when he asked about the doctor.

Finally, he found someone who nodded and said, "Yeah, my uncle took a doctor over to a small clinic where the regular doctor was unable to get in to see some patients there."

Blowing out a huge sigh of relief, he nodded. "Thank God! Listen, do you know who that doctor was? What's her name?"

Shaking her head, the woman lifted her shoulders as she passed another blanket out to someone in the shelter. "I've got no idea. The Red Cross has got people here. Lots of volunteers come from all over. The National Guard came in. Hell, I'm just glad we've got people willing to help!" She turned to keep handing out blankets to those coming in, and he tossed out his thanks as he walked away. With no more flights until morning, he drove to his parents' house, glad to find them safely ensconced in their home and hear the report that all relatives were safe as well.

Sitting at the kitchen table, his mom drank hot tea as his dad and he sipped Tennessee whiskey. "Mom, you keep up with everything around here. Do you remember that girl who helped me pass chemistry in high school? Lori Baker was her name."

"Of course I do," his mom replied, nodding emphatically. "Nice family. She was a sweet girl. So pretty, just like her mama. Real quiet. Super smart."

That was exactly how he remembered her. Well, partially. He also remembered a bright laugh, a wry sense of humor, and the prettiest eyes he'd ever seen in his life.

"As I remember, I kept wishing you'd ask her out instead of the parade of bimbos you so often took out to the movies."

"Jesus, Mom, that was sixteen years ago. How do you remember who I dated?"

"Because you didn't date!" She laughed, earning a smile from his dad that he attempted to hide behind his hand as his mother continued. "You never did. You went out with girls. Took them out but never *dated* anyone for more than a few weeks at a time."

He sighed heavily and prodded. "Let's get back to my question. Do you know what happened with Lori? I know she was going to Vanderbilt, but then I lost track of her."

"She did go to Vanderbilt. I remember her parents were so proud." At that, his mother sighed heavily, her eyes downcast.

"Are her parents still around here?"

His parents shared a look, the slight wrinkles in their faces deepening in tandem.

"What?" His one-word question shot out, the apprehension on their faces creating a concern inside his chest.

"Oh, Frank, I'm sorry to tell you because I know you got to know them when you and Lori worked together. They were killed in a car accident together. It was so sad."

He jerked back as though punched. He couldn't imagine losing one parent in an accident, but for her to have lost both was unthinkable.

His mother's face scrunched in thought. "Let's see, that would've been when you were serving in the Air Force, so I guess she would've made it through college by then."

"Why are you asking, son?" His dad peered at him over the whiskey tumbler.

He sighed, his shoulders slumping. "I saw a doctor today who had the same color eyes as her who reminded me of her. I didn't have a chance to talk to the doctor, so I don't know if it's her or not."

"I never saw her again after the funeral," his mom said, shaking her head, her voice giving away her sadness. "I didn't know what her plans were and wasn't close to her family, but I always felt guilty that I didn't do more. A couple of weeks after the funeral, I stopped by the house with a casserole. I always find that people do so much right at the time of a death and funeral, but the family often needs more help several weeks later."

Her hands fluttered as she spoke. "Anyway, the house was locked up, and there was a real estate agent sign outside. I talked to the minister of the church they went to, and he told me that she had come and talked to him. She was going back to school and selling the house. Lord, I tell you, his words 'bout made my heart hurt so bad I almost couldn't stand it. He said he talked to her about just renting out the house in case she ever wanted to come back, but she said at the time that it was too devastating to think of returning to the place where her parents wouldn't be anymore. To be honest, that's the last I ever heard of her."

"I kinda doubt that the doctor you saw today would've been her since she doesn't live here anymore," his dad said, standing to rinse his whiskey glass. "Although, I suppose she could have volunteered. Lots of good people helping out just like you." He winked at Hop as he walked over and placed his hands on his wife's shoulders before bending to kiss the top of her head. "We've got another long day ahead of us until that river peaks and starts receding. My old bones gotta hit the sack."

His mother nodded and pushed to a stand. Hop followed suit, hugging both of them. He yawned widely and was looking forward to crashing in his childhood room, knowing he'd be doing more runs tomorrow. After a long, hot shower, he climbed into bed. But sleep was evasive as he thought back to the girl who'd taken the time to tutor him and then became a good friend.

Their relationship wasn't like a chick-flick where the shy, nerdy girl tutored the jock, and they ended up together, or he rescued her from bullies. Lori had friends and participated in activities. She could have easily told Mr. Fox that she didn't have time to tutor anyone. Hop snorted as he stared up at his ceiling. He'd been conceited enough at first to think she might have agreed just to get close to him. But she'd never flirted, never acted coy, never tried to come on to him. Instead, they'd settled into an easy friendship. He remembered sitting at his parents' kitchen table or at the library after school going over equations until the chemistry clicked with him.

Looking back, he realized how it was rare for a teenage guy and a girl to be just friends. Lori had wanted to become a doctor, and nothing was going to hold her back. *Hell, I wanted to become a pilot and wasn't about to let anything divert me from that goal.* They had both been forward-thinking. *Then I left the area and never looked back.*

That realization stung, and he wasn't sure why.

Rolling over, he punched his pillow, his body finally settling. But for some reason now, as sleep overtook his exhausted mind, he found that the ice-blue eyes drifted through his dreams.

Morning came early, and Hop wished he'd been able to sleep a little better. As he got dressed, the scent of his mom's coffee wafted upstairs. He was ready to suck down a gallon just to make it through the day. By the time he was downstairs, the sight of bacon, toasted bread, and scrambled eggs, along with hashbrown potatoes, had his mouth watering. "Damn, Mom, are you sure there's no way I can convince you to move back to California with me?"

She threw the dish towel over her shoulder and narrowed her eyes in his direction. "Are you saying that you want me to move all the way to the other side of the country just so I can fix breakfast for you?"

He wrapped his arms around her, pinning hers to her side, and lifted, giving her a twirl. "Aw, Mom, you know I just want to have you around because I love you!"

"Frank, you were always a rascal and still are!" she said between giggles.

"Put my woman down." His dad grinned as he walked into the room. Jerking his head toward the front door, he said, "We've got some company coming in to see you."

"Uncle Hop!"

The *clickety-clack* of plastic heels on the floor sent a grin spreading over his face, and he swung his niece up into his arms. Her princess outfit, complete with a pink tulle skirt and tiara, was a perfect way to start the morning.

"Uncle Hop!" his nephew called out in greeting, darting into the room.

He high-fived his nephew, then reached over to hug his sister. "BethAnn, gorgeous as ever." With his niece still in his arms, he shook hands with his brother-in-law. "Larry, good to see you."

Soon they were all sitting around the kitchen table, their heads bowed as his dad offered a prayer for those whose homes, livelihoods, and families were affected by the storm. Then with a blessing offered for those volunteers helping, they dug into the comfort food.

As they passed dishes and filled up on his mom's good cooking, it didn't take long for their conversations to move from what was new with everyone to what they had on the agenda for the day. He, his dad, and his brother-in-law were heading back to the high school command center for their assignments. His dad and brother-in-law would go out in boats while he would utilize the helicopter. His sister and mom would take turns watching after his niece and nephew while helping at the shelter. His uncles, aunts, and cousins would all be doing the same.

Sitting at the table, he was once again struck with the notion that he came from good, honest, decent folks. His parents and grandparents always offered a helping hand, never knew a stranger, and wouldn't rest until everyone was taken care of.

"Whatcha smiling at, Uncle Hop?"

He shook his head as he leaned over and ruffled his nephew's hair. "Just thinking about what a good family we have."

"I want to be like you when I grow up. I wanna be big and strong, fly helicopters, be in the military, and catch bad guys!"

"Well, first, you better finish your breakfast," his sister quipped, giving her son the *mom* look, one he remembered their mom often gave when he was a kid.

It didn't take long to get to the high school, and from there, his first assignment had him on high alert. While the rain had stopped, the river continued to rise during the night, and the floodwaters were lapping around one of the smaller hospitals in a neighboring town. Much of the rescue work would have been executed by the National Guard, but considering the expanse of flooding covered such a vast geographic area, they accepted any help they could get.

"We're sending in helicopters to land on the roof to get the last patients and staff out," the emergency commander said to the volunteer pilots.

The Red Cross administrator looked over at Hop. "I've got a pilot for an air ambulance helicopter, but he's having chest pains. I know you're licensed in this aircraft and can take over for him. Are you willing?"

"Absolutely."

Making his way out to the airfield, he was glad to see that the helicopter was ready. He completed his checks, then lifted into the air, heading toward the small hospital. With the sun high in the sky, he could look down and see the flooded streets and fields. At least now that the river was close to peaking, he hoped the water would soon begin to recede. Twenty minutes later, he approached the hospital, and without another helicopter on the pad, he was able to land immediately.

A man in scrubs bent low and rushed over. "Good to see you! I'm Bob Trogden, hospital chief of staff. Thanks for coming!"

"Not a problem. What have you got for me?"

"We were able to move all nonemergency patients yesterday afternoon, as well as anyone who was awaiting surgery and all nonessential personnel. They've been taken to Bristol, Johnson City, and Kingsport, and a few were taken to Knoxville. We've been running morning lifts, and believe it or not, we're almost at the end. Right now, we've got three women who had babies during the night or this morning, and we want to get them to a nearby hospital. That'll leave me with only one woman who had complications during birth and their doctor who's with them."

Immediately thinking of Lori, he said, "How about if I take them?"

The hospital administrator shook his head. "No, I need you to take this group. The helicopter you've got is the size that can carry them, plus the last of my nurses who stayed. We've got one other Red Cross helicopter coming right after you that can get the doctor, myself, and the last patient and take them to Knoxville."

He knew not to argue and nodded his agreement. The sliding doors opened, and he watched as three nurses rolled wheelchairs out to the side of his helicopter, each filled with a woman clutching a blanket-wrapped bundle in their arms. Looking over, he asked, "Are the fathers here?"

The nurse closest to him shook her head. "No, we made them leave first thing this morning. They're all waiting at the Kingsport hospital."

With assistance, he gently lifted the first woman into his arms while the nurse held her baby. Offering his easy smile, he climbed aboard and settled her into one of the seats. Seeing her grimace, he asked, "What's your baby's name?"

The new mother immediately smiled widely, her eyes brightening. "Wilder Richardson," she said, pride oozing with the two words.

"Well, he's appropriately named." Hop continued to grin. "He's about to take his momma on a wild ride on his very first day."

She laughed, her discomfort seeming less. He moved out of the way to let the nurse sit next to her. He repeated the process with the next two women, asking about their babies and getting them to smile, and soon had them ready to fly.

The last nurse hopped out and looked toward the administrator. "I'll stay to assist with the last woman and the doctor."

Hop glanced up as the hospital roof doors slid open again, this time seeing someone in scrubs racing forward to hand a medical bag to one of the nurses already strapped in. His eyes never left her dark-haired ponytail, hoping she would look toward him. At the last minute, she turned to wave toward the others before glancing his way.

And ice-blue eyes met his gaze. His breath hitched just like yesterday as he stared at the beauty. A blast from the past met the present as he stared. This time there was no doubt as to who the beautiful doctor was. *Lori Baker.*

She showed no signs of recognition, but with his goggles on, he wasn't surprised.

"You're ready!"

He jolted at Bob's voice and jerked his head around. With a curt nod, he climbed into the cockpit. Having no time to waste, he knew he needed to get his aircraft off the hospital helicopter pad so the next one could land. He was forced to take off, leaving Lori behind once again. But this time, he was determined to find her again as soon as possible.

Why? It's been fourteen years. At the time, it had been easy to leave high school friends behind and immerse himself in college and then the military. *Hell, college had been a sex smorgasbord. And the bars off the Air Force bases had provided the same experience.* He winced at the indiscretions from his earlier years and sighed heavily at the realization that with her parents' deaths, she would have had a vastly different life than he.

But looking back at high school, there was no doubt

she'd made a good adolescent experience better, and he felt guilty that he'd let her drift away.

He had no idea why she'd crossed through his life again, but this time, he didn't want to squander the chance to catch up with an old friend.

4

Two days later, the floodwaters had significantly receded but left damaged streets and buildings in its wake. While there was a lot of work to be accomplished, no more rescue missions were left to fly, so Hop knew it was time for him to head back to California.

He'd tried to find Lori but had been unsuccessful. She hadn't shown up at the high school emergency command post, and he hadn't seen her around town. While he considered asking Jeb to get her information for him, he'd hesitated to use his coworkers' resources to find an old high school friend...despite how she'd filled his thoughts and dreams for the past few days.

Driving the truck one of his uncles had loaned to him while he was in town, he headed to a local restaurant's bar for his last night in Tennessee. He knew his relatives, a few old friends, as well as many of the first responders and volunteers would be gathering.

He glanced to the side as he neared the town's cemetery and slowed, then turned on his blinker as he pulled onto the lane that meandered amongst the headstones. It had been a long time since he'd visited his grandparents' gravesites, and he had no idea when he'd be back again. Thinking of his parents, he hoped it would be a long time before he had to bury anyone in the family plots again.

The cemetery was on high ground, and other than the hard rain and winds from several days ago, it was untouched by the floods. The mountains provided the background, and the lush grass was dotted with the stately headstones, some grander than others, but all standing as sentries to those who'd gone on before.

After parking, he smiled as he walked to the large section that held his family, recognizing the names of most. Coming to his Wilson grandparents, he squatted and rested his hand on their combined stone. "Grannie, you made sure I sat up straight in church when Mama was singing in the choir and then would let me get an extra piece of cake at Sunday dinner." He remembered her apron with little flowers sewn on it for everyday meals tied around her plump middle and the one with a little lace for special occasions. Looking at the other side of the stone, he added, "Grampa, you taught me how to fish, how to hunt, and how to take care of the nature around us. For all that you two were, I'm more grateful than you can imagine."

Standing, he turned and walked to his other grandparents' headstone and squatted again. "Mama Hopkins, you made the best chocolate bourbon pecan pie while pretending you didn't see Papa sneaking some of the bourbon," he said, his mouth watering at the memory. "You took the blue ribbon every year at the fair and deserved it, that's for sure. And Papa Hopkins, you taught Dad how to be a good man, and in turn, both of you taught me. I just hope I learned to be half as good a man as you." Chuckling, he added, "And you told the best jokes. Can't remember how many times I almost busted a gut laughing."

Closing his eyes, he said a prayer as more memories swept over him. Standing once more, he turned to walk back to the truck when a movement off to the side caught his eye. A woman dressed in jeans tucked into boots and a soft leather jacket was bending over a headstone with her hand resting on top. He sighed, understanding the emotions that can crash down on someone in a cemetery. Sometimes it was with fond memories, and other times it was with bone-crushing grief. He had no idea what the woman was feeling but wanted to give her privacy. He started to turn away when a breeze whipped her dark ponytail about her face, and he halted, his eyes wide. *No way! There's no way it could be her!*

He started forward, his feet moving silently over the grass while approaching, then hesitated. *Fuck... I can't just interrupt... I don't want to scare her... what if it's some random mourner—*

The woman turned, her gaze landing on his, and she startled for a second before cocking her head to the side, her ice-blue eyes piercing. His feet stumbled to a halt as he realized the person he hoped it would be, turned out to be her. As his gaze moved over her face, his chest depressed with a rush of air leaving his lungs. She was... *breathtaking.* Her features had matured perfectly. The teenage youthful cute was now replaced with a woman's beauty. "Lori? Lori Baker?"

She stared in silence for a moment, her head leaning back as her gaze moved from his hair down his broad body to his boots and back again before landing on his face. Recognition, mixed with incredulity, sparked in her eyes. "Hop? Frank Hopkins?"

He reached up and scrubbed his hand over his head, a grin spreading over his face. "Yeah, it's me."

"Wow," she said, shaking her head as she stood, her gaze glancing over the cemetery before returning to his face. "I never expected to see you here."

"I've been looking for you." Not wanting to sound like a stalker, he rushed, "I saw you the other day and wanted to see you again. This was just pure crazy luck to be here and find you here as well."

Blinking, she jerked her head back. "You... you're the pilot from... with Carrie and Thomas." He nodded, and her mouth dropped open. "Oh, Hop, I'm so sorry I didn't recognize you. But then, I can't believe you recognized me either."

"It's your eyes, Lori. I've never known anyone else with eyes so"—*special, unforgettable, brilliant*—"um, unusual." He inwardly winced at the word he chose. Giving his head a shake, he couldn't understand what about seeing her again seemed to short-circuit his brain.

She snorted as she nodded. "Most people wonder if I'm wearing special contacts. I'm not sure they believe me when I tell them that I don't." She looked behind him again as though searching for someone else, then brought her gaze back to him. "Is your family...? Are they...?"

He jerked his head back and forth. "I was just visiting my grandparents' gravesites. I don't get to Tennessee very often, so I came to pay my... um... respects." His gaze had dropped to the headstone near her, and his heart stuttered along with his words.

> Grace Baker and Carlton Baker
> Beloved wife and husband. Beloved parents

His shoulders slumped. "Shit, Lori, I'm so sorry."

She shrugged, the light dimming in her eyes. "You didn't know. Anyway, I don't get here often either, so I thought I'd take the opportunity to visit." Shoving her hands into her back pockets, she shrugged again. "Kind of like you, I guess."

"My mom told me about your parents just the other day. I was real sorry to hear about their accident." His words felt inadequate. He remembered she had no siblings and no other relatives in the area, so her parents' deaths had left her all alone. Between aunts, uncles, cousins, and other members, his family could fill half the church when they all got together.

She pressed her lips together in a tight line and nodded. "It's been years, but I'm not sure I'll ever get used to not being able to pick up the phone and call them." She then gave her head a little shake as though to dislodge her thoughts. "Anyway, it was nice to see you.

I'm glad you came over." She dipped her chin, then turned toward the only other vehicle in the area.

"Have you got plans tonight?" he called out, not wanting to lose their connection.

Turning back to him with lifted brows, she shook her head. "No, not really."

Pressing forward, he said, "A lot of the first responders who are getting ready to leave are meeting at the bar across town. Why don't you come?"

"Well, I don't know—"

He wasn't ready to walk away from her after just finding her. "Come on." He flashed her a trademark grin, one that had often caught many women's attention, but he noticed she eyed him with cool interest. "What were your plans?"

She chuckled. "Sitting in the hotel room, flipping channels for an hour, trying to find something to watch before realizing absolutely nothing was on. Then probably munching on bags of cheese crackers and drinking a beer before going to bed."

His brows lifted while choking back a snort. "Sounds hard to top, but let's see if I can show you a better evening. Come on, let's catch up." He watched as an indefinable emotion passed through her eyes. He prodded, "I'd really like to catch up with you, Lori." Suddenly filled with an unusual bout of self-doubt, he wondered what her response would be.

A slow smile made her even more beautiful as she finally shrugged. "Okay, sure. I'd like that. It would be nice to catch up with you, too. But I don't know where the bar is—"

"That's my truck over there. I'll pull around, and then you can follow me."

She nodded and pointed at a white car parked nearby. "Okay. My rental's just over there."

Another breath left his lips, followed by a wider grin. As he jogged to his truck, his movements were hastened by the excitement building at seeing her again, mixed with the uncertainty that she'd actually follow him to the bar. As he carefully turned around on the small lane in the cemetery, he breathed another sigh of relief as she pulled in behind him, thinking of the implications of what she'd just said. *She's staying in a hotel. Her vehicle is a rental. So she probably flew here... she doesn't live close.*

Curiosity filled him. *Where is this excitement coming from?* He had no idea what the answer to that question could be. He only knew that this trip home had brought him face-to-face with some good memories that he hadn't thought of in a long time and didn't want to forget again. Over the past few days, he'd realized how she helped him succeed in high school while being a good friend. But to his adolescent mind, ready to get out of the small town and take on the world, he'd easily walked away from almost everyone other than family. Grateful, as well as intrigued with finding out more about her now, he kept glancing into the rearview mirror to make sure she was following.

Arriving at the parking lot of the bar, he wasn't surprised to see how packed it was. Finally finding an empty spot, he passed it but waved his hand out the window to indicate she should take it. He watched as she pulled in, then drove onto the street and parked behind a line of other pickup trucks. Jumping down, he hustled over, arriving just as she was hitting the lock on her key fob.

She glanced toward the bar, then grinned. "I never came here when I was younger. I think my mom was concerned about a bar connected to the restaurant. But I was always curious about that name."

He looked up at the old sign with the letters burned into the wood. **End of the Road**

Laughing, she continued, "Since it's not at the end of this road, I always wondered where the name came from."

"Maybe this should be someone's last stop before they go home." They walked side by side toward the front door. "And while it's known as a bar, the restaurant has good food, and a lot of families with kids will be here, too." The noise from the bar spilled out every time the door opened, and he wondered if they would be able to have a conversation inside. Once they passed through the doorway, it took a moment for him to see over the masses. He hoped they'd be able to find a place to sit.

As they weaved their way through the crowd, he accepted back slaps, handshakes, and hugs from old high school buddies he still remembered and some of the first responders he'd just met over the past couple of days. He was even introduced to a few more cousins he didn't even know he had. Glancing to the side, he was glad to see that Lori was being greeted by other first responders she'd met as well.

He placed his hand on the small of her back and

guided her through the crowd, his height giving him the advantage of seeing over most people and his bulk giving him the benefit of maneuvering through everyone.

She tilted her head back and said, "This is where your size makes a difference. I can't see past the person in front of me!"

As his fingers flexed on her back, he lowered his chin to hold her gaze. "Glad to be of service." Finally arriving at the table that held his parents, a few aunts and uncles, and his sister and brother-in-law and their kids, he appreciated them shifting to the side on the bench so he and Lori could sit.

"Oh, my goodness!" his mom exclaimed, smiling widely at Lori. "It's so good to see you again. Frank was just telling us that he saw you the other day." She extended her hand across the table, fussing, "I'd give you a hug, but these booths don't allow much maneuvering!"

Lori laughed and reached out to clasp his mom's hand. "It's nice to see you again, Mrs. Hopkins."

"Uncle Hop! Who's the girl?"

"Hey, buddy. This is Dr. Lori. She's an old friend of mine."

"She doesn't look old. She looks like a hot babe—"

The adult heads at the table whirled around in unison, and BethAnn narrowed her eyes at her son. "Lawrence Junior!"

Lori's lips pressed together in an apparent effort to keep from laughing, and Hop prayed his nephew wasn't going to say that he'd learned that phrase from him.

"But that's what Corey at school says. He calls girls hot babes all the time—"

BethAnn shifted her glare from her son to her husband. "You need to teach your son that he shouldn't listen to seven-year-olds who don't have any manners!"

"Hey," Larry protested, his face scrunched as his hands lifted. "He didn't learn it from me!"

Before his family could devolve into a blame-game-manners lesson, Hop jumped into the breach. "Larry Junior, you're right that Lori is a very pretty lady, but let's not call her a hot babe. She and I were friends when we were in high school."

His nephew stared at Hop, hero worship evident in his eyes. Then with a worldly nod of his head, he looked over at Lori. "I'm sorry if I said something I shouldn't have. But you are pretty."

"I think you look like a pretty princess," Hop's niece said, grinning widely while dipping her chicken strips into barbecue sauce, then licking her fingers. "You just need a twinkly crown like me."

"Thank you," Lori said before turning her gaze to Hop. "Your niece and nephew are certainly good for my ego!"

"So you're a doctor. Always knew you'd succeed at whatever you wanted to do," his mom said, her smile both indulgent toward her grandchildren as well as directing bright-eyed interest toward Lori. Hop wondered how she managed both but figured it was a *mama* thing.

Nodding, she said, "Yes. My specialty is OB/GYN."

BethAnn looked over with curiosity. "You don't

practice around here, do you? At least you weren't with the group when I had my babies."

"No, I don't practice here," Lori said, shaking her head. She glanced toward Hop and shrugged. "I guess I'm like a lot of people who are in the area now. When the Red Cross put the call out, I responded. I work with the Red Cross as well as a large practice with multiple doctors. That allows me to go out on a lot of national and international Red Cross calls."

Hop wanted to ask so many more questions, but the crowd in the bar made it almost impossible. While there was still a lot of damage and work to be done from the flooding, most of the first responders who came from other places would be leaving soon and were taking tonight to kick back and enjoy some well-earned downtime.

After a while, BethAnn and Larry gathered their kids and said goodbye, soon followed by his parents. He was glad they had the booth to themselves, but it seemed selfish to take up a large space with just the two of them. He tried to think of a witty way to ask her out but couldn't think of a line that didn't sound like his usual cheesy pickup line. And he wasn't about to use that on her.

Going for honesty, he said, "I'd love to spend more time talking to you, but this place is so crowded it's hard to have a conversation. I wish I had a place to invite you to, but I'm staying with my parents. There's a diner not too far from here if you'd like to get something to eat in a less elbow-to-elbow establishment."

She held his eyes for a moment before nodding. "I'd

love to." Her soft smile was wide, and her words sounded sincere.

Once again, with his hand on her back, he guided her through the bar. He hated to give up her company for any time at all but knew it made sense for them to take both cars. Once again, she followed him, and they parked outside the diner.

"Believe it or not, I'm staying just across the street." She laughed, inclining her head toward a motel that had seen better days.

He scowled at the poor security he was sure the hotel provided. *Especially for a lone female.*

As though she could hear his thoughts, she added, "The owners have updated the inside, so it's not as bad as it looks."

A grunt was his only response as they made their way into the diner, finding it quiet this time of night. She shrugged off her jacket, exposing the soft blue sweater underneath before they slid into the booth. Nothing about what she wore was exceptional, but everything showcased her assets perfectly. The jeans were molded to her lithe frame. The color of the sweater brought out the unusual color of her eyes. The boots were practical yet stylish. Everything about her called to him.

The server walked over with a wide smile on her face. "What can I get you, good folks?"

"Is it terrible to say I'm starving right now?" Lori leaned forward, whispering as though hating for the server to hear.

Laughing, Hop patted his stomach. "I'm always in the mood for food. Order whatever you want."

"Then I'll take a strawberry milkshake and a cheeseburger with fries." She looked over at him and shook her head. "I might not sleep all night, but I'll be satisfied."

It was on the tip of his tongue to say he could come up with another reason to satisfy her, but he clamped his mouth shut at the last second. Looking down to hide the grimace that crossed his face, he knew the last thing she deserved was some dumbass, cheesy line.

The server looked at him and cocked her head to the side. "And for you?"

Blinking, he jerked back to the task at hand. "Yeah, ah, I'll have the same, only make it a double everything."

The server smiled widely and tucked her pen into her bun before walking back toward the kitchen.

They sat for a moment, both fiddling with the paper ring around the napkins and utensils, glancing up at each other as though neither knew what to say. Finally, he spread his hands open on the table and grinned. "I feel kind of stupid asking you to catch me up on the past fourteen years, but I really would like to know what you've been up to."

She chuckled while nodding, the hue of a light blush painting her cheeks. "That's funny because I was thinking the same thing about you."

"So who goes first?"

"We could always take turns."

He settled back and winked. "Okay, you start. The last time we saw each other was right after graduation from high school. You were heading to Vanderbilt… pre-med."

"Um…yeah. I went to Vanderbilt but stayed there during the summers so I could graduate in three years."

"Ambitious, but I'm not surprised. You always had a goal."

Her shoulders hefted in a shrug. "It's just that I knew I wanted to go into medicine, and facing all those years of school, I didn't want to drag out my undergraduate degree." She placed her hands on the tabletop also. "And you? College on a football scholarship. Maryville, right?"

"Yeah." He was surprised that she remembered. "I got recruited by UT, and everyone was surprised I went to a little college."

She nodded, a soft smile on her face. "I remember. But if you recall, I told you that I wasn't surprised. It suited you, even if most people didn't see it."

His gaze locked onto her, his breath halting. She was right… she hadn't been surprised by his decision to attend a small college. Lori had always listened to him, understanding him better than his buds or his dates.

He nodded, once again feeling pulled in by her attention. "I was able to play and had a good time, but more importantly, I got my degree without getting lost in a big university. Then joined the Air Force, did OCS, and got accepted into flight training. I already knew how to fly small planes and helicopters from my uncle, but the Air Force gave me the training necessary for their equipment. I flew Gulfstreams and a Twin Huey bird. I ended up doing Air Force special ops before getting out."

"And now?"

"I work for an elite private security and investigation business in California."

She fell back against the booth, but her hands stayed close to his. "Wow. How'd that happen?"

"I flew a special op and met some guys from different special forces, including a few on CIA ops. One of them reached out to me just to let me know that he was joining another security company and creating a California office. Offered me a position if I was ever interested." Sucking in a deep breath, he turned his hands palm up on the table. "I loved the Air Force but had felt restless for a bit. When the offer came in, the timing was perfect. Now, we run missions, I get to fly, and I'm no longer constrained by the military."

"I'm impressed! But then, I always knew you'd be successful."

He laughed and shook his head. "You're a doctor. There's no reason to be impressed by me."

"You're being modest. I remember that about you."

"Modest? Me?" he barked out, scoffing. "Hell, most people would say I was as cocky as they come!"

She slowly shook her head. "You forget... I knew the Hop that you sometimes hid from others. You were very self-assured, but that's not the same as being cocky."

The smart-ass comment died in his throat with her pale-blue eyes holding his gaze. As he stared at the woman in front of him, so familiar and so different all at the same time, he realized she was right—she really had known the adolescent him. He nodded slowly. "Yeah, you always *got* me." He cleared his throat as her intense gaze remained on him. "What else do you remember?" He couldn't help but ask, curious to see what she would say while holding his breath as he waited for the answer.

5

If she wasn't absolutely certain that she'd look ridiculous, Lori would have pinched herself. Hard. She couldn't believe she was sitting in a little diner back in her hometown with Frank Hopkins. *Hop.* It was hard enough to imagine that she'd come back to Tennessee at all, and in truth, if it hadn't been for the emergency flooding and Red Cross assignment, she wouldn't be here.

She also couldn't believe that she hadn't recognized him as the rescue helicopter pilot, but then she'd been solely focused on her patients. While she'd certainly had a quick glance of female appreciation for the muscular pilot, she'd been too involved with the new mom and baby to indulge in more than a passing thought.

But at the cemetery, the proof was right in front of her. Five days ago, when she'd walked into the high-school-turned-emergency-command-center and wandered through the halls, adolescent memories had hit her full force. Over the years, she had occasionally reminisced about Hop, but after so long, it felt foolish to try to reconnect. Social media wasn't a platform she spent any time on, but once, years earlier, when she'd searched his name, only a few mentions from his college days came up. In truth, though, she'd never forgotten the handsome boy who'd befriended her during chemistry tutoring.

A flash of memory hit her— sitting at his parents' kitchen table after school as they first studied, then eventually talked and laughed as a true friendship between them was forged. She didn't fall for him no matter how hard it was sometimes being so close to what she'd thought was perfection. She'd known nothing would ever come of an unrequited adoration, considering he had every girl in school panting to be with him. She'd accepted that their destinies were not on that path. But she'd loved being his friend. That was something no other girl could claim.

And now he sat across from her. His large frame was sculpted, muscles barely contained in a pair of jeans that had seen better days, yet the soft material clung to his thighs and ass perfectly. The tight black T-shirt emphasized his arms and chest. And a charmingly uncertain expression on his face as he ducked his head, his clear blue gaze looking at her, asking, "What else do you remember?"

Rolling her eyes, she flipped her hand in his direction, waving it up and down. "I remember you were bigger than most guys in the school. Still are. I remember that you had a killer smile. Still do. And I remember you had more girlfriends than you could keep up with." Lifting a brow, she silently dared him to refute her memories.

Shaking his head, he clapped his hand to his chest as though in agony. "I didn't have girlfriends. Just girls who were..." He hesitated, now blushing.

"Easy? Hot? Panting? Claiming? Desperate?" She ticked off her multiple answers with her fingers, then lifted her hand to cover her mouth, knowing there was no way to hide her wide grin.

"Damn, it's kind of embarrassing to look back, isn't it?" He huffed as he leaned back against the red faux-leather booth. His gaze stayed on her, and she felt drawn in, just like many years ago. "I mean, I had a lot of good high school memories and some really good teammates and guy friends, but you... you were different. You were the only girl who I was friends with. The only one I could really talk to. The only one I really cared about. The other girls? Damn, like I said, looking back is embarrassing."

A warm flush filled her, surprising her. She was no longer the quiet teenager with a secret crush on the hottest guy in school who'd cared for her as a friend but had never tried to kiss. Yet years later, it felt good to hear how much he'd cared.

"I think that's probably why I don't look back very often," she said ruefully. "High school was good, but I don't spend much time thinking of the past."

"Because of your parents?" As soon as the words left his mouth, he winced. "Christ, Lori, I'm sorry."

She pressed her lips together and then met his gaze.

"It's okay to talk about them. After all, you did just see me at the cemetery."

"Yeah, but… well…" He kept his eyes on her. "I'd like to know more, but only what you feel like telling me."

She chewed on her bottom lip for a moment, thinking how little she shared with others about anything personal. It had been years since she'd talked about her parents with anyone, and since no one she knew now had ever met them, it seemed overwhelming to try to get someone to emotionally catch up to where she was. *But with Hop…* she felt an ease move through her. "Well, I finished college in three years and then started medical school. I was in my third year when they were in an accident. They were coming back from Gatlinburg, and it was icy. No one's fault. Just one of those moments in life that changes everything. I was devastated but had to bury my grief at the same time that I had to bury them."

She sighed and looked down at her hands resting on the table. The words were so casual, almost as though she was speaking of someone else. Slowly shaking her head, she lifted her gaze to find him staring. A look of sympathy but not pity filled his eyes, and she appreciated that he remained quiet, not trying to fill the void with meaningless platitudes. "Of course, I know that's not a very emotionally healthy way to deal with grief, but I simply functioned on autopilot."

She continued to hold his gaze, and the comforting concern she observed in his eyes warmed her. "So I came home and dealt with the funeral, grateful that my parents had their affairs in order. I arranged to sell their house, auctioning off the contents I didn't need and moving the items I wanted to keep into a storage facility until I had a place of my own."

"I'm so fuckin' sorry, Lori." His voice was rough, scraping past the layer of fluff she used to cover the emotions. "I would've been overseas at the time, so even if Mom had told me, I'm afraid it wouldn't have given me a chance to get home."

She jerked lightly, shaking her head. "Oh, Hop. I wouldn't have expected you to come home. The funeral was a simple affair at their church with mostly people who knew them, not me. I did a piss-poor job of keeping up with anyone from high school. I was never very good with social media. After the first year of college, I kind of gave it up. Plus, besides a few girlfriends, you were the only person I cared about from high school." She scrunched her nose, casting her mind back. "At the time of their death, I wasn't in touch with anybody from high school."

"It might surprise you to hear that I was the same," he admitted. "Between football practice, games, my classes, and the mandatory tutoring for the team, I just didn't have time to post on social media about what I was doing after my freshman year."

She remembered that after they'd exchanged a few emails, their contact had slowed. She was busy with extra classes and knew his life was also full. The posts from his freshman year had shown him with his new buddies and at functions with his arm usually around a variety of cute blondes in tight dresses. At the time, she'd told herself that it didn't matter since they were just friends. But the truth was, it solidified in her mind that she and Hop would never be more than high school friends, destined to fall into the category of "that person I vaguely remember."

Pushing those thoughts down, she pressed onward. "I know. I would sometimes look at other people's posts, and everybody was drinking, laughing, pledging a sorority, or doing whatever it was that made them look special and amazing. I was just trying to get through college as fast as I could to start medical school. Once I was in medical school, everything else fell away except that goal." She sighed, the air between them as heavy as her heart. "Of course, if I'd known that my parents were going to be… taken away from me, then I would've spent more weekends coming home."

Hop leaned forward, placed his hand on her arm, and her gaze dropped to their connection. "You can't think about that, Lori. I used to worry about something happening to my family before I would go out on missions. Then I had a captain who once told me that if I can't do anything about the worry and can't change things, then spending time fretting about what might happen wasn't doing me any good and could put my whole team at risk. He said to basically shut that shit down."

Her lips curved upward slightly, a little snort slipping out. "Shut that shit down. Words to live by. Sounds like a good message to embroider on a throw pillow for my sofa." They both barked out laughter, the fog of heavy conversation lifting slightly.

She glanced again at his large hand on her much

smaller arm, unable to deny the continued warmth that spread throughout her at the simple touch. Suddenly uncertain what else to say, she couldn't help but notice the way his intense gaze stayed on her face. She swallowed heavily as her gaze dropped to his lips. His perfect, full, luscious lips.

"Here you go, folks!"

They jumped apart, an almost-guilty blush covering her face as the server set their plates in front of them. As the woman bustled away, they looked up at each other, their smiles spreading.

Blowing out a breath, she forced her eyes to take in their plates and gushed, "This looks great."

"Yeah... yeah, it does."

Looking up at the sound of his strangled voice, she found his gaze still on her. The noise of the diner faded away, and for a few seconds, she was transported back to adolescence, sitting near him at his parents' table, wishing they were more than just friends. *Jesus, I'm an adult... not some teenager!* Jolting back to the present, she picked up her cheeseburger and took a big bite, sure that it would take her mind off his mouth. As he took a bite of his, she watched him chew and swallow, discovering that nothing seemed to keep her mind off him.

They concentrated on eating for several minutes before finally chatting again. Sopping a french fry in ketchup, she popped it into her mouth and chewed. "Anyway, to finish what you'd asked, coming back here just wasn't in my plans without my parents around anymore. The house sold quickly. I went back to school and buried my grief by pushing myself academically."

Shrugging, she admitted, "Again, probably not the most emotionally healthy way to deal, but it worked for a while. I entered counseling a year later, and that made all the difference. I wanted to get away, so I accepted a residency in El Paso."

"El Paso? Jesus, you did go to the other side of the country, didn't you?"

Lifting a brow, she quipped, "This coming from someone who lives and works in California!"

"Touché." He laughed, finishing his burger.

"Anyway, I stayed in El Paso, got in with a hospital, got married—"

"Married!"

She noted his gaze dropped to her ring finger—her plain, bare, unadorned ring finger. "Yes... married.... and divorced," she proclaimed, each word punctuated.

"Whoa, I'm sorry," he said, his hand landing on her arm again.

His expression held another emotion, but she couldn't identify it.

She hefted her shoulders. "I married too soon after my parents' deaths. It was stupid, really. We met shortly after I moved to El Paso. Dated for a little while, and it's not like he changed after we got married. The signs were all there, but I ignored them. He loved the idea of a *power couple*. That we'd eventually become a physician duo who would command attention at a large hospital. Then I started working with women's clinics for patients who had little money and no insurance. The poor deserve to have quality medical care, deliver babies safely, and have gynecological cancer screenings like anyone else."

"And he didn't like that?" Hop's incredulity was etched on his face.

Lori snorted lightly. "God, no. He hated it. We argued. Constantly. I think he was truly shocked that I wouldn't change the scope of my practice. And then the final straw? I was invited to be part of a Red Cross international team of physicians for an area that had lost hospitals and medical care due to a natural disaster." She held Hop's gaze, seeing the unasked question in his eyes. "My husband *forbade* me to accept the position."

"Shit," he breathed, eyes wide. "What happened?"

"He became my *ex*-husband."

A second passed before Hop threw his head back, roaring out with laughter. "Holy shit, Lori. You go, girl!"

Now it was her turn to laugh, realizing she hadn't let go and laughed about her ex in... well, ever. And it felt great. A flashback hit her squarely in the chest. When she first began tutoring Hop, she'd assumed he might be stuck-up since he was part of the teenage *it* crowd. But, soon, they were able to share secret jokes and laugh at the antics of the truly stuck-up ones.

As their mirth slowed, she toyed with her napkin wanting to turn the conversation back to learning more about him. "You've still got so much family here. Do you come back often?"

His smile lingered for a few seconds before slowly dropping as he shook his head. "My family is amazing, but I don't get back very often. Between work and travel, it never seems like there are enough hours in the day. But we're all close and stay in touch."

"It was nice to see your parents and your sister. I'd forgotten how many aunts and uncles and cousins you have."

"I've got like twenty aunts and uncles and a jillion cousins. I can't even keep them all straight. Of course, a lot of them left the area, but there are still enough Hopkins and Wilsons here in the hometown to go around." A slight grimace crossed his face.

"What are you thinking?"

"Sorry, Lori, but I remember that other than your parents, I didn't think you had any relatives here."

"No, I didn't. My grandparents passed, and I have no siblings. That's why it was easier to leave after they died. I miss them but not necessarily this place. This is no longer home… just a place of remembrance."

They were silent for a moment, but she pushed past the solemnity of the subject. "Until this trip, and I actually walked into the high school. Talk about a blast from the past! I walked down the science wing and remembered how we became friends." She shook her head. "I can't believe I didn't recognize you as the pilot."

"As the doctor, I would've expected you to be focused on your patients, so I don't take offense that you didn't notice me."

"Oh, I noticed you, but more in the *wow, he's a really good-looking guy*, not in the *oh, I once knew him* way."

Hop laughed again, and the sound of his mirth reverberated through her. And she remembered how often he laughed and how much she loved to make him laugh.

"Hell, Lori, I like that description!"

"I'm sure you do!" She rolled her eyes, shaking her head.

He sobered slightly. "I noticed you, too, and then got a look at your eyes and couldn't believe it might be you."

She smiled at his admission, and they finished their food, slurping down the last of their strawberry milkshakes. Their conversation had been so easy, and now that their plates were clean, she hated for the evening to end. It had been a long time since she'd had such a pleasant time just talking to someone. And talking with someone who'd known her family, her hometown, and her past. "It was always easy with you." Seeing his tilted head, she realized the need for clarification was evident. "I remember how nice it was to just sit and talk with you."

He held her gaze for a long, silent moment, then nodded, his lips curving upward, more on one side giving his smile a bit of a quirk. Finally, he broke eye contact, glanced around, and then said, "I know the diner looks like they're ready to kick us out, but I don't want the evening to end. It feels nice just to be with you."

She nodded, his smile sending tingles throughout her body as though each nerve was electrified, and her own smile curved her lips. "I was just thinking the same thing." She hesitated, wondering if the idea that had just popped into her head made sense but decided it didn't matter. Before she lost her nerve, she inclined her head out the window toward the hotel across the street. "How would you like to come over? I've got some beer in the mini-fridge." She hoped her voice sounded nonchalant but felt sure he could read her like a book. And the story would be of the confident woman asking a man back to her hotel room, while underneath was the quiet girl who once loved spending time with the gorgeous boy who'd become her friend.

He'd turned to look out the window, and her heart pounded in her chest. Just when she expected him to make an excuse, a smile started slowly and then spread across his face. As big and muscular as he was, no one would mistake him for anything other than *all man*, yet when he grinned, there was a boyish expression on his face that she remembered so well.

"Lori, darlin', I can't think of anything I'd rather do more."

He tossed a wad of bills onto the table quickly as she let out a breath. She'd started to offer to pay, then realized it would be a waste of time. Glad she could provide beer once they got into her room, she allowed him to gently tug her upward from the booth and loved the feel of his hand on her lower back as they walked out of the diner, both waving to the server who'd just made a huge tip.

Not wanting to leave their vehicles in the diner parking lot, they drove across the street, where she parked near her room, secretly smiling as he parked next to her. She had no idea what the evening might bring— continuing to catch up with an old friend, chatting about plans for the future, or maybe an evening's recreation with a good man who she had no doubt could rock her world for a night. She'd be satisfied with any of those options, but the thought of the last one made her glad she'd showered and shaved before leaving her hotel earlier.

6

Hop was truthful when he'd told Lori that he didn't want the evening to end, but getting invited to her hotel room wasn't what he expected. It was more. More time to be with someone who'd meant a great deal to him many years ago. More time to be with the woman she'd become. More time to find out about her life. And he couldn't deny that he'd tried not to stare at her lips all evening but had failed miserably. The pretty teenage girl who'd befriended him had become a beautiful, accomplished woman, and he damn sure wasn't finished spending time getting to know her now.

It wasn't hard to notice the lack of security as he followed her inside but was glad to see that the room had been renovated. New carpet covered the floor, the walls were freshly painted, and a glance into the bathroom showed that it was modernly updated. The bed was made, but an open suitcase with clothes spilling out sat in the corner.

Lori hung up her jacket then glanced at the messy

suitcase and chuckled. "Sorry, I wasn't expecting company."

For some reason, knowing she'd been alone in the room with no one else coming over pleased him. "So I take it you haven't been throwing any keggers between rescue missions," he joked.

She rolled her eyes as she walked over to the fridge. "I'm afraid I'm about as social now as I was in high school. A couple of good friends, and that's it. I have little time for anything else, I'm afraid."

She bent over to snag the two beer bottles, and he couldn't help but stare at the stretched denim over her perfect ass. Blowing out a breath, he tried to pull his mind out of the gutter. *This is Lori. And I'm not some horny teenager.* Although, in honesty, being around her brought back not only memories but all sorts of feelings. Feelings that in high school had confused him, but as an adult, he processed them for what they were, even if the results surprised him and caught him off guard.

The reality was that he'd cared a great deal for her in high school and not just as a friend. He fantasized plenty of times and even wondered what it might be like to date her. But she was Lori, his tutor, and friend. And the last thing he wanted to do was cross a line with her that would blur their relationship and possibly ruin it. So he'd kept his hands to himself and reveled in their friendship. Something he was proud of for a horny teenage boy who didn't often restrain himself.

"Are you okay?"

Jerking, he looked up to see her standing close to him, her brow furrowed and a beer held in each hand.

"Yeah, yeah. Sorry, I guess my mind just went down memory lane once again."

She chuckled as she walked toward him, holding out a beer. "That can easily happen here. I've suffered that malady several times in the past couple of days."

He reached for the bottle, and his fingers glided over hers, sending an electric tingle and warmth up his arm that he hadn't felt with another woman. His gaze moved from their connection up to her eyes, seeing her pupils dilate slightly, and he knew that she felt it as well. Her mouth grabbed his attention, and the blood rushed south. *Shit.* Needing to divert her attention from the bulge behind his zipper, he cleared his throat and glanced around. Noting only one small chair at a minuscule table, he inclined his head to the other side of the room. "Why don't you sit on the bed and get comfortable." He turned to drag the single chair closer, then sat and propped his feet up on the mattress, giving her room to pile pillows against the headboard before she leaned back. With both her legs stretched out, their feet were close to touching.

"I saw our chemistry teacher, Mr. Fox, the other day," he admitted after taking a swig of beer. "Honestly, that's what made me think of you before I even saw you."

A smile brightened her already beautiful face. "Do you remember how surprised he was when you passed that first test after we started studying together?"

Snorting, he nodded. "I'm surprised he didn't send me to the office assuming that I'd cheated!"

She shook her head emphatically. "No, no. He

suggested tutoring, and I think he was very impressed with you!"

"Who knew that would be the start of a great friendship?" He leaned forward, lifting his beer bottle in a salute.

She clinked the neck of her bottle to his beer, and then he watched as she lifted her chin to take a swig, exposing her pale throat. He watched her swallow, strangely thinking how sexy the movement looked. She dropped her chin and smiled back at him. "We had a lot of fun, didn't we?"

A strange twinge hit the left side of his chest. They hadn't started their tutoring-turned-friendship until junior year, but by the time they graduated, he counted her as one of his best friends. "Yeah, we did, Lori."

"You know, the other girls were jealous. They couldn't stand that I had any of your time and attention and couldn't believe we were just friends."

"God, I know what you mean. I used to get ribbed all the time by some of my teammates because they couldn't believe we weren't… well, you know." His face warmed as he tried to think of a polite description.

She barked out a laugh. "I'm an OB/GYN. I'm pretty sure I know what goes on between men and women. It's okay to say sex. Or banging. Or fucking. Or—"

"I get it! I get it!" He reared back as though horrified to hear what she was saying, then couldn't help but begin chuckling as well. "Jesus, I'd forgotten how easy it was to be with you."

She bit her bottom lip, a slight smile still gracing her face, and he wanted to be the one to bite her lip instead.

So focused on her face, he almost missed her next question.

"Did you ever decide to settle on one woman, or are you still delighting the masses?"

A groan erupted from deep within his chest. "Delighting the masses? Never heard it put that way." Hefting his shoulders, he shrugged. "I guess that's one way to describe not making a commitment. But I assure you, there's not a lot of mass to the masses anymore."

"Oh, then you're more discerning than in high school?"

"Hell, Lori, you know what it's like in high school. Or even college! An adolescent male only thinks of one thing, and that's sex."

She wrinkled her nose. "But that's what's so weird. The other girls weren't jealous of each other, and you were actually banging more than one. But they were envious of me."

"Because you had what they didn't." Seeing her chin jerk back as her face filled with a curious stare, he continued. "They had my fleeting attention. You had all my attention."

"All?"

"Oh, yeah. I told you what adolescent males think about. So I had that, plus a good friend."

She lifted her brows. "Really? So that's what you were thinking when you and I were hanging out?"

Realizing she'd caught him in his own web of talking too much, he groaned again as he leaned back and stared at the ceiling for a moment. Then dropping his chin, he nodded as he held her gaze. "Yeah, even with you, Lori, I thought about sex. I also thought about asking you on a date, kissing you senseless, and taking you to prom."

Eyes wide, she dropped her mouth open. "So I guess the big question is, why didn't you?"

"Seriously? I was terrified it could ruin everything."

He had no idea what her response would be, but as she continued to stare at him, she nodded slowly. "Yeah, I get that. I crushed hard on you in high school, Hop. I was secretly nervous when Mr. Fox suggested that I tutor you, just knowing I would get to spend some time alone with you. But then, the more we talked and the closer we got, I discovered the guy behind the cocky persona you projected to everyone. I mean, you were definitely confident, but you let me get to really know you. It was just nice having you as a friend. And I figured the crush was one-sided anyway."

He lifted his legs from the bed and plopped his feet onto the floor. Leaning forward, he rested his forearms on his knees, still staring intently at her face. *Guileless. She was always so fucking honest. One of the things I loved about her.* "I assure you the feelings were not one-sided, Lori. Who knows, maybe we should've acted on them."

The air in the room thickened, and he watched her breathing change, knowing she could feel the emotions and memories churning around them. But she shook her head slowly, and he wondered what she would say.

"I think it's better that we didn't act on those feelings, Hop. I just don't think either of us would've had the maturity in high school to deal with those emotions and not fuck them up." She snorted, still shaking her head. "Fucking them up by fucking, I guess that's what I mean. So even though I felt as though I had unrequited love for my only guy friend, at least I knew you were in my life. And that was worth everything to me. I just wish I'd been a better friend when we went off to college. I should have stayed in touch."

"To the first part of what you said, I agree. I certainly didn't have the emotional maturity to handle feelings very well and would definitely have fucked things up with our friendship. But with the second part, I disagree. It wasn't that you weren't a good friend when we went off to college. Our lives went in different directions. We were taking different paths. But I am sorry I wasn't around when you needed me."

Now she leaned forward, scooting closer to the edge of the bed and letting her legs hang off, dangling them next to his. "And now, all these years later..."

The earth's spinning seemed to slow as they stared, barely breathing. He sucked in a deep breath and said, "I'd give anything to know what it was like to kiss you."

She blinked, and his heart stuttered. *Shit! Why the fuck did I admit that?* He opened his mouth to backtrack, to laugh, to make a joke. Anything to ease the thick silence that filled the room, blanketing them. But before he had a chance, she moved quicker than he could have imagined.

Leaning forward, she grabbed the front of his shirt with her fists and jerked him toward her. He went willingly, allowing her to pull him out of the chair, not wanting her to hurt herself with the effort. Uncertain if she was getting ready to kick him out, his brain barely had time to catch up when her lips landed on his.

The air that had felt thick suddenly crackled with electricity. The instant tingling as she pressed her body close to his short-circuited his ability to think rationally. His entire brain focused on her lips, his lips, and nothing else.

She fell backward, still clutching his shirt, and he toppled on top of her, barely keeping his weight from crushing her as he bent his arms and pressed his elbows into the mattress on either side of her. Her legs opened, and she immediately wrapped them around his waist, resting her heels against his ass. In this position, his erect cock was nestled right against her core. Warm, comforting, and mind-blowing all at the same time. Familiar, even though he'd never experienced it with her before. *Christ— it felt like coming home.*

Their mouths stayed sealed while landing on the bed, something he considered a true feat. That was the last coherent thought he had while giving over to the sensations rocketing through his body. His blood hummed. His cock swelled even more. There was a ringing in his ears. Warmth infused his already overheated skin. A delicate floral scent from her hair filled his nostrils. His hands cupped her face, the petal-soft skin meeting his rough fingertips before his fingers tangled in her silky tresses.

They twisted their heads, desperate for the perfect angle as their tongues delved deeply—tangling, exploring, tasting. She grasped the material of his shirt, trying to pull it upward. As he slid one hand down to slip underneath her shirt, allowing his fingertips to trail across her soft skin, she dug her short fingernails into his back. He didn't care if she broke skin— he'd wear the marks as a badge of honor as well as pleasure.

She rolled, catching him off guard so that he was now under and she was on top. Hell, he didn't care, loving the feel of her pelvis grinding against his aching cock. She jerked upward, her legs straddling him, and her chest heaved just as he groaned at their mouths losing contact.

"Please tell me you have a condom," she begged.

Once more, his brain short-circuited, taking a moment to catch up to her request. "Yeah... yeah, I do."

Her smile was brilliant as it beamed down, and for a second, he thought he could live happily just with the glow from her face. Then she whipped her T-shirt over her head and had her bra off faster than he could've managed. Considering he'd had more than enough experience with removing bras, her quick movements shocked the shit out of him. Her breasts were full with dusty-rose nipples that begged to be sucked. He stared, his hands digging into her waist as his mind caught up to what his eyes were seeing. "Damn, Lori babe."

She grinned, her pale-blue eyes sparkling in the dim illumination of the old lamp sitting on the nightstand.

He flipped her back underneath him and mimicked her movements, his T-shirt now tossed behind him. Pressing his chest to hers to rekindle their kiss, he felt her naked breasts and hard nipples against his skin, which had his cock fighting to break away from the confines of his jeans.

Kissing had always been something he'd preserved for a girlfriend, not that he'd had many of those. In truth, growing up in a loving family, he'd always seen his parents kiss each other good morning, goodbye, or just for fun. Same with his grandparents, aunts, and uncles. Kissing was associated with someone you cared about, not a fuck buddy, and sure as hell, not a one-night stand.

But kissing Lori had become as important as taking his next breath. In fact, if anyone asked him if he'd rather kiss her or breathe—hands down, the answer would be to kiss her.

Finally, the desire to taste more of her body, his lips slid away from hers but stayed in contact with her pale, soft skin as he nuzzled his way over her cheek, around her jaw, down her neck, to her fluttering pulse. Sucking gently, he shifted his body as his mouth continued its trail over her chest and circled her breasts before pulling a taut nipple deeply. The moan that erupted from her nearly undid him, but he was determined not to rush. He wanted to discover her woman's body the way he always wanted to discover her as an adolescent.

Moving slowly, he pressed his cock against her core, hating the material that separated them. After giving each breast equal attention, his hands moved to the waistband of her jeans, but he halted, peering down into her eyes, feeling as though he could see into her soul. He hesitated, giving control to her even though his cock wanted to demand its own time and attention.

Their gazes locked, unspoken words and questions, longing and desires, fears and excitement moving between them, communicating everything with just a look. *Please, just say it, babe.* Without her telling him what she wanted, he wouldn't take it further.

She nodded and smiled. "I want you, Hop. I suppose I want you because it was never something I could have done when I first met you. But it's also because of the man you are now. You don't have to worry about me, though. I'm not clingy. This is tonight only. I know that. You know that. Tomorrow we go our separate ways, back to our lives and work. But if all I can have is tonight, I'd like to make it last, and I'd like to make it memorable."

Time stood still as they continued to stare into each other's eyes, the air in the room both heavy and hard to drag into his lungs and light as though no worries could pass between them.

He nodded slowly, unable to keep the smile from curving his lips. "I couldn't have said it better. Tonight can be for the friendship we had many years ago and who we are now, meeting again. But if you think you're getting away from me without giving me your phone number..." He leaned down, dragging his tongue over her lips and sweeping it through her mouth before lifting again. "Then you're crazy."

She laughed, her breasts moving slightly with her mirth as her hands glided over his biceps and clutched his shoulders again. "Agreed. Now, how about showing me what you've got!"

"Your wish is my command. Hell, babe, your command is my pleasure!"

7

When Lori decided to stop at the cemetery, she'd thought it would be a quick visit and then back to her motel alone. Meeting Hop was a complete surprise. Then accepting his offer to get drinks at the bar and to spend time with him and his family had never crossed her imagination.

Walking down memory lane at the diner had also never entered her mind as being in the realm of possibility. Inviting him back to her hotel? Loving their conversation? Surreal. She felt as though she'd fallen down the rabbit hole into Wonderland.

But now, as he looked down at her, his heated gaze firing off all her senses, she once again thought about pinching her arm to see if it was real. She was nowhere near the adolescent girl she'd been many years before, but she couldn't help but grin at the idea that she had a night to enjoy the adult Hop.

He scooted off the bed, and while he shrugged down

his pants and boxers, she did the same with her jeans and panties. Her gaze landed on his erection, and she sucked in a quick breath. No doubt about it—he was well endowed. More than any man she'd been with. Glancing up, she was sure he'd have a cocky, *I-know-what-you're-admiring* expression on his face, but instead, his gaze was roving over her now naked body, appreciation gleaming in his eyes.

A drop of pre-cum was on the tip of his cock, and without hesitation, she leaned forward, licking him.

"God, almighty," he groaned, his hands clutching her head, his fingers slightly fisting her hair. She moved to take him all into her mouth, but he pulled her back. "No, babe. You do that, and I'll come too soon. I want to make this last."

Sliding her mouth from around the tip, she looked up and grinned. He dropped to his knees, his face now between her legs. His tongue darted out to lick her slick folds. A gasp left her lips as she fisted the sheets. *Shit... it's been a while... talk about coming too soon.* He added in his finger, sucked her sensitive nub, and continued the assault on her senses until she thought she'd fly off the bed when her orgasm finally rocked her. When the inner quivering eased, he stood, towering over her. Chest heaving, she dragged in oxygen as her gaze roved over his delicious body.

His muscles were model-worthy and well-defined, and she had no doubt they were honed from hard work, not just a gym. A lighthouse tattoo covered his shoulder, making her want to trace it with her tongue as well as her fingers. His biceps were massive, and she could have sworn that swooning was a real thing at the sight of his arms. She used to stare at him in high school, imagining what it would feel like to be embraced by him, but she never thought she'd have the opportunity to find out. Now, she knew he was about to ruin her for any other man—and didn't care.

He reached down to his jeans and jerked out his wallet. Sliding out two condoms, he tossed one onto the mattress and ripped open the remaining foil packet. Rolling it over his erection, he climbed back onto the bed, his hips between her spread legs.

Her gaze never wavered from his as he entered her in one swift thrust. She gasped at the fullness, then immediately felt her body surround him, each nerve tingling.

"You okay, babe?" he asked, the words torn from deep inside his chest.

With her fingers digging into his biceps, she barely managed to nod, her focus not only on his cock but on the way his biceps bulged as he held his weight off her chest. *Just the way I imagined.* "Oh yeah. I'm more than okay."

With that, he pressed forward, each thrust feeling as though it slid farther than the one before. She gave herself over to the combination of sensations. Friction. Electricity. The sounds of their bodies slapping together. The bounce of her breasts. The tightness of his arms as he held his chest over her. The hard muscles of his ass underneath her heels. The hiss of air that slipped between his clenched teeth.

She was surprised at how quickly her body tightened in readiness of her release. Usually, it took more. More foreplay. More clit stimulation. But Hop had her body firing on all cylinders. He was skillful, playing her body like a fine-tuned instrument. Hard, fast strokes that sparked the friction she craved, then long, slow ones where his cock dragged over her clit as she began to fall apart.

"Are you there? You close?" he grunted, his words sounding pained as though it took all his effort to hold back. His face was red, his jaw tight. The veins in his neck were standing out in stark relief.

"Yes!"

The word had barely left her mouth when the coil inside sprang loose, and she felt the inner vibrations as she clenched around his cock. With her head thrown back, she cried out her orgasm as he kept his eyes on her and roared through his own.

He continued to pump until she felt sure every drop must've left his body. He lowered himself onto her as he rolled, and they lay side by side, arms around each other, legs tangled, and his cock still deep inside as they gasped for breath.

"Holy shit, woman," he moaned. "I don't think I've ever come so hard in my life."

Those had been words she'd read in the occasional romance novel she'd found time to devour but hadn't really thought it was something a man might feel. "I assume that's a compliment, right?"

"Hell, yeah. I thought my head was going to explode, and I'm talking about the one on my neck, not my dick, which fuckin' did explode."

She laughed, then snorted as she could still feel him deep inside her. The movement of her mirth seemed to squeeze him even more as he groaned once again. "Would you believe me if I said I saw stars?"

"Lori, I'd believe anything you told me 'cause I'd know if it was coming from you, it was real. And if you did see stars, then I might have to get cocky over that."

She smiled as her hands glided over the satin warmth of his skin, feeling the steel of his muscles underneath. "God, you're beautiful."

"That's my line, babe," he murmured, burying his face in her neck. "And thank God I've got another condom because there's no way we're stopping after just that."

She wiggled slightly. "Speaking of condoms, I really hate to kick you out of bed and especially out of me, but you'd better deal with that."

"I know, I know," he groaned. "Usually, I take care of it right away, but damn, I don't think my cock wants to leave your body."

"Well, tell him that as soon as you take care of it, you can come back and get reacquainted with my body."

He cupped her jaw and peered into her eyes, and she sighed, remembering that she used to stare into his eyes so often when they were in high school, whether studying, telling jokes, or just talking. But now, holding his gaze after rocking each other's worlds was pretty damn amazing.

He finally slid his cock from her channel and rolled to the edge of the bed. He stalked into the bathroom, and she heard the toilet flush and the water running in the sink. Stretching, she smiled at the delicious ache between her legs.

She rolled to her side and propped her head up on her hand with her elbow bent. Watching as he walked out of the bathroom, she admired his obvious comfort with nudity. Damn, with his cock still at half mast, she admired his nudity, as well.

"See anything you like?" His lips quirked up on one side.

Lifting a brow, she swept her free hand down along her body and threw back, "Do you?"

"Hell, yeah."

She laughed and nodded. "Me, too. I thought you were a really cute teenager, but holy moly, Hop. As a fully grown man…" She cut her eyes down to his cock, noting it was erect again. "And I do mean a *fully grown man*, you are gorgeous."

"Fuck, Lori," he growled, stalking closer.

"That's the idea," she quipped, then watched as he climbed back onto the bed after rolling on the remaining condom.

"You're the one who's gone from pretty to knockout."

"If that's the last condom, let's make it count."

His face scrunched in frustration. "One thing about this town is that streets still roll up by midnight. But I could probably find an all-night market around here somewhere."

"I'd be afraid the condoms would be past their expiration date!" She laughed. "I'm on birth control but never take chances."

He settled between her thighs again, his head lowering until his lips were a whisper away from hers. "Then we'll just make this count, won't we, babe?"

He didn't give her a chance to answer, but it didn't matter as soon as his mouth sealed over hers and his hips thrust his cock deep inside. Coherent thoughts were nonexistent as she gave over to the tingling, electrical current that moved between their bodies, fusing them together.

When they finally tucked in for sleep, they lay wrapped around each other, both having confessed that they didn't want the night to end alone. With her cheek pressed against the warm muscles of his chest, she smiled. What she'd just shared with Hop would never be more than one night, but it was a night she'd remember and cherish forever.

The following morning dawned bright and sunny, all traces of the previous storm clouds long gone. Lori had woken in Hop's arms, and shimmying down his body, she wrapped her lips around his morning wood. Between her mouth and hand, she managed to work all of his impressive length.

"God, what a way to wake up." The words were dragged from his chest as his hands fisted in her bed head. Just before he came, he reached down to pull her up. "I'm gonna come."

She shook her head and kept going, working his shaft until he groaned again, this time louder and longer as she sucked through his release. Looking up, she licked her lips while grinning. It struck her that she'd had more fun with Hop than with any other man she'd been with. *Not that there'd been many*, she thought wryly. A few in college. Her husband appreciated perfunctory vanilla sex, and at the time, that was fine with her. She wasn't into random sex but had had a couple of lovers over the past few years, and while the relationships had ended amiably, she always felt lacking.

She had no problem admitting she was a romantic. *I want what my parents had... what Hop's parents have.* Love, marriage, children, family. But she certainly had chosen poorly with her first husband, and now looking up at the expression of absolute pleasure on Hop's face, it struck her that she'd love to see that look every day. Blinking, she shook her head slightly to dislodge the thought that had bolted through her. *Jesus, girl, get a grip. He's an old friend. This is just sex with an old high school friend.*

"You okay down there?"

She blinked again, then focused on his gaze staring at her. "Yeah, yeah... just taking in the view."

He bolted upward while laughing, and before she knew what was happening, he'd flipped her, tossed her legs over his shoulders, and returned the morning favor in full. With his lips, tongue, and fingers working magic, she soon cried out her release as well.

They rose from the bed, tired but sated, both with grins on their faces, and she wondered what would happen now. She hated goodbyes and, in her line of work, said them often.

As though reading her mind, Hop said, "I can't believe it's goodbye already." He held her close, their naked bodies pressed tightly.

He nuzzled her neck, and she moaned while tilting her head to give him greater access. "I know. But it's been great to reconnect."

"And what a reconnection it was!" He leaned back, peered into her eyes, and cupped her face with his hand. "I've just got to run over this morning to say goodbye to my parents and grab my bag. Then I'm heading to the airport where my plane is waiting. If you wanna come with me, then I can take you to the airport."

It was on the tip of her tongue to agree. Even though she'd just seen his parents yesterday, it would be nice to see them again. She wasn't a dirty secret to keep, but since nothing would be continuing between her and Hop, it didn't seem fair for his parents to think that was a possibility. Reaching up, she wrapped her hands around his arm that was holding her tight and squeezed. "As much as I hate for our time together to be over, I think it's best if you go to your parents' house alone."

If she thought he was going to argue, he didn't. Instead, he nodded slowly. "You're probably right. My mom always thought you were perfect, and if she saw us together, she'd be making plans."

A flash of *making plans* caused her breath to hitch, but she cleared her throat, hoping to cover the initial sound.

"I'd still like to take you to the airport. You stay and get showered and dressed, and ready to check out. I'll go to my parents' and then get my cousin to drop me off here. Then we can take your rental to the airport."

Her smile slipped out unbidden as she nodded her agreement. With another quick kiss, he pulled on his discarded clothes and headed out the door.

Once out of the shower, she swiped her hand over the condensation on the mirror and stared at her reflection. She looked the same. Same dark hair, kept long so she could unceremoniously pull it back when needed. Same face that her ex had often mentioned would be enhanced with more makeup. Same body, but now it hummed with the appreciation of good loving from a man who knew what the hell he was doing. The same, yet something felt different. More alive. More vibrant. More fun. *And now it's over. But that's okay... I have a career... people who need me. I get to travel and care for others.* All that was true, but it also left little time for a relationship. Sighing, she turned away from the mirror, dried off quickly, and then dressed.

Two hours later, as she stood by the ticket gate at the airport, she held his gaze as his arms encircled her, pulling her close. They kissed again, this time with a touch of sadness from her, and she wondered if he felt the same. *Longing for what would never be is dangerous.* "Listen, if you're ever in El Paso—"

His arms tightened. "Fuck that, Lori. I'm not waiting until I happen to be in El Paso to check in with you. We've got each other's phone numbers. We've got each other's emails. I don't want to lose having you in my life again."

"Agreed," she said, wondering if he could tell how much the past day had come to mean to her. She continued to hold his gaze for another moment, neither speaking while volumes were being written by their eyes. She'd never had a night like last night. With Hop, everything felt like more. Perhaps it was the connection from long ago that had rekindled the adolescent feelings she once had. Maybe, it was just that he was the most handsome man she'd ever been around, and their sexual energy radiated all around. But he had a life, and so did she, and now it was time to get back to reality.

"For the record, Lori, I wouldn't mind making plans with you. At least plans that say we'll get together again as soon as we can."

Those words scored through her, finding them both frightening and intoxicating at the same time. "I never know when I'm gonna get called somewhere," she said. "But I promise to stay in contact, and we can figure something out."

He pulled her close, and she wrapped her arms around his neck, tilting her head for the kiss she knew was coming. He didn't disappoint, and a few seconds later, his mouth sealed over hers, his tongue delving through her warmth, their bodies plastered to each other. She knew it was goodbye even though she tried to tell her heart it was only farewell. And when they finally separated, and she walked through the security line, tears threatened and she had to swallow past the lump in her throat. Turning, she kept him in her sight until the last second.

A heaviness filled her heart as she walked toward her gate. The success of her Red Cross mission and the safety of the mothers and babies she'd been with had always been enough to make a mission memorable but now took a back seat to the new memories she had of her night with Hop.

8

"Damn, man, I can't live where it's that cold!" Leo said, shaking his head.

Hop grinned as he landed his plane, chuckling at the jokes from Dolby, Leo, and Chris from the passenger seats.

The trio of Keepers he was transporting had spent time in Alaska, working a case with the DEA dealing with drug runners using fishing boats. The mission was successful and completed just in time for Hop to fly in to pick them up a week after getting back from Tennessee. Now, on their way back to California, their moods and spirits were high.

"I gotta agree," he said. He'd been all over the world but preferred warmer weather over the bitter cold.

"So…" Leo began, "Natalie told me that you came back from Tennessee with a big ole smile on your face."

"No one lost their lives in the flood. I got to see my family and caught up with some old friends. I figure that's reason enough for a big smile."

"Well…" Chris began, "Stella seemed to think it was because you hooked up with one of those old friends."

"Don't your women have anything better to do than gossip about me?" he grumbled.

"When we're home, we can keep 'em busy. But we've been gone the last couple of weeks, so they've had to search for gossip wherever they could find it," Leo quipped, stretching his long frame as they coasted to the hangar.

"I'll tell Natalie that you're accusing her of being a gossip just because you're not around like she doesn't have anything else better to do. She'll have your balls in her grip before you can scream," Hop groused.

"Damn, man, you're right," Leo agreed, his smile immediately dropping.

"Hell, now you've got me curious 'cause I don't have a woman to keep me up on the gossip," Dolby tossed out.

Knowing he'd have to give them something, or they'd make up shit just to mess with him, he said, "I just had a good time meeting up with an old friend. She works for the Red Cross—"

"She? So was it a meetup or a hookup?"

"Not gonna kiss and tell—"

"Hmmm, there was kissing." Dolby laughed.

"Fuck, you guys *are* worse than the women."

"I think this *friend* has got you tied up in knots. You're usually more cavalier about your conquests," Dolby pushed.

"She's not a conquest," he growled, bringing the plane

to a stop once inside the hangar. Realizing with every word he spoke, he was simply giving away more of his feelings, he sighed and scrubbed his hand over his head. Glancing at the other Keepers, he admitted, "In truth, she was an old friend from high school but not an old girlfriend. Just a friend who happened to be a girl. Anyway, she was special then, but we hadn't stayed in touch. She was one of the doctors from the Red Cross who came in, and it was an unexpected surprise to see her. Gotta admit she was even more special now than she was back then."

"So unexpected but not unpleasant."

"Let's just say that we had a really good time catching up. At least now, we have each other's contact information."

"You don't usually go back for a repeat, so that tells me she is special," Leo quipped.

"Yeah, she is." He turned and shot a glare toward Leo. "And I'm not that bad!"

"You wouldn't be the first Keeper to fall for someone on a mission." Chris laughed.

"I didn't fall for her. Well, not like that. I mean, she's wonderful, but... well, she's got her life, and I have mine."

"Why should that matter? Only a couple of us are with women on our team. Everyone else is with someone who has their own career and their own life."

"I mean, she doesn't live around here. And as a Red Cross doctor, she's always traveling."

"You're always traveling, too."

"Yeah, and that's exactly why something like this

wouldn't work out. Anyway, we're better off as just good friends."

"Keep telling yourself that, but from the look on your face—which, by the way, I've never seen that particular look before." Dolby laughed. "I'd say whoever this old friend is, she made quite an impression on you."

They climbed from the plane, and as the others unloaded their equipment, he ran checks over his aircraft to make sure it would be ready for the next time he needed to fly out.

Piling into the SUV he left at the hangar, they drove back to the Lighthouse compound. Their conversations rolled from the missions they had just completed to ones currently being worked on. His mind drifted to Lori, glad that the others had moved on to different topics.

He had decided not to waste any time contacting her after they'd said goodbye at the airport and had texted her that first night they were apart. Since then, they had chatted and texted often, and she'd emailed what her typical schedule looked like unless she was called for an emergency somewhere. For him, he had no regular schedule but told her he'd let her know when he'd be gone, even if he couldn't tell her where he was going.

As he and the Keepers arrived at the compound, it didn't take long for them to debrief with Carson and the others. Bennett was on a security assignment in Arizona. Adam was working with Jeb on the surveillance for a new lab being built several hours away. Natalie was already reviewing the mission Leo had just come from, looking for areas that she could improve for the next time. Abbie and Rick were preparing geometric analyses for an upcoming security mission that Poole was slated for.

The afternoon passed quickly, and Hop turned down offers for drinks at the local bar, wanting to hurry home in case Lori had a chance to call. *It's been less than a week, and I already look forward to hearing her voice.*

Not long ago, he would've found the idea of having spent one night with a woman and then looking forward to something as simple as a phone call ludicrous. But then, it wasn't one night with just *any* woman—this was Lori. And even though they hadn't seen each other in fourteen years, there was an ease and comfort with her that had been lacking with anyone else he'd spent time with.

Even their conversation several nights ago was about people they remembered from high school, teachers they'd had in common, remembering where their lockers had been, studying at both her house and his, and places in town that were still in business. He discovered how nice it was to have a conversation with someone who had a shared sense of history.

He'd barely walked through the door with his sack of Chinese takeout when his phone chimed. Looking down, he grinned widely as he answered. "Hey, Lori girl. How are you?"

"Crazy day, but I'm fine. How was your trip?"

"It was good, but Leo and I decided that we would *not* be moving to Alaska."

She laughed, and the sound reverberated through

him, keeping the grin on his face. "I didn't realize that relocating to Alaska was a possibility."

"It's not, but we were just talking about the cold. It's gorgeous country, and I like to visit, but I sure as fuck can't move that far north."

"I've never been to Alaska," she said. "Maybe I should put it on my bucket list."

"Well, if you decide to go, let me know, and I'll go with you."

"As long as we don't go in the dead of winter, right?"

"Damn straight!" He set the containers on his counter, grabbed a beer from his refrigerator, and pulled the chopsticks from the bag. It struck him that he'd just made hopeful plans to take a vacation with her to Alaska sometime, and that didn't bother him. *Hell, I've never entertained making plans with any woman before.* Lori had wormed her way into his thoughts so quickly without trying, but thinking back to high school, the same thing had happened then.

"Do you remember that winter of our junior year that was so cold?" she asked. "The one when we kept getting snowstorms, and they finally closed the school for a week?"

"You're right. The old mill pond was frozen, and my uncle took me ice fishing. I hated it just because it was so fuckin' cold out there in the early morning." He settled at his kitchen counter, eating and talking, remembering the past and sharing about the last couple of days.

When Mr. Fox suggested tutoring, Hop didn't mind because he wanted to pass the class. And when their teacher suggested Lori, Hop still hadn't minded because she was a nice girl, and he figured spending time with her would be pleasant enough. He knew she wouldn't talk down to him or hold it over his head that he was struggling with chemistry. But almost immediately, her sweet personality and calm manner, her patience, and humor, not to mention her beauty, had made it easier to spend time with her. Within a few days, he didn't care if they got together daily and whether they were studying or not. *And history repeats itself.*

Tonight, they talked longer than they had the other evening on the phone, and he found he wasn't ready to end the conversation even after he finished eating. Putting his leftovers away, he then moved into the living room and propped his feet up on the coffee table. But after an hour, he could hear the fatigue in her voice, and she had already yawned several times. He glanced at the clock, but it was only a little after eight. "You sound like you're ready to fall asleep."

"I was at the clinic late last night and early this morning." She'd explained that she was a relief obstetrician for a group that worked with uninsured women, giving her some stability between her Red Cross callouts. "I have tomorrow off, so if you've got any time, you can call me. I've just got errands to run and an apartment that I need to clean. Although it's so small, it won't take long to accomplish that task."

He'd never asked about where she lived, but hearing it was a small apartment surprised him. He assumed she and her husband had lived in a large house and even divorced, she'd probably stayed or moved into something equally as nice. As he glanced around his own home's living room, he was curious. "Tell me about your place."

A snort followed an eruption of laughter. "I'm not sure what I can tell you. It's a small one-bedroom apartment. I can practically shower, brush my teeth, and pee without moving in my bathroom. It's in a decent complex with a pool that I rarely use, a gym that I think I've been in once, and a grassy courtyard for parties that I've never actually attended."

While her description was amusing, it also struck him that it seemed a bit lonely. "So you don't have any friends at the parties?"

"There's not a lot of time," she admitted. "I guess that's why I never looked for anything larger and certainly not more permanent. El Paso is fine for now, but I don't know that this is where I want to put down roots forever. I'm gone days or weeks at a time and don't want a house where I have to worry about the yard or maintenance. And since the divorce years ago, the friends we had together stayed friends with him but not me. I've discovered there's very little that I really need to be happy."

A myriad of thoughts hit him with what she said. A glimmer of satisfaction that she had no real reason to stay in El Paso. A touch of sadness that she had no reason to put down roots. And a strange longing filled his chest, but the reason eluded him. *Or perhaps, I don't want to think about it because it would make me sound crazy, considering how she fills my thoughts.*

Clearing his throat, he joked, "All the more reason

for you to be able to take a vacation with me to Alaska anytime you want. Hell, it doesn't have to be Alaska. You get a hankering for taking a trip, let me know, and I'll be there with my suitcases packed."

Her laughter rang out, warming his heart as she agreed. "You're on, but I can pack quick and light. Next vacation, we'll figure out something!" As their mirth slowed, she yawned again.

"I'll let you go, Lori girl. Sounds like you need a good night's sleep."

Disconnecting after saying good night, he tossed his phone onto the sofa and grabbed the remote. Finding a game on TV that he wasn't interested in but made good background noise, he dropped the remote next to his phone and leaned back. With his beer in hand, his eyes stayed glued to the television, but his mind was far away on the woman he couldn't stop thinking about… and didn't want to.

Lori disconnected the call and walked into her kitchen, a smile still on her face. In the week that she'd been back in El Paso, she and Hop had begun talking and texting more. In fact, every day except for one day on his mission when they didn't have a chance because of her work schedule as well.

Since the night they'd spent together, he'd invaded her thoughts during the day and her dreams at night. *This is nuts!* She chuckled to herself as she walked through her tiny apartment and flipped off the lights, making her way into the bedroom. But it had been so long since she'd talked to anyone who knew her past. Their hometown. The same childhood memories of schools, friends, and places. Someone who knew and remembered her parents. *Is that all it is? Someone to connect to my past?*

As she climbed into the shower, she continued to ruminate over the question of why Hop had been so easy to talk to and so easy to *keep* talking to. And the only answer she could come up with was that it was just him. The infatuation she'd had with the teenage boy morphed into an adult infatuation with the funny, smart, dedicated, gorgeous, and oh, so sexy man.

After her shower, she climbed into bed and read for a few minutes, trying to settle her mind. As tired as she was, she should have been able to fall asleep immediately, but images of Hop continued to drift through her mind.

After reading the same paragraph three times, she shut down her e-reader and turned off the light next to her bed. She flipped and flopped for several moments, pushed off the covers when her body was too hot, then finally reached over to her nightstand and pulled out her vibrator. It didn't take long for her primed body to come, but it was a poor substitution for the real thing. *Hop has ruined me not only for other men but also for my battery-operated boyfriend!*

Sighing, she closed her eyes and finally drifted to sleep, her dreams filled with memories of the distant past mixed with memories from the previous week and swirled together with strange visions of the future.

9

Two weeks later, Lori had to admit that her conversations with Hop were becoming a highlight of her evenings. They now chatted daily unless he was out of town or she was at the clinic. And last night, he'd mentioned his friends were wondering what was wrong with him, considering he almost never went to the local bar with them anymore.

"You don't have to stay home because of me!" she'd exclaimed while secretly pleased. He'd hastened to add that bars had lost their appeal when he'd much rather talk to her. Warmth flooded her being at hearing those words, but she'd rolled her eyes, still wondering what they were doing. Long-distance friends were great, but that shouldn't keep him home if he wanted to go out. Of course, the idea that he'd stay home to talk to her was fine with her.

She sighed and shook her head. *I'm a thirty-three-year-old professional woman. Why do I feel like talking and flirting with Hop is the highlight of my days?* She dropped her chin to her chest. *Because it is the highlight.* With each passing day, she was pulled in more and more by the thought of him in her life.

Her phone vibrated, and she grinned, refusing to worry about the risk of being so happy that the caller was Hop. "Hey, how are you?" she chirped.

"You sound good." His ever-familiar voice was full of humor.

"My day was easy. Three deliveries, all routine. Next week, I'll be at Red Cross meetings, and those are much more boring."

"Ugh, I'll be on a mission for the next week, and we probably won't be able to talk," he added, his voice now growly.

"Oh." The one-word reply sounded simple to her ears, and she figured it did to him as well. But it felt strange to give into the urge to say how much she'd miss talking to him. He had only intimated what his job duties were when they'd been together in Tennessee, but over the past several weeks, she'd come to realize that the company he worked for offered a very specialized service for government contracts, private citizens who could afford their skills, and even some pro bono cases for those who couldn't. She was impressed and had told him so, but now wasn't sure what to say.

"I guess it sounds dumb to say that I'll really miss talking to you," he continued.

At those words, the air left her lungs in a whoosh, and she wished she'd been brave enough to say them first. "Me, too."

He chuckled. "Well, that's good to know. But I do have some news. At least, I hope it's good news to you."

"Oh yeah? What is it?"

"When I get back after next week, I have to fly to Arizona for a day or so. I thought I could make a quick trip down to El Paso on the way back to California and have a chance to see you again."

This time there was no denying that her heart leaped at his words. "I would absolutely love that! I'll take whatever I can get. If it's only for a few hours, I'll order takeout. If you can spend the night and don't mind sleeping in a double bed with me, then that's where I'd like you to be."

Laughter roared out, and for a second, she wondered if she'd misinterpreted where he'd like to sleep.

"Hell, we could sleep on the floor, and it'd be fine with me as long as I was with you."

"Damn, Hop, you always say exactly what I want to hear. Yet," she continued to admit, "I'm always afraid that we might not be on the same page."

"Tell me what page you want us to be on," he demanded gently.

Deciding to risk it all, she said, "I know we only spent one night together, but it meant a lot to me. And I know we decided to continue our friendship, and I don't wanna fuck that up. But when we can be together, I'd love for us to *be together*. If that's okay with you."

"I couldn't have said it better myself. So yeah, when I come to see you, I'll make sure to come for at least one night, and we can order food because I don't want to leave your place the whole time we're there."

Even though they'd just agreed they were on the same page, she still wasn't sure they were. She'd never been in a friends-with-benefits relationship before and was uncertain if that described what she and Hop were doing. She couldn't demand they be exclusive but knew she was and hoped he was, too. Even though she had no need to place a label on what they were right now, she considered him a friend. If the benefit was that when they got together, they could have more amazing sex, she was all in.

They continued talking for a while, sharing bits of their lives from the past fourteen years as well as now, finding things they had in common and jokingly arguing over things they didn't. By the time she said goodbye, knowing she wouldn't talk to him for almost a week, she felt a little pain in her heart. "Please be safe," she said.

"Always. In fact, that's been my motto in the past, but I'll amend it now. I'll always be safe, just for you."

Disconnecting, she thought of how wonderfully things were going… and smiled.

Oh shit, what a disaster! How on earth could this have happened? As soon as that thought went through Lori's mind, she snorted, knowing exactly how it happened. But that didn't make it any easier or any better. Squeezing her eyes closed, she tried to quell the nausea that rose in her throat. *I'm a doctor. A woman's doctor. How the fuck...*

She hastened to the toilet, barely having time to kneel before losing the contents of her stomach. Thankfully, she hadn't eaten much for breakfast, and her hair was in a ponytail, out of the way of what was hurled from her mouth. Reaching up, she felt for the toilet handle and flushed, then rose to her feet and leaned against the bathroom counter. Grabbing a cloth, she ran cold water over it and squeezed the excess before patting it over her face and lips and then placing it on the back of her neck to cool her overheated body. She filled the bathroom cup with more cold water and sipped, willing the nausea to pass.

Finally, she allowed her gaze to move back to the counter where the pregnancy test stick was resting. The two clearly visible pink lines glared back at her, almost daring her to deny their existence.

Finally, she continued to lift her gaze to the mirror, staring at her pale complexion. "Pregnant. You're pregnant," she whispered to her reflection.

How many women had she said those words to over the years? Countless. How many had burst into happy tears, fists pumping into the air, and shouts of praises leaving their lips? And how many had met her gaze with shocked, fearful, angry, or despondent expressions, some with tears sliding down their cheeks? She'd recognized the varied responses to pregnancy but had never considered them as much as she did at this moment.

Four weeks... I'm four weeks pregnant. She'd spotted during her last period, which wasn't abnormal.

Therefore, she'd never considered pregnancy. Swallowing deeply again, she hoped worshiping the porcelain god wasn't about to occur again.

It had been a week since she'd last talked to Hop, and he wasn't expected to arrive in California until tomorrow. Then he'd travel to Texas several days after that. Her head continued its path upward, and she stared at the ceiling for a moment, trying to still the thoughts that churned as much as her stomach. Only a few days ago, she'd felt nauseous for two mornings in a row. And then she'd only spotted when her regular period should have started.

We used condoms. And birth control. But I'd been on an antibiotic for some dental work the week before I went to Tennessee. Christ! I'm a gynecologist! I know the percentages... the risks... almost a two percent chance of becoming pregnant.

Blowing out a long, shaky breath, she stared at the stick again. *Pregnant. I'm a month pregnant.* For a few more minutes, she let her thoughts drift. *A baby. How does a child fit into my life now? I'm not going to abort, but my whole world will change. And what about Hop? How do I tell him? When do I tell him? I need to take a blood test at the clinic. I'm not going to tell him over the phone. It can wait until he comes here. By then, I'll have things more figured out.* Her mind continued to race.

She walked out of the bathroom and stood in her small bedroom. More thoughts hit her. *There's no room for a crib here. And this is a one-bedroom apartment.* She walked into the living room that was separated from the kitchen by a counter with space in the corner for a small four-seat table. Since it was always just her, she had the table pushed into the corner and only had two chairs. *Where would I put a high chair?*

Standing in the middle of the living room, she turned around in a circle, and reality hit her squarely in the face. *I'll have to move to a bigger place.* She was a doctor, but contrary to popular belief, she didn't make a ton of money. She'd walked out of her marriage with her freedom and no alimony, just the way she wanted. Her salary from the clinic was primarily funded with grants. And as a Red Cross doctor, she was lucky to have a salary from them as well, but that meant she was on call to travel the world when needed. *That won't work with a baby.* More realities slammed into her. *I'll have to look for a different clinic and possibly give up my Red Cross work for a while.*

She turned her back to the sofa and plopped down, her ass landing on the soft cushion. Sucking in a deep breath, she let it out slowly. Her hands slid naturally to her stomach, and she looked down. *A baby. My baby. Hop's and my baby.* She couldn't imagine what his reaction would be, and the nausea threatened to come roaring back.

For a second, her role as a physician sounded in her ears... *it's early... anything can happen... you haven't had a blood test yet to accurately prove pregnancy...*

Then a slow, tiny smile curved her lips. *A baby. My baby. Hop's and my baby.* She turned off the other voices in her head and closed her eyes. Whatever the future held, she would do whatever needed to be done for her baby. And prayed for the nausea to pass.

Two days later, she left work with the blood test results in her purse. Pregnant. Not that she was surprised, but having the diagnosis made it feel more real. She'd driven home early, knowing that Hop was supposed to call that evening. She'd just made it inside and changed out of her scrubs when her phone vibrated. As she glanced at the caller ID, her heartbeat jumped even though it was expected.

Taking a deep breath, she connected. "Hey, stranger." The words were normal, but her strangely falsetto voice sounded fake. *God, can he tell I'm freaking out?*

"Hey, gorgeous. Damn, I've missed talking to you," he said.

Keep talking normally. "Um... did your week go well?"

"Yeah, no problems. And best of all, I'll be in Arizona the day after tomorrow." He laughed, adding, "Carson said I could skip the Arizona trip, and he'd send someone else if I needed a break, but I told him no way! Then I confessed that I'd take an extra day to go see you."

"You told your boss you're coming here?" she squeaked, then immediately cleared her throat, hating to sound more adolescent than when she was an adolescent.

"Yeah. I said the friend I'd connected with in Tennessee lived in El Paso. He just grinned, and I took some shit from the others. I finally told them that I'd stayed in touch with you and that we were seeing each other. Of course, considering I've poured it on them at times, I guess payback is fair."

"Oh." *Oh? All I can think of to say is 'oh'?* "Um... so seeing each other?"

"Well, I guess that technically we haven't seen each other since we met up in Tennessee, but... yeah, Lori... I... well, we can talk when I get there, but I've got to tell you that I'm not fighting my feelings any longer. I want to see where this is going between us."

Her heart stuttered in her chest. *Oh God... I know where this is going... a baby in less than eight months!* "Um... when do you think you'll get here?"

"I'll get to Arizona on Thursday, and my plan is to be finished by Friday afternoon. I'll fly to El Paso and should be able to get a rental and be at your house by early evening. We can go out to eat if you'd like."

"No, I think that staying in would be good."

"Me, too," he said, his voice deepening. "Honestly, Lori, we can do whatever you'd like to do, but I can't wait to see you again."

"I've got some things I need to talk to you about," she blurted. Wincing, she scrunched her nose, wishing she hadn't said anything.

"Yeah? What about? Nothing bad, I hope."

"Um, no... not bad. Just... well, just some things going on with me. Um... it'll be easier to talk about it when you're here," she said, hoping he wouldn't try to get her to say anything, or God forbid, guess what she needed to tell him.

"I trust you, Lori. We'll talk when I get there," he agreed readily, and she let out a silent sigh of relief.

"Listen, I hate to call and run, but I've just gotten home, and it looks like my neighbor is bringing over some shit I've had delivered."

"Oh, that's fine," she rushed. "I'll be working, and I'm on call tomorrow, so I'll just see you on Friday."

"Can't wait. Bye, babe."

"Bye," she barely whispered before they disconnected. Blowing out another long breath, she tried to still the pounding of her heartbeat. *Okay, this was good. He's still coming. And I can tell him on Friday about the baby. I'll make sure he knows that I don't expect anything from him but that I'm keeping it, and we'll work together however we need to as long as the baby's needs come first.* As much as she'd reconnected with Hop, she truthfully had no idea how he'd take the news.

She placed her hand on her stomach again, swallowing several times to once more quell the nausea. Looking down, she whispered, "I've got you, sweetie. I might not know anything else, but I've got you."

10

"We're going to send in a team."

Of all the words her supervisor could've said, Lori did not want to hear those right now. She'd listened to the reports of the impending flooding in Quito, Ecuador, and now hearing that mudslides threatened to sweep through a populated area, cutting residents off from electricity, water, medical care, rescue services, and food, she knew what was coming.

"Dr. Baker, the city has a large hospital but also has a separate maternity clinic from the main hospital. It was started by a doctor trying to bring modern medical care to women who might not have sought care for deliveries. It was his hope to cut the maternity and infant mortality rates. It's not near the flood zone but is struggling with staffing. We'll send you in with the first team."

Normally, she would nod her head, agree without hesitation, and look forward to getting boots on the ground in an area she knew needed her and her skills.

But now, all she could think of was that she'd be leaving before Hop had a chance to get to El Paso. *Damn... that interferes with telling him about the baby.*

Realizing her supervisor was still staring at her, as well as several people around the table, she jerked slightly and nodded. "Yes, I'll be ready to leave in a couple of hours."

She tuned out the rest of the planning, knowing that her supervisor's notes on the area and the disaster would go to her tablet, and she could read them on the plane. Still battling nausea, she prayed she could keep it under control. As soon as the meeting ended, she took to her feet and walked briskly down the hall.

"Are you okay?"

Turning at the question coming from behind, she spied one of the Red Cross nurses she'd be traveling with. Jackie Blackmore and Marilyn Sanchez almost always traveled with her, and they'd built a camaraderie over the last few missions. Marilyn was petite, dark-haired, bilingual in Spanish, and smiled easily. Jackie was taller, with strawberry-blonde hair and a serious disposition. And both, two of the best nurses she'd served with.

Offering a quick smile, she nodded. "I'm fine, Jackie. I just haven't been sleeping well, so I'm tired."

"You know, if you're sick, I'm sure Dr. Weston can always send someone else." Jackie's eyes were full of concern.

Giving her head a shake, she said, "No, I'm fine. Anyway, he has plenty of things to worry about, and I'm one of the few OB/GYNs he can send in quickly. I'll be fine, I'm sure."

Even as the words left her mouth, she wondered how much truth there was to them. She wasn't worried about herself or the baby. She'd be well taken care of as a Red Cross doctor and knew that her time in Ecuador would not last long since they would rotate other doctors in, and then she could come home. *I just wanted to talk to Hop. I needed to talk to Hop.*

Forcing her lips to curve, she said, "I've got to go home first, as I'm sure you do, too. I'll meet you at the airport." With that, she turned, not wanting to prolong the conversation while her mind raced in multiple directions. Glad it didn't take her long to get to her apartment, she dialed Hop as soon as she stepped through the door.

"Hey!" he answered, excitement resounding. "I can't wait to see you tomorrow."

"Uh... that's why I'm calling. I'm not going to be here tomorrow, so I wanted you to have enough time to change your plans so you wouldn't include El Paso."

"Damn. Are you being called out?" Before she could answer, he jumped in, "It's Ecuador, isn't it? I was listening to the news about the flooding."

Not surprised that he was aware of world situations, she replied, "Yes, that's where I'm heading. I leave in a couple of hours."

He was quiet for a few seconds, then sighed heavily. "I can't believe the suck-ass timing. I really wanted to see you."

"I know. Me, too. We have things to talk about and

catch up on, but I… well, I… I'll plan on making a trip to California as soon as I get back from Ecuador."

"That'd be great, babe. And if you can't make it, then I'll fly down to El Paso for a weekend."

They were silent for a few seconds, her stomach clenching and her heart pounding. Before she could stop the words, she blurted, "I should've known when we met up in Tennessee that we couldn't have just one night without rekindling our friendship." She winced, uncertain where those words came from, but then in the last few days, she'd had so many thoughts flying around her head and pulling at her heart that she was surprised she was able to get anything done.

He chuckled, the deep sound wrapping around her. "I know what you mean, and you're right. I thought maybe we could when we were just talking, but after being with you that night, Lori, I've thought of you constantly. I kind of tried to fight it at first."

"Really? Why did you try to fight it?" Once again, she winced, wishing she could just keep from blurting out her thoughts.

"Honestly? I didn't think I had time or room in my life for anyone but me right now."

His words sent chills through her. She knew how he felt—after all, she'd felt the same. She glanced down at her stomach, once again the reality hitting that she had no choice but to have someone in her life now. Someone who would depend solely on her. And whether or not Hop would want to be part of that was up to him. Suddenly, she couldn't think of anything to say, and tears threatened to spill over. Clearing her throat, she finally managed, "Well, I have to pack and get to the airport."

There was a slight hesitation. "Are you okay?"

"Yeah, sure. Just have a lot on my mind. I'll call when I can, and we'll talk when I get back in a few weeks."

"Damn, I hate this," he muttered. "I really want to see you. Please take care of yourself and call me when you get there."

"I'm not sure what the phone, internet, or electrical services will be like, but I'll do my best. At least I can text when the plane lands."

"Okay." He sighed. "And Lori?"

"Yeah?"

"I'll miss you."

A tear rolled down her cheek and dropped onto her shirt. "I'll miss you, too, Hop." With that, she disconnected before he heard her sob.

Hop stared at the screen of his phone for what seemed like the millionth time, desperately wanting to see Lori's name pop up on caller ID or for a text.

"Man, what is going on with you?" Dolby asked, tossing a balled-up towel at him.

He'd made it back to California and was sitting on a weight bench in the Lighthouse compound. Dolby, Bennett, Poole, Adam, and Rick were in there as well, all working out.

He managed to duck the towel as it landed near his shoulder. "I'm waiting on a call or a text."

"Well, the way you're acting, you'd think you were waiting on a girlfriend, but since you haven't had one since I've known you, I can't imagine you're expecting a call from a one-nighter."

The others chuckled, and he looked around the room and groaned at their smiling faces. At first, he'd only mentioned that while in Tennessee, he met up with an old friend, but considering that since he'd been back, she was all he thought of, he'd finally mentioned that they'd stayed in contact. *Of course, that made fodder for their jokes.* That was only fair play, though, considering that he'd ribbed Leo and Rick when they got together with their women. Carson had met his now wife, Jeannie, on a mission to Mexico, but he wasn't about to poke fun at his boss. Plus, he really liked Jeannie and thought she was good for their iconic leader.

"Yeah, yeah, laugh it up. But it's Lori that I'm waiting to talk to."

Poole lifted his brows. "You sure you're not *just* friends?"

The others grinned as though they'd already guessed his feelings, so he admitted, "Yep. We're more than just friends. Although I haven't got a fuckin' clue what we are."

Bennett reared back. "Damn, man. Didn't figure you'd be ready to give up your freedom."

He opened his mouth to protest but didn't know exactly what he'd protest. *My one-and-done reputation or that caring for Lori was a bad thing?*

He sat up on the weight bench and grabbed the towel,

swiping it over his face before flinging it around his neck. "At first, it was supposed to be one night. Hell, it wasn't even supposed to be one night. She was a friend from high school that meant something to me. We never dated, but she was just a really cool girl who helped me out with a few classes. She was easy to talk to and fun to be around. And while I liked her, there was no way I would take the chance of messing up our friendship by acting on that."

Shaking his head, he continued, "We lost touch, and it was pure chance that we ran into each other fourteen years later, both working rescues. It wasn't until the last evening that we actually spent time together. We talked and went to a bar to hang out with my family and some others. Ended up at a diner and talked for a few more hours."

He looked around, wondering what their expressions would hold but found nothing but interest. Grabbing the end of the towel to wipe more sweat from his brow, he continued. "We caught up on what we'd been doing, and I found she was just as beautiful and easy to talk to as ever. She's a Red Cross doctor and would be flying back to her own life the next day, and I was coming here. We went back over to her room at the hotel to talk, and then…"

"And you thought it was one night only." Rick had finished with his reps and was sitting on another bench wiping the sweat from his face, as well.

He nodded slowly, but his brow was furrowed. "Yeah. She had a life to go back to, and so did I. But we were attracted to each other and spent hours talking and sharing. Anyway, I stayed the night and figured that would be it."

"So what happened?" Bennett asked.

"I made sure I had her phone number because I didn't want us to lose contact. But the reality was, I couldn't wait to talk to her again. I thought about her constantly. So for the past several weeks, we've been in contact. I was going to fly to El Paso on my way here to visit her again."

"That sounds serious," Dolby said. "Or are you just planning on keeping things fun and friendly?"

"Hell if I know exactly what she is. But she's no fuck buddy. She's no piece on the side. And she sure as hell isn't a one-and-done. She meant something to me years ago, but I'd relegated her to the mental box where we place all those old adolescent memories. Running into her as an adult changed all that."

"So what happened to keep you from visiting her in El Paso? Is she not on the same page as you?"

He shook his head. "She got called out yesterday. Flooding in Ecuador, and according to the news that I've been glued to for the past twenty-four hours, it looks like mudslides are threatening the area, as well."

Just then, Teddy popped his head in and said, "Gentlemen, Carson's moved the afternoon briefing up by half an hour."

Glad for the reprieve, considering he'd never spent so much time talking about a relationship—hell, about any woman—he was up off the bench quickly. He and the others headed into the locker room for quick showers. They were back in the main compound early, and since no one seemed to care, he pulled up the international news channel on one of the computer screens. It didn't take long for the news to roll to the devastation in Ecuador. And just on cue, his phone vibrated. Fumbling as he jerked it from his pocket, he looked down to see a message from Lori.

Here. Don't know when I can call again. Hopefully, I'll talk to you soon.

"Was that her?" Dolby asked.

Hop looked up and saw most of the Keepers' eyes on him. "Yeah." The ones who had not heard his explanation in the gym had curiosity written on their faces.

Deciding it would be easier to get the situation out in the open, he offered the abbreviated version. "The friend that I met up with in Tennessee has become someone important to me. We're not together, but she's someone who I'm very close to. And, truthfully, I hope that she's in my future in whatever way works out. She's a Red Cross doctor, and I was supposed to see her today, stopping by El Paso on my way back from Arizona. But she got called yesterday to head to the flooded areas in Ecuador."

Murmurs of both sympathy and congratulations were heard as everyone's gazes turned toward the computer screen that now flashed on the main wall. Streets were flooded even in the main city. And mudslides were threatening several urban areas near the mountains.

The newscaster announced, "Quito is Ecuador's capital and cultural epicenter. It is located in a valley on the eastern slopes of Pichincha, an active stratovolcano in the Andes. Unfortunately, this is now the third flooding of the region this year, and since the ground and structures are already destabilized from the two previous floods, they are unable to withstand the heavy rains and overflowing rivers coming from the mountains. Many people have been reported missing, and there are at least fifty-seven confirmed deaths. The Ecuadorian government has stepped in to send aid to the affected area, grateful for the support of neighboring countries, as well as the International Red Cross and the International Rescue Mission. To find out how you can contribute to the Red Cross support…"

"Is she already there?" Carson asked, cutting in through the newscaster.

"Yeah, I just got a text from her saying she'd arrived early this morning. Looks like from the news that the worst is yet to come."

"As always, if you need our help, you say the word," Carson added.

Hop looked over his shoulder at the other Keepers, recognizing the expressions on their faces. It was one he'd had when one of them needed assistance, and he'd been ready to jump in with both feet. Being on the receiving end of that offer felt strangely comforting. "Will do," he said, with a chin lift. As the group turned back to their cases at hand, he couldn't help but continue to gaze at the computer screen and pray Lori would stay safe while there.

A few minutes later, Natalie and Abbie sat down in the chairs on either side of him. His head swung from one to the other, uncertain of what they needed to talk to him about.

Abbie began, "I just wanted you to know that I've been looking at the geospatial imagery of the area in Ecuador where your friend is located. I've sent the information to Natalie, who's been looking at logistics. We thought we'd keep up with what's going on just in case you need to make a trip and need the most up-to-date intel going in."

His breath caught in his throat as a feeling moved through him that Hop couldn't remember having before. Yes, it was gratitude but so much more. Knowing that these two Keepers not only had his back but were also pre-planning in case it was needed moved him almost more than he could say. Finally, clearing his throat, he offered another chin lift and managed to say, "Thank you. Seriously… fucking thank you. I hope to God I don't need it, but knowing you have this information makes me feel a hell of a lot better."

The two women stood, patting his shoulders before they walked to their stations. He noticed that Carson had not sent a new assignment for him to work on and wondered if that was to keep his schedule clear. Deciding not to look a gift horse in the mouth, he continued working on the security issues from Arizona while still keeping an eye on what was happening in Ecuador.

He thought over the last phone conversation he'd had with Lori, remembering that she'd wanted to talk to him. Having little relationship experience to fall back on, he had to admit those words sounded a bit ominous.

Yet, she'd seemed glad to talk to him. Sighing heavily, he squeezed the back of his neck as he tried to push any negative thoughts from his mind.

The truth was Lori meant something to him. Something deep. Something special. Something more than friendship. And as crazy as it seemed, he could see her as a permanent fixture in his life. And just that thought had his heart beating faster.

11

The plane had landed outside Quito in the wee hours of the morning, not allowing Lori a chance to see any of the terrains they were flying over. *Not that it would matter.* Nausea had nearly knocked her on her ass, but at least her fellow medical teammates assumed she simply had a bout of air sickness when she had to escape to the toilet several times. As gross as it was to throw up in her own toilet at home, throwing up in an airplane was a million times worse. She'd closed her eyes and held her nose as she retched, then cleaned the area and scrubbed her hands. *Nasty.* She shivered, certain that she'd entered one of the levels of hell.

Once on the ground, she fired off a text to Hop. They moved through the airport customs as a group, gathered their luggage, and were grateful that the Ecuadorian Red Cross had a van and driver to meet them. In many countries she'd traveled to where natural disasters had decimated resources, they had to catch taxis or even donkey carts to get to the affected areas.

As soon as their sparse luggage was stowed in the back, she, Jackie, and Marilyn climbed into the older model van, grimacing at the stale cigarette smoke smell. Breathing through her mouth, she barely listened as the driver rattled on about the rains and the floods, her ears only perking up when he specifically mentioned the facility he was taking them to.

"The area we're going to has a maternity clinic built away from the main hospital. It's farther up toward the mountains to assist with the women who can't or don't want to go into the city to the main hospital."

Since she'd worked in huge hospitals, small clinics, and even tents and outdoor shelters, Lori figured she could handle whatever situation they were assigned. But hearing the clinic was still functional was gratifying news.

"Because mudslides are threatening," the driver continued, "the closest hotel has been evacuated. But there will be rooms at the clinic set up for you and your comfort."

Normally, she would look out the window at the passing views, taking in the scenes of the country. But now, even in the early dawn light, nausea continued to threaten, so she kept her eyes closed. While she felt she could lie down and sleep for hours, she knew there was a good chance they would have to hit the ground running. Hoping the obstetrical clinic stayed out of the way of the floods, she also knew it was possible that the building could be compromised if the mudslides came to fruition.

For as long as she could remember, she'd wanted to

be a doctor. Her parents had encouraged her to follow her dreams. Like most things, she'd remained focused, giving one hundred percent toward her goal. She'd valued her independence without feeling the need to be single. And when she divorced, it wasn't because she was against the institution... just the man and his dictates. Working with those who couldn't afford the most advanced medical care had called to her, and discovering the excitement of Red Cross assignments had been the icing on the cake. *Until now.*

Now, all she could think about was how miserable she felt, how she wouldn't want to work at this pace once her baby was born, and wondered how on earth she was going to manage it all. Thinking of her parents brought the sting of tears to her eyes, knowing she couldn't share the grandchild experience with them. *And Hop... how will he react to the news?* She held no illusions of happily ever afters and riding off into the sunset with him, but she hoped they would be able to work together for the baby's sake. *God, just a few more weeks, and then I can see him and tell him—*

"We are almost here!" the driver called out, his voice cheerful despite the ravages of the flooding in his city.

She opened her eyes to see the sun had risen a little more and prayed that they would arrive soon. Some streets were underwater, but their driver darted toward the higher roads. While on the plane, they'd been briefed on the situation and knew that the areas closer to the rivers coming down from the mountains had overflowed the banks, and many houses were now under the floodwaters.

As the van climbed higher toward the majestic volcanic mountains, she observed the modern downtown buildings in the distance. Where they were going, the houses were built much closer together, and the area was poorer. By the time they got to the clinic, she had looked around at the structure, surprised to see that it was three stories tall but was squeezed into a small lot with roads on either side. *When real estate isn't plentiful, up is the way to go.*

They alighted from the van, and she gratefully sucked in a deep breath of clean air, not caring that the rain pelted her raincoat. With their luggage in tow, she and the nurses followed the driver through the door into the clinic's reception area, where they were met by a small, gray-haired man. His suit was rumpled as though he hadn't had a chance to change clothes during the last day or so. The driver introduced them to the local Ecuadorian Red Cross medical director, Dr. Paulo Casta. Lori held out her hand toward Dr. Casta, liking his warm but tight smile, understanding the pressure he felt trying to ascertain the city's medical needs were met.

She turned to thank the driver, who was bowing and nodding as he called out that he must go back to the airport to pick up more arriving Red Cross volunteers and personnel to be taken to other areas of need.

She, Jackie, and Marilyn followed Dr. Casta through the front door of the clinic, entering a wide reception area staffed by several women behind the counter. Nodding their greetings, they continued down the hall as he led them into an empty room.

He appeared harried and apologized for rushing them through the tour. "I'm so sorry, but the clinic's director isn't here to greet you, and I'm needed elsewhere. The first floor is for reception and intake. The second floor is the birthing rooms and surgery. The third floor is the pharmacy, labs, and where the staff has their locker room and lounge. We've added cots in there and apologize that it is not more comfortable."

Lori waved her hand dismissively. "Please, don't worry about our accommodations. We'll make do. What is the status of the clinic?"

"It's safe. Still functional. The biggest threat is mudslides farther up the mountain, but if the rain stops soon, that won't be a problem. Right now, as soon as a woman gives birth and the staff is sure she and the baby are stable, they are discharging them back to their relatives."

"And if their houses have already been affected?"

"We can't keep them at the clinic just for that. We have another Red Cross liaison who works with the family in case they don't have a home to return to. Of course, due to displacement, we have more than our usual number of women coming to the clinic. Some would have given birth at home but have come here instead."

Lori knew the drill. She's been through it enough times in the last several years. The geography and the country change, but the situations in crisis are often similar. "If you can show us where we can put our luggage, Dr. Casta, we'll do so now and get to work."

"I can't thank you enough for coming, Dr. Baker," he

said. "Some of our staff have flooded homes and can't make it in. Our clinic's founder, Dr. Alfonso Rocha, will be here later today. I understand that his house is in a possible flood zone, which is why he's not in yet today. Having you here will help ensure that these women and newborns have the best care we can give them under the circumstances."

He led them to the elevator, and she, Jackie, and Marilyn shared a look. "Are your electricity and generator stable?" she asked.

"So far, yes. But I don't know how long that will last. I realize that you will probably prefer to use the stairs, but I thought with your luggage, the elevator would be fine for now."

She held her breath while the elevator moved to the third floor, letting it rush from her lungs when the doors opened. They stepped out into a wide hall, and Dr. Casta continued his tour. "This door remains locked at all times. It leads to our pharmacy, which is well-stocked for all needs. You will be given a key, and the nurses on staff also usually have one. Dr. Rocha's office is around the corner."

"Do you have enough pharmaceuticals?"

"Dr. Rocha was able to get more ordered when we knew the rains were coming and feared for more flooding as we had several months ago."

Nodding her approval, she followed as he turned in the other direction. "Here is the lounge, which contains the staff bathrooms and showers, as well as a kitchenette. I have also had the refrigerator and cabinets stocked with food for your arrival." He opened another door and waved them forward. "We have cots in here for you and for any of our staff that has to stay. We still have two women who are on the kitchen staff preparing meals for the patients, and they will fix extra for you, as well. Also, we are down to two janitorial staff members. The laundry service is halted, but the duty is rotated during this time."

"Dr. Casta, it looks like you've taken care of everything. My nurses and I are going to stow our belongings, make sure we're hydrated, and head down to the lower floors to begin work. Will we be expecting an increase in cases from the other hospital?"

"Because of the flooding, several small clinics have sent their expectant mothers here if they suspected a problem. Of course, many women will just give birth at home, but we hope to be able to take care of those who need extra medical services."

Before she had a chance to ask any other questions, a knock on the door revealed a middle-aged woman, her black hair pulled severely away from her face, but a smile softened her expression.

Dr. Casta waved her in. "I'd like to introduce Elisa Silva. She is the head nurse of the clinic and will be assisting you during your time here."

"I'm Dr. Lori Baker." She stepped forward, extending her hand. "Please understand that we are not here to take over but to assist you."

Elisa's smile widened, and she nodded. Speaking English, she said, "It is my pleasure to welcome you to Ecuador, but I wish it was not under such circumstances. Without our doctor, we are grateful for you to be here."

"The Red Cross nurses with me are Jackie Blackmore and Marilyn Sanchez. Marilyn is bilingual in Spanish, and while I don't consider myself to be bilingual, I speak and understand enough to be functional in the hospital, although having nurses translating will be good."

"I am also bilingual and have several nurses who will translate for you," Elisa assured me.

Thanking Dr. Casta again before he left, Lori turned to her nurses and said, "Choose a bunk and go ahead and leave your things. Let's grab some water and a snack and then be ready to head down."

Elisa walked over to the refrigerator and opened the door, giving Lori a chance to glance inside, seeing it was fully stocked. With bottles of water and bags of cheese crackers in hand, she and her nurses ate quickly, then followed Elisa down to the second floor. It didn't take long to become acquainted with the clinic, make the rounds of the women in active labor, and meet the clinic nurses there.

One stepped forward, her face pinched and lips thin. "I'm Rosa Matos. Nurse anesthetist."

Lori had no doubt that the nurse was overworked and exhausted, especially with the clinic's doctor not in residence. "It's nice to meet you. We'll work together to make the women as safe and comfortable as possible." The lines emanating from Rosa's eyes seemed less deep as she nodded.

Lori glanced out one of the windows. The rain was

still drizzling, but according to the last weather report, it should be slowing even more during the day. But as she knew from experience, the rivers would continue to rise, and the ground would continue to soften. And there was the threat of more approaching rain.

She looked down the street as a car and a van pulled up to the front of the clinic and a nurse wheeled out a new mother. Lori smiled at the idea of the mother and baby going home but hoped they had a safe house to return to. A woman alighted from the car and carried the baby carrier with her while the mother climbed gingerly into the van and waved to the nurse who re-entered the clinic. She was glad relatives were stepping in to help, especially if the new mother's house was compromised by the floods. *I need to ensure that our future discharges have a safe place to go.* As the two vehicles drove away at the same time, she glanced up at the raindrops that continued pelting the glass.

Clearing her mind from the weather, she walked into one of the birthing rooms, following Elisa. Meeting the woman lying on the bed, she ascertained this was her third child, and her husband was home with the other two. The woman was grateful to meet Lori, and after she examined her, she reported that the labor was progressing normally.

At the nursing station, she looked at the dry-erase board where the patients were logged in and nurse assignments were given. Nodding toward Jackie, she said, "You divide the assignments. Decide which one of you wants to sleep first, and the other takes what's going on now. I'm going to check on the breech baby in room 202."

Her team worked like a well-oiled machine, for which she was grateful. Moving down the hall with Elisa, they stepped into another birthing room, and she smiled while greeting the very young mother. Discovering she was a first-time mom and a C-section had already been planned for the day, she listened as the patient spoke in rapid Spanish. Elisa turned to interpret. "She's fearful without the doctor she was expecting."

Rosa stepped into the room. "I have already been in to assure her that even without Dr. Rocha here, all will be as promised."

The wording from Rosa sounded off, but Lori assumed that some concepts were lost in translation. After her examination, Lori looked over and smiled at the young woman. "Since she was scheduled for a C-section today anyway, I think we should go ahead and perform the procedure."

"But I know Dr. Rocha would want to be here," Rosa protested.

"Everything with the patient looks good, and the impending flooding can only worsen. If the delivery is today, we can see if she can go home tomorrow."

The young girl's eyes were wide, but Rosa bent low and spoke to her, finally gaining her nod.

Not knowing how Dr. Rocha had prepared the teen mother for the procedure, she headed to the OB surgical room while the nurses finished their prep. Rosa sat at the girl's head, monitoring the anesthesia. Once it had taken effect, Lori made a transverse incision, then separated the muscles until coming to the uterine wall. With a final incision, she opened the amniotic sac and delivered the baby boy through the opening.

Rosa looked up and directed one of the nurses to take the baby, but Lori interrupted. "Hand him to the mother so bonding can take place."

Rosa's lips were pinched tight again, but she acquiesced. Assuming the nurse didn't like having her orders overturned, Lori sighed, knowing she was the interloper in the clinic and yet responsible for the patients.

Finishing the C-section procedure while the mother cried as she held her baby, Lori smiled at the scene before her, ignoring Rosa's sour expression. Pressing her lips together, she couldn't help but think of what it would be like to hold her own baby. Forcing her personal thoughts away, she nodded toward Rosa and hoped to salve the nurse's obvious displeasure. "Good work. I suggest you rest as often as possible until we get more relief."

Rosa nodded and let out a long breath. "Thank you. It feels much better to have your assistance now." She looked down at the new mother and said, "I believe someone will be coming for her tomorrow."

"Dr. Casta mentioned something about more Red Cross nurses from other locations, and we might get another nurse anesthetist," Lori said.

"I'll be fine," Rosa replied sharply. She glanced down at the mother and lifted her brow before turning to walk out of the room.

Lori blinked, uncertain if she had insulted Rosa or if

she was always prickly. Not having the time or energy to consider what it might be, she smiled at the new mother, who was still crying as she kissed her newborn. *How many times have I done this so far? How many babies have I seen come into the world? Even under the most horrendous circumstances, the miracle of life shines through.*

She had also seen gut-wrenching tragedy and sadness beyond belief when things didn't go well, but she was pleased that the great percentage of deliveries brought great joy.

As the nurse cared for the new mother, she moved to the sink to toss her gloves and wash her hands. With her surgical gown off, she once again glanced down at her stomach and felt a rush of warmth at the idea that she'd be holding her own baby in eight months. Closing her eyes for a few seconds, she sucked in a deep breath and let it out slowly. *Christ, I hope I'm ready because this baby will come whether I am or not.*

The rest of the afternoon passed with little fanfare. A few more expectant, ready-to-deliver mothers checked in, and the clinic discharged several others. The rain was finally slowing, and just like she remembered when she was in Tennessee weeks earlier, the heavy dark clouds were finally lifting. Standing at one of the windows again, she looked out over the mountains in the distance behind them and wondered how swollen the rivers would become.

Thinking about Tennessee obviously made her think of Hop, and her hand moved to her stomach. Dropping her chin, she stared down for a few minutes, hating that their impending visit had been canceled. While it was still very early in the pregnancy, she had no plans to keep her condition a secret. She wanted to let him know because he deserved that much. What he chose to do or say about the situation wasn't something she would worry about, but her integrity would not let her hold on to the fact that she was pregnant with his baby.

Sighing heavily, she wondered how long it would be before she would see him. *Another month? Is it fair to wait that long just to try to see him in person?*

"Dr. Baker?"

She turned to see a middle-aged man, his neat dark hair swept to the side, wearing dark pants, a light-blue shirt, and a white lab coat with *Dr. Rocha* embroidered over the chest pocket. He appeared very dapper for a man in the middle of flooding who'd been watching after his house, and she was very aware of her own somewhat haggard appearance.

"Dr. Rocha, it's nice to meet you. I'm Lori Baker, Red Cross OB/GYN."

They shook hands. "It's delightful to meet you, Dr. Baker. We are most appreciative of the assistance you and your nurses can bring."

"I understand your home is threatened by the floodwaters?"

His eyes flashed, and he nodded. "Yes, I apologize for not being here when you arrived. My wife does not handle decisions well, and I thought it best if I was there to assist."

"I see," she murmured. "We've been well taken care of by your staff and Dr. Casta. I'm sure Elisa will have records and charts for you to look at from what we've done since arriving yesterday. We just performed a C-section and—"

"Yes, Rosa has informed me. I'll see the patient myself and then review the records in my office. Thank you."

With that, he said goodbye and walked away, leaving her standing in the hall staring after him. *He'll check in on the patient I just delivered? He'll be in his office after that? The clinic is full of women ready to deliver, and he's going to go sit in his office?*

Sighing, she shook her head. She'd served in many situations as a Red Cross doctor in facilities that were run in a variety of ways. She wasn't there to question how he operated his clinic but simply to give medical care to the patients who walked through the door.

Hearing someone getting off the elevator, she turned and looked behind her, seeing Marilyn, who said, "I was going to lie down for a little while and take my rest shift, but if you'd rather do it now, that's fine with me."

Lori was dead on her feet, which she knew was because of the pregnancy as much as the job. She'd often worked thirty to fifty hours straight when she was an intern in a fully staffed hospital and even as a Red Cross doctor working in the field. But now, the little one was already zapping her energy.

Plastering a smile on her face, she shook her head. "No, no, you go ahead and rest. I'll take the next shift." With that, she patted Marilyn on the shoulder as she walked past her and headed back down to the second floor, ready to make her next rounds.

12

Hop had risen early that morning, his feet pounding the dirt as he ran trails along the compound grounds. With his earbuds in, he listened to the news, glad that Jeb had set him up with an English-speaking Ecuadorian station so that he could stay abreast of what was going on.

When a new security contract came in yesterday, he noted that Carson didn't give him one that took him away. Instead, he assigned him to compound duty so he could stay close to home. By the end of the day, he'd spoken to Carson, assuring him that he didn't expect special treatment. "I have no idea how long Lori will be in Ecuador, so you can't keep me off active missions based on that."

Carson had shaken his head. "I'm not. You've taken several missions recently, including flying others to their locations, so it's your turn in the rotation to spend some time in California. Believe me, there's plenty of work for you to do around here."

He knew his boss was right and appreciated the

gesture. It appeared that the rain had slowed in the Quito area, but the rivers would still be rising. And the latest word was that more rain might be on the way, as well as the still-looming possibility of mudslides.

He and Abbie had spent time yesterday looking at some of the satellite pictures, along with Natalie. In the past year, that area of Ecuador had had flooding and mudslides coming down from the volcanic mountains, decimating entire villages and towns. He studied the town she was in, remembering that she'd mentioned a maternity clinic. From what he could see, the clinic appeared to be on the side of the hill and not close to the river. That should keep her safe from any flooding. But landslides? That was an entirely different nightmare scenario.

As he'd lain in bed the previous night, he'd kept turning their last conversation over and over in his mind, still wondering what she wanted to talk to him about. *Has she decided that she'd rather not try to have a relationship? Or wants a relationship but doesn't know if I'm on board? Fuck, if only we could have met up before she left.*

He'd finally fallen asleep, but it had been a fitful rest. And now, as the fog lifted over the mountain trails, he ran to chase out the thoughts swirling in his head. When he finally came to an outcropping of rocks that overlooked part of the mountains that fell away below him, he plopped down onto a flat stone and breathed in the cool air deeply. Pulling his phone from his pocket, he fired off a text.

Thinking of you. Staring at the news and hoping

you're OK. I know you're working and exhausted. Take care and call when you can.

After resting for a few minutes, he shifted on the rock and stood. Looking around at the breathtaking scenery once again, he then turned and began the run down the trails toward the lighthouse. Arriving early, he stopped and chatted with Rachel and Teddy in the lobby.

She lifted her brow and said, "You're out early. Either you slept great last night or didn't sleep very well at all."

Laughing, he shook his head. "You're not wrong. My confession is that I didn't sleep well."

"I understand that you're concerned about a friend of yours who's working with the Red Cross in Ecuador right now," she said, her business demeanor slipping as her warm gaze held his.

He nodded, no longer feeling the desire to keep his personal business separate from what was going on at work. "I'm sure she's fine. I'll just feel better when I hear from her."

"That area has had it rough," Teddy said, his brows lowering. "I can't say I pay much attention to that part of the world unless there's a mission nearby, but I was watching the news last night, and this is the third time in the past twelve months that they've had flooding. And a lot of those places weren't built to withstand that much water or the shifting earth that occurs."

"That's my biggest fear," he admitted. "She's an OB/GYN, and they've got her at a smaller maternity clinic that's not with the larger hospital. From what

Abbie and Natalie have been able to find out, it should be safe from flooding but not mudslides."

"Well, you know Carson," Rachel said. "If he even thinks there's a possibility that you're needed, he'll have me making the arrangements while you make the flight plans!"

"I hope it doesn't come to that because that would mean she would really need me. Hell, though, I'd just like to go and make sure for myself that she's okay."

With a chin lift, he walked back to the locker rooms and took a quick shower. By the time he was dressed, other Keepers were coming in.

A few hours later, his phone vibrated, and he slipped it out of his pocket again, trying to still his racing heartbeat as he saw her name in the messages.

Fine so far. Just tired. Working with a skeleton crew right now. Rain has stopped, and the clinic isn't in danger of floodwater. Have to admit, mudslides scare me. Maybe we can talk soon.

Not willing to let her get away, he immediately typed a reply.

Call me anytime. I really wanna hear your voice. Miss you. Can't wait to see you again.

His heart continued to pound as he watched the bubbles of a new text being written bounce around for a moment until her next message came through.

Sounds good. I should have a chance to call tomorrow. I'll text first to make sure it's a good time. Miss you too.

A sigh of relief escaped his lungs, and he closed his eyes for a few seconds. *She misses me. Surely that means she doesn't wanna call things off.* While a text wouldn't replace the sound of her voice, he felt as though he could breathe a little easier.

By the end of the day, Lori and the staff were dead on their feet. She had no idea how long they would be expected to work at the same level as they had on this first day in Ecuador.

"Jesus, I wish we were connected to the main hospital," Jackie said, circles underneath her eyes. They were sitting at a table in the lounge as they took a hasty break to eat dinner. "At least then, the hospital would be able to shift some of the other nurses to the maternity floor since they wouldn't have any elective surgery patients."

"I didn't want to make any major decisions until the director, Dr. Rocha, got here, but I'm not overly impressed with what I'm seeing from him. He stayed in his office most of the afternoon and early evening, only coming out to check on a couple of the patients. It was as though he had his favorites, and the others who came in were relegated to us."

"I noticed that and thought it was weird, but maybe he's used to relying on his staff to take care of everything. But speaking of staff, what about the shortage?" Marilyn asked.

"I've got a call in to Dr. Casta to see when we can expect more Red Cross nurses. Again, I was expecting Dr. Rocha to make that call, but he left after seeing those select patients and talking to Rosa." She sighed.

"I'll talk to him about it tomorrow. Of course, that's assuming he comes in, but then I'm sure he will. I'm honestly not certain why I'm feeling so bitchy toward him."

"Maybe because in the middle of his country's disaster, he didn't seem to pull his weight. Hell, he hardly seemed to do anything," Jackie continued to grouse, pulling her hair out of the ponytail and running a brush through its length.

"One way or the other, either through him or Dr. Casta, I'll put in for more nurses."

"What about midwives?" Marilyn suggested.

Nodding, Lori replied, "I was going to ask for those, too. Although, if there are women who can't get in or are planning on having a home birth and their home is not compromised, the midwives may be busy with their own cases. But if any of them could spare some time to come in, that would help."

"I overheard Elisa mention some British Red Cross volunteers coming as well. I'm hoping some get assigned here."

Lori reached out and rubbed her brow, glad the rice, beans, and bread were stilling her nausea from earlier. Now, if she could just keep the fatigue-induced headache at bay, she'd consider that a win for their first day in the country. "Let's get some rest since several new night nurses have arrived. I'm gonna try to sleep for a few hours, hope there are no labor complications overnight, and tomorrow, we'll face the situation with fresh eyes."

Not wanting to sleep in the same scrubs she'd worn

all day, Lori took a shower and changed into fresh scrubs, knowing pajamas would be a waste of time. She'd started taking prenatal vitamins, making sure to keep them tucked into her luggage and not take them on an empty stomach. She towel-dried her long hair, then braided it, not worried about what it would look like the next day.

Eyeing the hard cot with no covering or sheet, she was grateful for the pillow. Letting out a sigh of relief, she stretched out and rested her aching head. She both looked forward to and dreaded trying to call Hop tomorrow, having wished now she hadn't promised to do so. She knew the situation at the clinic would be hectic based on the day they'd just had. But the desire to hear his voice was overwhelming.

Will I be able to talk to him, knowing that I carry his child but can't say anything? Her duties as a Red Cross doctor had never lasted more than three to four weeks before she was rotated out, and two weeks was the norm. *It's not that long. I'm sure I can wait until I make a trip to California to tell him.* With that assurance in her mind, she closed her eyes. She fell almost instantly asleep as utter exhaustion overtook her body.

13

By the time Marilyn gently shook her awake on the fourth morning in Quito, Lori had managed to get six straight hours of sleep. She considered that to be a miracle, considering the last few days had been a constant round of intakes, deliveries, and discharges. She hoped the night's sleep portended a good day. Splashing cold water on her face, she moisturized, pulled her hair out of the braid, and re-brushed it before tying it back into a wavy ponytail. Shoving her feet into Crocs, she hustled into the kitchenette, avoiding the coffee and fixing a cup of herbal tea instead.

"Jesus, how can you not be dying for a cup of coffee?" Jackie asked, sipping the hot brew. "Especially Ecuadorian coffee!"

Glad that her back was to the other nurses, she inhaled deeply, enjoying the smell of the delicious coffee but simply shrugged her shoulders. "I'm afraid too much caffeine might make me jittery."

Carefully nibbling the eggs and toast that one of the other nurses had cooked, she prayed the morning sickness would abate while knowing she needed the energy to make it through the day. After eating, she quickly headed down to the second floor for rounds. Most of the rooms were full, but only two deliveries presented with possible complications. The others appeared to progress normally.

"Good morning, Dr. Baker."

Turning, she watched as Elisa approached. She'd tried to get Elisa to call her Lori, but the nurse had shown surprise as she'd shaken her head. *"I'm afraid Dr. Rocha would consider that informality to be unacceptable."* Not willing to argue, Lori had simply acquiesced.

"Good morning." She started to head down the hall, then turned back. "By the way, do you know if we can expect Dr. Rocha to be here today? I know I've only been here for a few days, but we will definitely need assistance. I wanted to wait until he made it in today before I asked for more nurses and volunteers from Dr. Casta."

Elisa pressed her lips together tightly and shook her head. "That was the reason I was coming to see you. I just got word that there is more flooding in one of the areas of Quito that houses quite a few of our wealthier citizens. Dr. Rocha's house is in that neighborhood, and he may not be back for several days."

That was not welcome news, but Lori quickly made an executive decision. "Thank you for telling me. I'm going to call Dr. Casta now and see when we can expect to get more nurses, another doctor, and perhaps some volunteers. I'll use Dr. Rocha's office and—"

"Oh no, you can't."

Lori's brows rose to her hairline. "I'm sorry?"

"I don't have a key to Dr. Rocha's office. In fact, no one has a key to his office except him, and I suppose the cleaning staff. He's very private and considers that to be his professional sanctuary."

Lori opened her mouth to retort, then snapped it closed, giving her head a little shake. "Well, I suppose I'll leave his little sanctuary alone. But we'll need more pharmaceuticals and supplies if he won't be in for another week. Will you be able to assist me, or should I go through Dr. Casta for that?"

"I'm very sorry, Dr. Baker... Lori. Dr. Rocha handles all of those responsibilities."

It was clear by Elisa's wringing hands that the head nurse was discomfited. Hoping to alleviate some of the concerns, she said, "We can't wait for Dr. Rocha to return to take care of the clinic's needs, so I'll talk to Dr. Casta about that as well."

"I know that Rosa would appreciate the help, but I also know that she has a special relationship with Dr. Rocha."

"Special?" Lori wondered if that was code for sexual or romantic.

She quickly shook her head, her cheeks blushing. "Oh, not like that. Or... I don't think so. I just mean they work closely together, and she's usually the only one who spends any time in his office. She might be able to assist with some of the pharmaceutical records for what needs to be re-ordered if he doesn't come back soon."

"Thank you for the advice," Lori said, finally turning to head into the next patient's room, deciding to call Dr. Casta as soon as she had a break.

An hour later, Marilyn met her outside of a room with a scowl on her face. "We have a patient who's insisting that they must deal with Dr. Rocha only. But she's not in labor yet. And yes, I've explained to her that he's not in and won't be in!"

"Well, they're just going to have to deal with me," she replied, unable to shed the grumpiness that threatened to overtake her.

"I can take care of her," Rosa said, stepping around the corner, her narrow-eyed gaze darting amongst the others in the hall. "I'm sure I can deal with her."

"Thank you, but I'll have a word with her, as well," Lori said. "She needs to understand that she's still in good hands." She turned and walked into the room, interrupting Rosa's insistence.

The expectant mother was sitting on the edge of the bed in one of the birthing rooms. Glancing at Rosa, she said, "If you'll translate, please." Then looking at the woman, she explained, "I'm Dr. Baker, an obstetrician, and even though Dr. Rocha is not here, I assure you that your needs will be met. But I'll need to examine you to see if you are ready to be admitted."

"You don't understand," the woman bit out. "I need to see him. I haven't received my payment!"

"Your payment?" She understood that word and

glanced toward Rosa, shaking her head. "She must mean her bill."

"I want him! Dr. Rocha!" the woman cried.

"I'm afraid he's not coming in today. But we will do everything we can to make sure you're as comfortable as possible for a safe delivery for you and your baby. But you cannot stay if it is not time for you to deliver or have a medical condition that doesn't needs monitoring."

The woman opened her mouth, then snapped it closed as she looked beyond Lori. Turning around, Lori noted Rosa was shaking her head.

Rosa shifted her gaze to Lori. "I believe the new nurses have just arrived. I'll continue to talk to this woman and find out what she needs."

Inclining her head, Lori started out of the room, frustrated, but with a clinic to run, she hardly had time to argue. Heading downstairs, she was greeted by the same driver who had brought her, Jackie, and Marilyn to the clinic.

His rain slicker was dripping water on the entrance floor, but with him, he had three women in Red Cross jackets, each with a suitcase at their feet.

"Hello! Hello! I bring you more help!" he called out, a smile on his wet face.

Hurrying forward, she greeted him warmly and wished him safety before he turned and left through the door again. Looking at the new arrivals, she introduced herself, thrilled at having more help.

The oldest, with a pleasant smile and no-nonsense

manner, was an obstetrics nurse from London. The youngest was a nurse anesthetist, also from London.

"Oh my God," Lori exuded. "We are in desperate need of your help." Turning to the third woman, she smiled as she was introduced to a midwife from Rome.

"You are all very welcome. I've been here for less than a week, but I can tell you that things may get confusing very quickly if they decide to evacuate us. So please follow me, and I'll introduce you to the head nurse here."

Quickly showing them where they could stow their luggage, she gave them the rundown on the clinic, the possible evacuation happening later that day, and the procedures. The Ecuadorian and other Red Cross nurses quickly introduced themselves, and they immediately began rounds, pitching in with the women actively in labor and checking on those who had already delivered.

Much of the day passed like the previous ones. The electricity flickered several times, but each time the generators kicked on. She and the other staff kept an eye on the news as they watched the floodwaters rise in the areas of town closest to the river. The threat of mudslides still filled the news, making her wonder whether it was a possibility or a probability.

After several more deliveries, including a few difficult ones, she talked to Dr. Casta, then finally took a break in the late afternoon, deciding to attempt a call to Hop. Desiring privacy, she found a door leading to the stairs that took her to the rooftop. Since the rain had stopped, it was the perfect place to have a private conversation.

Enjoying the quiet, she walked to the edge and leaned her elbows on the brick wall that surrounded the roof. The air was fresh, and the green mountains appeared lush. It was hard to imagine the majestic beauty creating such devastation if the steep sides began to crumble downward.

She glanced down to the streets below, glad that while wet, they weren't flooded, making it easier for them to discharge patients. A vehicle pulled up to the front, and she smiled at the sight of another new mother being wheeled out. *Strange that there's no excited father or family rushing out to greet her.* Continuing to watch, she spied the mother getting into the vehicle after waving to the nurse, who went back inside.

Another car pulled in front of the clinic, and a woman alighted from the passenger side. She walked to the new mother and took the bundled baby from her. From her rooftop viewing place, Lori was too far away to see if the new mother was surprised, but she didn't act upset. She simply closed the vehicle door, and her driver drove them away as the car with the baby left in a different direction. *Was she a relative? Some kind of caregiver for the new mother? Or...*

A snake of unease now moved through her. This was now twice that she had witnessed someone else leaving with the baby besides the new mother. Pressing her lips together, she wondered if something was happening that might involve the clinic. Snorting, she shook her head. *Like I have time to figure out why some babies are in a different car than their mothers. Let me add that to all the other things on my plate!*

She looked down and patted her stomach. *You're my primary responsibility, little one. And it's time to talk to your dad.* Walking over to an upturned bucket, she sat down and pulled out her phone. As promised, she sent Hop a text to see if he was available. He texted his enthusiastic acquiescence almost immediately. Blowing out a deep breath, she dialed.

14

Hop had been on pins and needles, waiting to see if Lori would have a chance to call. When the text finally came through, he couldn't reply fast enough. She was only three hours ahead, but he was taking a late lunch break, hoping she'd be able to call at the end of her day. It looked like the timing was perfect.

Sitting in his car at a gravel overlook, he took in the view of the Pacific Ocean on one side as it glistened in the sunlight, and a burger food truck that he'd just eaten at was off to the side.

His finger hovered over the accept call button, jabbing it quickly as soon as her name came through. "Hey, Lori babe, how are you?"

"I'm fine. What about you?"

Her voice soothed him. He'd take a text if that was all he could get, but listening to the sound of her gentle voice was even better than he remembered. "Hell, darlin', you don't have to worry about me. You're the one in the middle of a disaster."

She chuckled ruefully. "Well, at least the rain has stopped, although they're calling for more in another day. I really hope it misses us because I don't know how much more this area can take."

"How's the hospital?"

"Since it's higher up on a hill just outside of town, it's not flooded. But not being connected to the main hospital has its drawbacks, particularly with staffing. I hope to get more Red Cross nurses and volunteers tomorrow. Right now, I'm acting as the director because the regular doctor in charge is at his home, which is threatened by floods."

"Hasn't he got someone else to watch over his house? Shouldn't he be at the clinic?"

She hesitated, then sighed.

It hit him that she might be surrounded by others and wouldn't want to be overheard as being critical. "You probably can't answer that, depending on who's around."

She laughed, and if he thought her voice sounded lovely, her laughter filled him with longing. "What's so funny?"

"Actually, I'm by myself, and nobody can hear me. I'm up on the roof."

"On the roof?"

"Yeah. I wanted privacy to be able to talk to you, and right now, we are packed full of pregnant women, and the nursing staff is running around. I'm taking a break and discovered that I can sit on the roof and have a private conversation since it's not raining."

"Would you be offended if I said please be careful?"

"I promise I'll be careful, and hearing you say that is nice."

"Listen, Lori, I've had something on my mind since we last talked. You said you had something you wanted to talk to me about, but you'd rather do it in person. To be honest, my mind has come up with all sorts of crazy shit, especially since it might be a while before we see each other."

She didn't reply, and a strange unsettling in his stomach began. Pressing on, he said, "I thought maybe you weren't sure of our relationship. Or... um... wondering if I was interested or maybe if you weren't interested or..." There was continued silence, and the unsettling in his stomach turned into a full-blown riot of nerves. "I guess I just didn't want to have things hanging out and not know what was going through your mind."

She sighed heavily. "I'm sorry, Hop. I shouldn't have said anything and dragged this out. It's not about any of those things, or rather, it's not just those things. I mean, it's just that I had something to tell you, and I... well, it's not the kind of thing I want to say without thinking about how you might take it, and um... it would be better if we could see each other... shit, I'm not making any sense."

"I get it, Lori. Whatever it is, you'd rather do it face-to-face, which I respect. I just need you to know that I care about you, and I don't want you wondering or worrying about anything. But waiting to find out what you're thinking is kind of driving me crazy."

Another few seconds of silence seemed to stretch

into forever, and his breathing shallowed as he wondered if she was going to speak again. Another heavy sigh met his ears, and his heart beat an erratic pattern in his chest.

"Hop, this isn't how I wanted to tell you, but it's only fair that you know. And I don't expect you to say anything because I've had a week to process it, and you need to have that, too. Maybe it's better this way so that when we see each other face-to-face, we both will have come to grips with our feelings."

Every word she said ratcheted up the nervous fear that was now coursing through him. Part of him wanted to tell her to just wait, but if they were going to have any kind of a relationship, they needed to be able to communicate. "It's okay, Lori. Just say whatever is on your mind."

"Well… um… it's not really something that's just on my mind. It's actually a reality that we're going to have to face. But there's no right or wrong way with how we face it, so… oh, hell, Hop, I'm pregnant. And in case you're wondering, there's been no one else but you. I certainly understand that you'd want a paternity test, and as soon as I get back, we can take care of that."

Pregnant. *Pregnant?* Pregnant. *No way. She can't be. We used protection.* His mind blanked, and no words came forth. He waited, almost expecting a panicked response to hit him, but instead, he felt calm. Shocked but calm.

"Lori…" he stumbled, trying to find the right words… *any* words to say.

Suddenly, he could hear shuffling and voices in the

background. Lori's voice was low, and it appeared she was speaking to someone.

"Shit, Hop. I can't believe this. I've got an emergency downstairs, and I've got to go. Christ, I'm so sorry to dump this on you and run. I should never have said anything until we could talk face-to-face. Please, just... I'm sorry. We'll talk soon."

Before he could think to speak or even say goodbye, the connection was dead. He sat with the phone still held to his ear for a long moment, not moving. Finally dropping his hand, he continued staring at the ocean in front of him.

Pregnant? How the fuck did that happen? Pregnant? Even with protection? Fuck, even I know that's not one-hundred-percent effective. Shit, she's pregnant... with my baby.

Unable to form a coherent thought, his mind raced as he stared out upon the churning ocean waves as they crashed onto the rocks below. The sun shone through the blue sky, and the ocean glistened with diamond sparkles. It was the kind of day that he had been admiring a few minutes earlier as he finished his lunch. Now, all he could think of was Lori, pregnant with his child, battling floodwaters and possible mudslides, functioning with little sleep and a lot of work.

The next thing he knew, he was pulling into the parking lot at the compound, stunned that he'd driven there on autopilot. He needed to go in and finish the workday but had no idea how he could manage to keep the others from seeing his tumultuous thoughts. He wanted to call her back. He wanted to assure her that she would never face this alone. But right now, all he could do was get his shit together enough to walk into the compound. After all the successful missions and special ops he'd run, he wondered if getting through the next few hours was going to be his greatest feat.

He was grateful when he got inside the compound and found that most of the other Keepers were gone or occupied. Natalie and Abbie were at their computers, typing away. They seemed to be coordinating something with Jeb. He remembered a few Keepers were leaving for a local security check. Rick and Chris were probably home packing to get ready to travel to Idaho, checking in with the DEA to assist with a drug-running mission.

Moving to a computer station on the other side of the room where his screen would be hidden, he spent the next couple of hours researching more of the area where Lori was staying. With one eye on the news and the other on a new internet search on pregnancies, he managed to fly under the radar of his fellow coworkers.

By the end of the day, he felt as though he was crawling out of his skin and left quickly, calling out a good night to the others still there. Driving home, he forced his mind to focus on the drive. *Getting into an accident won't help my situation.*

Walking into his house, he tossed his keys onto the counter and stalked directly to the refrigerator, pulling out a beer. With his hip leaning against the counter, he downed it quickly. Reaching into the cabinet, he grabbed the whiskey, poured a shot, then slammed that back, too.

Fuck, this isn't going to change anything. Knowing he

needed to stay levelheaded, he pulled out his phone and called for pizza delivery, adding in an Italian sub and wings, before he walked through the living room and plopped down onto the sofa to wait.

"She's pregnant. She's pregnant with my baby. *My baby.*" He said the words out loud now that he was alone in his own house, and even hearing them aloud didn't seem to make it any more real. *What else had she said?* Searching his memory of their shortened call, she'd mentioned a paternity test. *A paternity test? Fuck that!* He'd do whatever she wanted but knew the baby was his. "It's mine. My baby." Hearing that declaration once again finally seemed to settle something deep inside.

As shocking as the news had been to hear and as tumultuous as the feelings that had slammed into him, he realized he wasn't upset. Surprised, shocked, stunned. But not angry, upset, blaming, or even uncertain.

"But we were cut off before she had a chance to tell me how she felt about anything," he muttered. *Shit! And she's probably wondering what I'm thinking!* Frustrated with their separation more than ever, as well as the time difference, he grabbed his phone and typed out a text.

I hate that our conversation was stopped. I don't want you to worry about anything. Please call again as soon as you can. I want to know you're OK. You're not in this alone.

Having no clue what else to say, he hit send. He waited, desperate for a return text, but it didn't come. A knock on his door jolted him from staring at the phone in his hand, and he remembered he'd ordered dinner.

Jumping to his feet, he pulled his wallet from his back pocket, accepted the food, and tipped the young man well. Grabbing another beer from the kitchen, he set the pizza box on the coffee table, turned on the television to a game he wasn't interested in, and placed his phone front and center so he could see as soon as she replied.

He continued to stare at the phone while eating, barely tasting his food. Finally, it vibrated, and he jumped again. *Jesus, I'm never this tightly wound, even on a mission!* Grabbing his phone, he quickly looked at the returning text from her.

I'm OK. Wish we had more time to talk. I have no expectations from you but wanted you to know. Don't worry about me. I should be home in a couple of weeks, and we can talk then.

He read her message several times, still trying to define her emotions from the words she'd written. He hated the separation. Hated that they couldn't talk easily. He knew even if he called her right now, she wouldn't talk if she was surrounded by other people. Grinding his teeth together, he was surprised his jaw didn't crack. Refusing to remain silent, he typed another text.

It's important that you know that while your news was a surprise, I'm not upset. I know we can work things out together. Just please stay safe, come home as soon as you can, and call me when you get a chance. Don't worry about anything.

He reread his words before hitting send, wishing that he could have said everything that was on his mind. *Now, I understand why she wanted to wait until we were together before she told me the news.* Trying to put thoughts and emotions into simple texts left so much out, and he was terrified that she wouldn't understand what he wanted to say. But more than anything, he wanted her safe and healthy. *Her and our baby.*

Having eaten half the pizza, half the sub, and most of the wings, he wrapped the rest in foil and put it into the refrigerator, then tossed the beer bottles into the recycle bin. Glad that tomorrow was Saturday and he wasn't assigned a weekend duty, he was determined to stay close to his phone in case she could call. Now that the news had settled in, he wanted to hear her voice more than anything else. Whatever happened between them, he wanted her to know how much he cared for her and their baby. *My baby. Our baby.*

Holy shit... Lori is having my baby, and I'm going to be a dad.

15

Lori hustled down the stairs from the roof, having heard her name being called. She stopped at the bottom of the stairs and shoved her phone into her pocket, grimacing with self-anger at the way she'd handled the phone call with Hop. *Why did I do that? I wasn't going to tell him I was pregnant until I could see him!* She was proud of her self-control and her carefully thought-out process for difficult situations. And with that one call, she'd blown her good intentions to smithereens.

She wanted to scream out her frustration but was forced to walk out onto the floor and become the doctor who was one-hundred-percent focused on the women who depended on her. Squeezing her eyes shut, she swallowed deeply to keep the tears from flowing. Silently chanting, *"You got this; you got this,"* she had to move forward because she sure as hell couldn't put the genie back into the bottle now.

The concern in his voice still rang in her ears, making her want to reassure him that she was really okay. *Christ, I could've handled the news in so many other ways!* Having to end the call before they had a chance to talk was just another rotten thing she'd been forced to do.

As she hurried down the stairs and pushed through the door onto the second floor, she realized that perhaps giving him time to be on his own while he considered the news and their situation was not a bad thing. But she still felt guilty as hell for the way the conversation had ended so abruptly. Sighing heavily, she shook her head, knowing she couldn't do anything about it now. Seeing Jackie, she hustled over. "Sorry, I was taking a break."

"You deserve it, so I'm the one who's sorry to have to disturb you, but a woman's just come in, and things are not going well."

Pushing all other thoughts to the side, she hurried into the birthing room, instantly sliding into professional mode. Glancing at the young, wide-eyed mother lying in bed hooked up to monitors, Lori headed to the sink. Once washed and gloved, she examined her, looking at the charts and the monitors. Turning to the terrified woman, she offered a smile to hopefully ease her fears. With the Ecuadorian nurse translating, she explained the fetal distress and the need for a cesarean section. At first, the patient burst into tears, but when she understood that her baby was in danger, she nodded, begging Lori to take care of them.

The nurses rolled her into the surgery, where Rosa handled the anesthesia, and Lori efficiently performed the surgery, observing as the healthy baby was handed to the still-sobbing mother. Lori stitched her up while the baby was nuzzled by his mother, who was now smiling through her tears, causing Lori to smile as well. Finishing, she left the baby and mother with the nurses as she walked out of the surgery room. Wiping her brow, she began her rounds, pushing down her own personal situation. There were new mothers to discharge, expectant mothers to evaluate for delivery, and for right now, no more cesareans on the board.

Once out into the hall, she walked past a door and glanced inside, seeing Rosa talking to the pregnant woman who'd come in early, demanding to see Dr. Rocha. She started to walk inside, determined to make sure Rosa was not promising that Dr. Rocha would come. The harshly whispered words caused her feet to halt as she understood most of what was said.

"I want my money. I haven't gotten anything since the last installment!" the patient bit out.

"I assure you that Dr. Rocha will take care of everything when he returns. But you can't stay now."

"I was supposed to get my money upon delivery. If I'm going to go through this, how do I know he's going to live up to his side of the bargain?"

"He has never reneged on an agreement," Rosa said. "So let me take care of you, and I promise he'll be in touch."

"And the baby? Who will come to take the baby?"

"I'll contact him now and find out what he wants us to do. If they are ready, we'll make arrangements for tomorrow. You have to understand that with the flooding and possible evacuation, we are in a situation that was not considered. But the agreement will be upheld."

"It better be. I'm not carrying this child for nothing—"

The woman's tirade grew softer as Lori hastened down the hall so she wouldn't be caught listening. Lori turned their conversation over in her mind. While her Spanish was imperfect, she felt sure she understood the hastily spoken conversation between the expectant mother and Rosa. *Agreement? Contract? Payment? Dr. Rocha and Rosa? Is someone taking the baby?* She didn't like the sound of the conversation but wasn't about to ask Rosa because she could no longer trust her.

Stepping into the staff restroom, she locked the door and gripped the sink, breathing deeply. She was acutely aware of various baby-selling schemes in most countries, especially third-world countries, where young mothers could be lured by the idea of receiving payment for their babies. Sometimes the babies were given up for adoption outside the legal channels. And sometimes for exploitation and trafficking purposes. Staring into the mirror, she sucked in a ragged breath. *Is that what's happening? Or am I making up a scenario from an innocent mistranslation?* Wetting a paper towel, she swiped her face before stepping back into the hall.

Seeing Elisa, she approached cautiously, trying to think of how best to bring up the subject. As Elisa turned her expectant face toward her, Lori cleared her throat. "I happened to notice a patient getting into a vehicle without the discharging nurse staying with her and the baby to make sure they were secure."

A furrow marred Elisa's brow. "We usually have an aide wheel out the mother and baby, but I don't know about them coming inside the clinic too soon. Of course, we are down most of our aides. Perhaps they are in a hurry to return to their other duties, but I will certainly talk to them."

"Thank you. I think that would be appropriate. I'd like a staff member to stay with the discharged patient and baby until they are securely in their vehicle. I know we're working under extreme circumstances, and Dr. Rocha isn't here to direct the clinic, but I'm concerned to see babies leaving in one vehicle and the mothers in another."

"What do you mean—"

"Elisa? You're needed in room 215," another nurse called out, interrupting Elisa's question.

"No rest for us, it seems," Lori said, patting Elisa's shoulder. Watching Elisa walk away, she thought of what she'd seen. Now, more than ever, she wanted to look inside Dr. Rocha's office. Whatever was going on filled her with a suspicion that she couldn't ignore, especially if Elisa didn't know what was happening.

Hurrying down the stairs to the first floor, she moved to the back, where the cleaning staff had a small room. Slipping inside, she found the room unoccupied, but what she was looking for was hanging in plain sight. A small ring of keys that she assumed they used to get into the various rooms. Grabbing the keys, she slipped them into her pocket and dashed up to the third floor, panting by the time she arrived. Chastising herself for running, she calmed slightly when she observed the hall was empty.

It took several moments, but she finally discovered the key that unlocked Dr. Rocha's office. Sliding it off the key chain, she hastened back to the first floor and replaced the key ring on the hook once again before it would be missed.

Taking a slow walk around the second floor, she made note of her patients' progress, and since no one needed her services at the moment, she glanced at Jackie and smiled. "I'm going to check in with Dr. Casta."

She returned to Dr. Rocha's office and felt no guilt over her explanation since she fully intended to check with Dr. Casta very soon to check the status of their possible evacuation. With no one around, she used the key and slipped into Dr. Rocha's office, shutting the door behind her.

She stood in his office for a moment, casting her gaze at the minimal but elegant furniture. The office wasn't ostentatious, but the polished wooden desk and leather chair appeared to be of quality. A bookcase lined one side, and at a quick glance, she could see the volumes were mostly medical books. A computer was on his desk, but she had no idea how to get into it or figure out his password.

The only other piece of furniture in the room was a matching wooden credenza behind his desk. Walking to it, she was surprised to find it unlocked. Opening the drawers, she quickly flipped through the files but found nothing that would indicate anything worthy of a second look. Snorting out loud, she shook her head. *Of course, if he's involved in something that he shouldn't be, he'd hardly leave it in plain sight.* A heavy sigh left her lips. *I guess it's a good thing I'm a doctor and not an investigator.*

She thought back to the woman who'd indicated Dr. Rocha owed her money while at the same time appearing not to have plans to take the baby home with her. The inkling of unease that she had felt earlier continued to slither through her, growing as her imagination ran wild. *Was the woman a surrogate for another couple that should be coming in? Was the woman part of a medical study that she was being paid for? Was Dr. Rocha giving kickbacks for someone using his facility?*

No matter what question she posed, she couldn't come up with a good reason the woman would be demanding to see him for reasons of payment. Not finding anything else in his office worth searching, she cracked the door just enough to make sure no one was in the hall and then slipped out, locking the door behind her. Pocketing the key, she went down to the second floor.

She stopped into several rooms to examine the women and babies who were ready for discharge, not willing to send them home unless she knew they were healthy and had safe homes to return to. She also reminded the nurses to make sure that those discharged had family members show up to assist them as they left.

Coming to the room Rosa had last been seen in, she spied the young woman who was so adamant about seeing Dr. Rocha, still sitting in one of the birthing rooms.

Checking her chart, she could see Rosa's name at the bottom and was furious that a bed was being occupied by a woman not in active labor. Deciding to see what she could discern from the woman while no one else was around, she attempted the best Spanish she could manage. "Dr. Rocha will be pleased when you have your baby."

"He owes me for baby," the woman replied, and Lori was glad she was able to understand what she had said.

"Uh... what is he paying for?"

The woman's brow furrowed as she stared up at Lori. "For baby! I have baby, and he pays. Gives baby to someone when I get money."

She sucked in a hasty breath, wishing she could push aside her growing suspicion that Dr. Rocha was involved in some kind of pay-for-baby racket.

Rosa rushed in, but Lori speared the nurse with a hard glare. "It appears you admitted this patient who is not in labor. You will need to send her home—"

"I can't," Rosa said, her gaze darting back and forth between the woman and Lori. "Her home is flooded, and she's alone. No husband. No family. That's why she wanted Dr. Rocha. I called him, and he said to admit her."

She held Rosa's gaze for several long seconds, debating if she should continue to insist, but ultimately, she couldn't see possibly harming the young woman. *Plus, if she's here, I can see what happens after she has the baby.* Offering a curt nod, she turned and walked back into the hall.

Once her rounds were complete, she decided to take the opportunity to call Dr. Casta and headed into the nurses' office. She wanted to ask about getting more assistance and see if he had any insight into Dr. Rocha. But the conversation quickly moved in a different direction.

"I've been told we may need to move you to another location."

"Another location?" She rubbed her forehead as her senses heightened. "To where? And when?"

"The minister of health is looking at your area for stability and is considering moving the patients and staff to another hospital away from the possibility of landslides."

"Dr. Casta, why wasn't this considered before now? Are we in immediate danger?" There was a hesitation after her question, which sent a nervous snake of anxiety slithering through her. "Please, Dr. Casta, if we need to evacuate, I need to know so I can plan. I've done this before in similar situations, and it can't just happen without planning."

"He said they would make a decision first thing in the morning. If evacuation is needed, then it will happen tomorrow. They are looking to make room at a hospital away from both the floods and the mountains."

"What about Dr. Rocha? I know his house is in a flood zone, but when can we expect him?"

A heavy sigh met her ears. "I'm sorry, Dr. Baker. I don't know."

Pressing her lips together in indecision, she finally blurted, "What can you tell me about him?"

"About Dr. Rocha?"

"Yes... I've only met him once, and while the clinic seems professional, I have questions about some of the patients he sees—"

"Oh, as I told you, his clinic often sees the patients that might not go to see a doctor or those who avoid hospitals—"

"Yes," she interrupted, not in the mood to listen to a litany of Dr. Rocha's virtues. "But have there ever been any concerns about how the clinic is run?"

"Oh no, I've never heard anything negative."

Inwardly scoffing, she sighed. *No doctor and no clinic has only satisfied patients, so to never have heard anything negative isn't realistic!* But arguing wasn't going to meet the needs she was facing.

"Then, as acting medical director for this facility until he returns or someone from your medical department or Red Cross tells me otherwise, I'm formally requesting more assistance, especially someone with anesthetist certification. And I want to be kept abreast of every decision concerning this clinic."

"I agree, Dr. Baker. I have a few more Red Cross nurses on their way and will have them assigned to you. They should arrive tomorrow and can assist if you have to evacuate."

She hoped tomorrow wouldn't be too late, though she had no choice but to accept his word. Hanging up, she battled the desire to slam the phone down. Taking a moment to calm down, she then walked into the hall and called for Rosa, Elisa, Jackie, and Marilyn, giving them the rundown on what Dr. Casta had told her.

"Well, hell," Jackie bit out. "It's supposed to start raining again tonight, and that couldn't be a surprise to the ones in charge. So they let us sit up here and now decide we might need to move the women and babies, hell… everything to somewhere else?"

"Why can't they just move us to the hospital on the other side of town now?" Marilyn asked, her dark eyes snapping with anger.

"They are overfilled with casualties from the flooding," Lori said, fatigue once more pulling at her. "They will have to make room for our patients and for us to direct the ones who planned on coming to us to go there instead."

"I don't understand why they can't get ready for these contingencies," Elisa said, anger written on her face, as well. "We keep having floods. We keep having mudslides. The government knows climate change is making everything different, but they can't seem to make policies to help. And the minister of health can't keep up with the demand."

Lori nodded at Elisa's accurate words, but nothing they could do was going to settle the situation at the moment. "We need to rely on the few new nurses who came in for the night shift to do as much as they can so that the ones on the day shift can get some rest. It looks like tomorrow will be a busy day, one way or the other."

Rosa had remained quiet but muttered, "I will talk to Dr. Rocha to see—"

"No," Lori said, cutting her off. "As acting medical

director, I will talk to him." She was immediately aware of the undercurrent of anger pouring off Rosa, but the nurse wisely remained quiet. Turning, she walked down the hall.

By the time she'd finished evening rounds, she was exhausted. And pissed. Her attempts to call Dr. Rocha had been unsuccessful. As she showered, thoughts of Hop slipped back into her mind, and she sighed heavily. Staring down at her belly while the water sluiced over her body, she whispered, "I'm sorry, little one. Seems like I'm messing things up right from the beginning, doesn't it?"

16

It was only eight o'clock when she climbed into bed, but she was taking an early shift and planned on rising early in the morning. Her phone vibrated with an incoming message. Seeing it was from Hop, she squeezed her eyes shut for a moment, wondering if what he had to say would make things better or worse. But she'd never been a coward, so she popped open her eyes and clicked on the message.

Thinking of you. I'm watching the news and am concerned. Please let me know how you're doing. I can't stand thinking of you and our baby being there and in danger.

She read the message several times, poring over every word. *He's thinking of me. He mentions our baby. He's worried.* No matter what spin she tried to put on the words, she couldn't help but feel that he was reaching out to let her know he was okay with the news she'd dumped on him earlier.

I don't know when I can call. We might evacuate

somewhere else tomorrow. I don't know how that's going to go. I'm still acting medical director of the clinic since the real director has gone AWOL, and I'm pissed about that. But I'm fine, so please don't worry.

She hit send, and in less than a moment, her phone rang. She couldn't help but smile as she hit connect. "You didn't have to call, you know."

"I hated the way our call ended earlier and have been wanting to talk to you. Getting your text now has me even more worried," he confessed.

"This isn't the first time I've had to do this, Hop. I just wish the health department and government had decided earlier if they wanted the clinic patients to be moved. Now, we're at full capacity with women coming in who are afraid that something might happen, and that just gives us more people to be responsible for if we try to evacuate."

"What's the situation with the medical director?"

She leaned back on her cot and sighed. "I've only met him once. His name is Dr. Alfonso Rocha, and it's my understanding that he left the clinic the other day when he was afraid his house was in a flood zone. It seems he lives in a wealthy neighborhood near the river. He's decided to stay there and protect his house, although I'm not sure what he thinks he can do if the floodwaters reach his property. It's not that I'm unsympathetic, but he had a duty to the staff and the clinic here. He showed up yesterday and did little, only seeming to check on a few of the patients. On top of that, he seems secretive... oh, I don't know. Maybe I'm making up shit because I'm tired. But he and the nurse anesthetist go into a few of the birthing rooms and just seem secretive about their conversations with the select women he's attending to. On top of that, we have no idea if he's coming back in the next couple of days, so I've had to assume the position of acting medical director."

"And that means you're in charge of evacuation if it happens?" Hop growled the words pulled roughly from him. "That's bullshit. You shouldn't have that kind of stress on you."

"The job is stressful, Hop. As I said, this isn't my first rodeo."

"Yes, but before, it was just you. Now you're carrying a baby, and the stress is that much worse."

She wanted to argue that she knew exactly what was happening but realized he was still in the early stages of getting used to the idea. Sighing again for what felt like the zillionth time that day, she rubbed her forehead. "I'm taking care of myself, and it's early days in the pregnancy."

An idea popped into her head, and she blurted, "Listen, I know I don't know much about what you do for a living, but you did mention investigations, right?"

"Um... yeah. But if you're trying to draw a parallel between my job and yours, you can't—"

"Oh, hush, Hop, and listen! I just need to know if you can find out some information on someone from another country, that's all."

"Well, yeah... I mean, if they have some kind of a record or digital footprint. Who are you asking about?"

"Dr. Rocha, the clinical director."

There was a second of hesitation, but she quickly filled the silence. "This has nothing to do with me being irritated at him for not being here. It's just that I've come across some suspicious activity, and when I tried to investigate—"

"You investigated?" he shouted. "What the hell are you doing?"

"If you can't help me, then there's no reason to continue this discussion," she huffed, now sorry she'd opened the can of worms.

A growl met her ears, then he said, "Lori, please. We're separated by time zones and countries. I'm worried about you, and now you've dropped this on me. You've gotta cut me some slack, babe."

She rubbed her lips together, glancing around to ensure no one was in her proximity. "Okay, you're right. I overheard something that made me think he might be involved in something illegal. Baby selling."

"What the hell? Shit, Lori, this is serious."

"I know. That's why I'm asking to see if you can find out anything about him. I've tried looking in his office, but it's almost boring in its efficiency."

"Stop. Absolutely stop looking into him at all!"

"But—"

"No, Lori, no! If he's truly involved in a baby-selling ring, then he'll stop at nothing to keep anyone from discovering what he's doing. I'll look into it. Whatever I can find out, I'll get everything I can on Dr. Rocha. But you stay away from him."

"Well, you don't have to worry because I didn't find anything in his office. I tried to question the patient, who I think might be selling her baby to him, but I think a nurse might be in on it as well."

"Babe, this is fuckin' dangerous! You've gotta stop!"

"That's why I'm asking you, Hop. I know I'm in over my head with whatever he's doing. I'm working my ass off just to take care of the clinic."

"Dammit, Lori, I'm coming down there."

"Coming down here?" She gasped. "Hop, that makes no sense. I'm just doing my job." He was quiet for a moment, but she had no idea what he was thinking. "Seriously, I'll be fine. I'll work on evacuating tomorrow and let you know how things are going."

He huffed loudly. "I'm talking to Carson tonight. Nothing I'm working on now can't wait a few more days. I'd rather be there, helping where I can and making sure you're okay."

"But that's nuts! You can't possibly halt your job every time I go somewhere for the Red Cross."

"After you have the baby, you won't be going everywhere—"

"Excuse me?"

"Shit, Lori, don't get all pissed. I just mean that it'll be different."

"Hop, I—"

"Dammit, Lori, I don't want to wait around anxiously trying to guess what's happening or watch the news. And if I can get down there, I can help. I'll text you to let you know when I'm coming."

It was on the tip of her tongue to say that she didn't need him. That she was a professional who could handle her job without him flying down. That he needed to stay in California and get used to the idea of being a dad without telling her what to do. *Christ, what a fucking mess.*

Squeezing her eyes shut for a moment, she breathed deeply before letting it out slowly. "Hop, I can't tell you what to do any more than you can tell me. Tomorrow will be busy, but I'll call or text to let you know what's happening."

"I'm still coming," he said. "I just... I want you to know... well, I... oh, fuck, Lori. I've got a lot of things going through my mind, but you need to know that I'm okay with everything. I know for a lot of guys finding out unexpectedly that they're going to be a dad isn't good news, but all I can think of is that we're going to have a baby. And when you get home, we can talk and figure everything out, but just know that having a baby with someone as wonderful as you, someone who I care about, makes me a happy man. Unexpected doesn't mean unwanted."

His words caught her off guard. She swallowed past the lump in her throat, and she swiped at the errant tears that fell. *Unexpected doesn't mean unwanted.* Those words crept into the cold crevices that had been forming since she'd first discovered she was pregnant and warmed her deeply. Though she hated to speak with a choking voice, she didn't want to wait since she had the room to herself and no one else could hear her. "That means a lot to me, Hop. I care for you too, and I promise to take care of myself and the baby."

She sat for a moment when they disconnected,

allowing his words to ease the nerves that fluttered through her veins.

She had no misconceptions that he was going to declare vows of love and proposals of marriage. Still, she hoped they would be able to work out an amicable co-parenting situation. *We're friends. If nothing else, we can offer that to our child.* But while she could easily call Hop her friend, her feelings toward him ran deep even in the brief time they'd reconnected. And she knew unrequited love could be a difficult life sentence as co-parents.

Pushing those thoughts away, she placed her hands on her rumbling stomach. Knowing it wasn't the time to make life-altering decisions, she grabbed some cheese crackers from the table next to her cot. After munching on her late-night snack before brushing her teeth, she then crawled into bed.

Her head hit the pillow, and she stretched out on the hard, uncomfortable cot, but as tired as she was, sleep came soon.

17

Hop paced outside their compound for ten minutes after his call with Lori ended, but he was no calmer and definitely not ready to sit and wait to see what might happen. Stalking past Rachel's desk, he hesitated, then turned and looked directly at her. "Rachel, I'm going to be making a trip just as soon as I pass everything through Carson."

She held his gaze with an assessing one of her own before nodding. "When you have the details, just let me know."

"It'll be to Ecuador."

Her expression stayed the same, although he could have sworn her lip curved ever so slightly upward for a second. "I assumed as much."

Opening his mouth, he snapped it shut and simply lifted his chin before turning back to the security door that led to the rest of the compound. Stepping into the room, he didn't hesitate even when every eye landed on him.

"Hop?" Carson called out as soon as his gaze met Hop's. "What's up?"

"Boss, I'm sorry as fuck, but I need to talk to you. I need to take more leave."

"No worries. Whatever you need, you can have."

"I hate to pull this on you, but I need to get down to Ecuador. Lori told me the maternity clinic might have to evacuate. She's having to—"

Carson lifted his hands. "Hop, it's okay. You don't have to justify the trip to me. All I need to know is if you need our assistance. We're at your disposal."

His jaw tightened, then he cast his gaze about the room, seeing the concern on the other Keepers' faces. Swinging his gaze back to his boss, he pressed on. "And there's more. I need to ask for our resources to find out everything we can about Dr. Alfonso Rocha from Quito, Ecuador. She thinks he might be involving the clinic in baby selling."

The room resounded with murmurs of cursing as Jeb turned back to his computer, immediately typing. "I'll see what comes up," Jeb said without hesitation.

Hop planted his hands on his hips, emotion pooling in his throat as he watched his fellow Keepers jump into action.

"Initial intel coming up on the screen," Jeb announced.

Hop looked up, seeing the photograph that must have come from a hospital or clinic badge. Thin face. Neatly trimmed dark hair and dark eyes. He digested the information as he read aloud. "Forty-six years old.

Medical degree from the Central University of Ecuador, Quito. OB/GYN."

"I pulled up the info on the clinic yesterday when we were gathering initial info in case it was needed," Natalie said. "According to their mission statement, he started the clinic five years ago to meet the needs of the surrounding area, particularly assisting those who might not seek prenatal medical care. Ecuador has a universal healthcare system, so no one pays for their care. But with his clinic, his maternal mortality rate is below the national average."

A whistle sounded out from Poole. "Look at his house."

The Keepers' gazes swung to the next image on the screen of a large mansion. The aerial view showed it nestled amongst other similar estates. "Seems mighty fine for someone who works at a clinic in a poor neighborhood," Rick added.

Hop looked over at Carson. "I'm going down to assist with Lori's possible evacuation but have no idea what I'm getting into. This isn't a mission for us, but I need to be prepared that there could be a problem with the clinic and Dr. Rocha."

"This *is* a mission for us," Carson retorted.

"What's up?" Leo asked, his voice belying his intense stare. "You seem more anxious than... well, than I've ever seen you."

He looked around the room again, unused to the nerves spiking through him. Torn between keeping his private life separated from work, it hit him he'd never had to do that before. He considered all the Keepers to be friends, and they certainly knew each other's business. But in the past, he'd considered himself an open book, but now he was no longer certain. He barely had time to get used to Lori's news and couldn't help but wonder what the others might think.

But in the midst of all the uncertainty swirling around him, he was filled with a sense of pride and protectiveness for both her and the unborn baby. No shame. No awkwardness. No denying.

Lifting his chin, he swept his gaze around one more time before landing on Carson. "Lori and I got together in Tennessee, and despite our protection, she's pregnant. With my baby. I know in my heart that even if this was just Lori alone facing danger, I'd want to be there for her, but knowing she carries my child makes this trip even more necessary." Because everything had happened so quickly, he hadn't had time to consider what his friends' reactions might be to the news. But in typical Keeper form, they instantly rallied.

"Holy shit," Rick said without hesitation. "I'll go with you."

"Natalie and I will run the geospatial and satellite images from here," Abbie volunteered, shooting him a smile before she turned to her computer with her fingers flying over the keyboard to assist.

"If you fly down, you'll need transportation once you get there," Leo said, turning toward Carson. "Where can we get a secured vehicle?"

"The International Rescue Committee should be able to help us, knowing we're coming to assist," Carson said. "We'll see what ground transportation we can arrange."

"I've already got them on the line," Rachel said, standing just inside the door, her warm expression on Hop.

"Count me in," Dolby added. "I'll head down with you."

"Same for me," Adam tossed out.

As the Keepers went into planning mode, Hop felt an unfamiliar stinging behind his eyes and swallowed several times before gaining control. "I…" His voice faltered, and he cleared his throat before trying again. "I don't know what to say other than thank you."

Natalie walked over and laid her hand on his shoulder, giving a gentle squeeze. "No thanks needed between friends, Hop. No thanks are needed between Keepers. You've always had our back. Now we have yours."

"Quito has had a ton of pounding rain," Abbie called out. "It's the heaviest rainfall they've had in almost twenty years, surpassing the previous floods they've had this year. The valley of Guayllabamba River, where Quito lies, is flanked by volcanoes. The nearby Pichincha volcano is covered in a layer of mud and rock without much vegetation to anchor the soil. This makes the area unstable. The rain cannot soak into the ground, so it creates new rivers of mud that flow straight down toward the city. Water is already flowing down the streets on the western side of the city, and now it's taking on the mud as well. The clinic is close to the path."

"Got it," Jeb said. He glanced over at Hop with a grimace on his face. "It's located just north of the city... northwest. Which puts them in a dangerous place."

Over the next hour, they looked at the area, and he filed his flight plans once Carson had secured the transportation Hop would be able to use once he landed at Quito. It was decided that he'd only take two Keepers with him since he wanted to have room for Lori on the way back to the States. While she hadn't given any indication that she'd return and not stay in Ecuador, he hoped his powers of persuasion would have her agree to return. Plus, he wasn't opposed to begging if necessary. Adam and Dolby were flying down with him, with several others as backup if needed.

With a plan in place, he clasped hands, was pulled in for hugs and back slaps, and accepted congratulations from the others. Stalking into the equipment room and armory, Teddy made sure he had the communication devices and guns necessary.

"Third-world countries in a natural disaster can become hotbeds for gangs and criminals," Teddy growled. "Take what you need to protect yourself and the clinic, if necessary."

He hoped he wouldn't need them but accepted the weapons gratefully. After arranging to meet at first light with Adam and Dolby, he stepped out onto the stone patio outside of the lighthouse and glanced down over the water, sliding his aviator glasses onto his face. He sucked in a deep breath of fresh air and let it out slowly.

In less than twenty-four hours, his life had altered dramatically. A woman he cared for deeply was having his baby. And it didn't matter that he had just found out. An ache buried in his chest squeezed tightly at the thought of anything happening to them, and he was determined to do whatever he could to protect them. He fired off another text.

Coming. Will see you tomorrow. Stay safe.

He wasn't surprised not to receive a reply, hoping that meant she was getting some sleep. Filled with a sense of purpose that eclipsed the most important mission he'd ever participated in, he climbed into his vehicle. Heading home to pack and grab a few hours of sleep, he tried to blank his mind... but failed. All he could think about was Lori. The girl he'd relegated to his memory as a high school friend who had become no more despite his attraction to her. The friend he'd lost touch with after graduation. The woman he'd stumbled across purely by happenstance, finding her to be even more desirable and rekindling a friendship. And the woman who now carried his child.

It seemed he'd just fallen asleep when his alarm sounded. In the dark, pre-dawn of the next morning, his Cessna aircraft lifted off the runway, Adam as co-pilot and Dolby in the back. The night sky was comforting as they flew south. They wouldn't arrive in Ecuador for about nine hours, and that was with a stop for refueling. They'd arrive in the early afternoon, and that should give them time to get to the clinic. While he didn't have a specific plan, his goal was to assist with the evacuation, hoping to take some of the work and stress off Lori.

18

The next day, Lori woke to the sounds of Jackie's grumbling and the once again familiar patter of rain against the window. Standing, she groaned as she stretched, her body aching, and glared at the offending cot. Sighing, she shoved down the inner complaining, knowing that many in the city would give anything to have a dry cot to sleep on. She swiped the sleep from her eyes and dressed quickly. Sipping the herbal tea, she was grateful for the toast and cheese left in the staff lounge. Looking at her phone, she spied Hop's text and inhaled quickly, nearly choking on the hot drink. Sputtering for a moment, she leaned back in her chair, her mind swirling with the idea of him coming to Ecuador. Her finger hovered over her phone as she typed and deleted several texts. Finally deciding on a bland reply, she typed **Be safe. See you when you arrive** and pressed send.

Downstairs, Elisa pulled her to the side. "We are

gaining more patients than expected. Those who had planned on home births are afraid of being at home under the weather threats or delivering on the road somewhere if they have to leave their houses. We're taking them in if they are in active labor."

She nodded, patting Elisa's shoulder. "That's all we can do. We'll run out of supplies quicker, but hopefully, we can start moving them within a few hours to the other hospitals that are not in danger."

Passing one of the windows, she stopped and looked out through the raindrops that slid down the glass. The rain had started in earnest again, and she wondered how high the river had overflowed its banks. She'd tried to keep the televisions off in the birthing rooms, but the one at the nurses' station captured the staff's attention as they watched the news in worried fascination. She glanced at her watch and thought of Hop. *I wonder how close he is now.* The fact he was coming to assist made her heart skip a beat. She wanted to see him but knew he was putting his life at risk just by attempting to fly through the messy weather to get to her.

Seeing Rosa coming out of a patient's room, she recognized it as the room of the woman who wanted payment from Dr. Rocha. She waited until Rosa disappeared around the corner, and with a quick glance around, she darted into the patient's room, glad to find her alone. Looking at the chart, she cocked her head to the side. "I see you still have not started labor."

"I stay. He needs to pay first."

Walking to the side of the bed, she smiled gently,

softening her voice. "So, um… do you know who will come for your baby when it's delivered?"

The woman's brow furrowed, and she shook her head.

"Dr. Baker?"

Lori jumped slightly and whirled around to see Elisa standing at the door. "Dr. Casta has called for you."

Lori stared but couldn't discern if Elisa had heard the conversation. *Or is it part of a scheme?* Clearing her throat, she nodded. "Yes, thank you. I was hoping he'd call." She hastened to the nearest nurses' station, her mind torn between the need to learn about the possible evacuation and confiding her suspicions. *But I have no proof.* She'd barely had a chance to say hello when his words came.

"Dr. Baker. The minister of health has decided to evacuate the clinic. You will discharge all patients possible and prepare for the evacuation to Hospital Metropolitano, about five miles from your location. They now have room after discharging their latest round of patients and postponing any elective surgery patients from arriving. We will be sending volunteers to assist." He continued to speak, but her mind had already shifted to what needed to be accomplished in a short amount of time. And life became infinitely more complicated, pushing everything else to the side.

She waved her hand for Elisa to come back over and whispered, "Evacuation. Gather the senior nurses and tell them to be here in five minutes." Elisa nodded and walked briskly down the hall, poking her head into various rooms.

"Dr. Casta, when will the ambulances arrive? We have over ten women in active labor with two possible C-sections."

"You should be ready to move the first patients in an hour."

"And Dr. Rocha? Can we expect his assistance?"

Dr. Casta's hesitation once again told her everything, but he finally admitted, "I have not heard from Dr. Rocha. Please continue with the leadership role you have assumed."

As she disconnected, she turned to look at the television screen behind the desk where other nurses had gathered. The streets on the northern side of Quito were running with dark, muddy water, the tremendous force already pushing cars, trees, and anything in its path downward. "Fuck," she whispered, wondering how they would manage.

As soon as the nurses gathered around, she spoke just loud enough for them to hear without alarming the patients in their rooms. "We need to continue to discharge everyone we can. Elisa, I'm putting you in charge of your nurses, making sure they follow the protocols we have in place. Jackie and Marilyn will assist with the surgeries. Rosa and Angela, the new nurse anesthetist, will get ready to take the two scheduled C-sections so that I can do them one right after the other. By the time I'm finished, we should have discharged over half the women in the clinic. The others will start being picked up soon."

The next hours passed in a blur as Lori focused on

each task at hand, thanking God that the two C-sections provided no unseen difficulties.

By the time she made it down to the first floor, she was pleased to see an ambulance carrying two new mothers and their babies to one of the hospitals on the eastern side of the city where they could stay and be evaluated for several more hours until released.

"We have had many mothers and babies discharged, each going home with their husbands or family members to areas not in immediate danger," Elisa reported. "We have also sent three of the new arrivals who were not close to delivering in ambulances to the hospital so that they could make it in time to deliver there."

Nodding, she said, "What about the staff? I'd like to move as many of them out as safety allows."

"Our cleaning staff was dismissed this morning, and we only had Mr. Ochota left, but I sent him home an hour ago. We had two staff members fixing food for the patients, but one of them had asked to leave, and I sent them both home as well."

"Excellent. We can do without the cleaning or food staff since we're all leaving, and that gives them time to hopefully get to their homes or safety. I'm going back to the second floor to check on the others."

Lori had barely turned when a rumbling in the distance could be heard. "Shit!" she barked, her gaze shooting out the window as she watched trees and debris rush down one of the nearby streets several blocks away from the clinic along with fast swirling muddy water. Her gaze shot up to the other nurses standing around, their eyes wide with fear. She was sure that her face registered the same expression as her heart pounded.

19

"Shit, look at the terrain around the airport," Dolby said, looking out the window.

Hop expertly flew over the mountains of the nearby volcanoes. "Yeah, from what I studied, this airport isn't exactly a pilot's dream. Houses encircle the airport, and mountains surround the whole area. Major airlines only have two approaches. We'll be fine, but this rain makes visibility a bitch." The others stayed quiet as he approached, breathing easier as the wheels touched down.

The airport was still functioning, although it appeared more planes were flying out than coming in. "Looks like most people are trying to get out of here," he said to Adam. Taxiing to the assigned hangar, he rolled to a stop once inside, the sound of the pounding rain now lessened as it hit the metal building above instead of their windshield.

He was tired but wired, reminding him of untold missions he'd run over the years. Eight hours of flight time and a half hour for refueling and a break, on top of the little sleep he got the night before. But knowing that just a few miles away, Lori was working her ass off under difficult, if not treacherous circumstances, gave him the fire in his gut that he needed to get to her as soon as possible.

Just before they landed, Abbie had relayed that mudslides were already coming down from the Pichincha volcano. In the lower part of town, many first floors of buildings were already flooding with mud, debris, and water.

"I've got the clinic on satellite imagery and am sending it to you," Abbie said when he called in. "Check your tablets. Some streets that run to the side of them already have flood water coming from the mountains, but because the clinic is built on a fairly steep incline, I would assume that the water is not entering the building. But that also means that the roads for getting to them will be dicey and soon impassable."

"Shit," he cursed. Looking toward the others, he shook his head. "If I'd just made up my fucking mind two hours earlier, it would've been a hell of a lot easier getting to the clinic. As it is now, we're gonna have problems."

Adam looked up. "Carson has the contact for the International Rescue Committee. They welcome our assistance in securing the maternity clinic. Plus, he's talked to the Red Cross and told them we're here to help. They are currently evacuating the clinic."

"Hop, it's Natalie," she radioed. "I've sent logistics to Adam. A slightly elevated, flat parcel of land that's part of a schoolyard is only three blocks away from the clinic. Right now, it's your closest shot to getting to them. Carson has the IRC offering a helicopter. It's at the airport where you are, and I've downloaded all the information and sent it to you."

Relief filled him. It didn't matter how many rescue missions he'd been on to help others, the personal aspect of this one made his previous missions pale in comparison. Turning to see Adam already pulling up the information on his tablet, the three hustled out of the hangar, following the directions Natalie had sent to where the IRC had a helicopter ready.

While the others looked over Natalie's logistics, Hop pulled out his phone and dialed Lori. Not knowing if she would answer, his heart leaped when she picked up and he heard her voice.

"Hello? Hop?"

"Hey, babe, we're here."

"We? Who's we?"

"Me and a couple of friends… coworkers. We've got a helicopter, and we're gonna be leaving the Quito airport soon to get to you."

"I don't know what you'll be able to do here. There's water rushing down the street immediately to the west of the clinic. We've managed to evacuate everyone we could, but I've still got several patients. I've dismissed most of the Ecuadorian staff and reassigned the three International Red Cross nurses who showed up today to the hospitals where many of our patients were taken. I'm here with my two Red Cross nurses and two of the nursing staff from the clinic."

"Don't worry about it, Lori. We'll be able to land about three blocks away from you. Decide who you want to evacuate first, and we'll get them out of there. I just need to coordinate with the rescue committee."

"So you're coming? You're going to come to the clinic?"

"No flood or mudslides will keep me away from you." As soon as he said the words, he knew they sounded like a movie cliché, but they couldn't have been more true.

"Then I'll see you as soon as you get here," she said, her voice uncharacteristically shaky. "I can't believe you actually came."

He felt her relief in his gut. "Believe it, Lori. See you soon." Disconnecting, he let out a rush of breath.

"She okay?" Adam asked.

His attention jerked toward the other Keepers. "Yeah, I think so. She's busy. Got a lot of stress, and things are only gonna get worse."

"Not true, brother. With you and us here, things will only get better." He clapped Hop's shoulder before they both turned and headed to where the available bird was waiting.

Having to meet the IRC official in charge of the helicopter, go over the plan for landing at the school near the clinic, and transfer their equipment meant they didn't lift off for almost an hour. Frustrated with the lost time, Hop cursed lightly under his breath as he followed the directional coordinates, glad that the rain had ceased once again. Flying over the crowded but more modern downtown, he headed toward the northwest neighborhoods, where it was evident the buildings were wood and stucco. Several minutes later, he pointed downward. "There's the school, and with Abbie's intel, the clinic should be that building just over there."

From their vantage point, they could see water racing down the streets but no apparent flooding in the buildings. The clinic appeared to be the most modern building in the neighborhood, the multi-story brick building was squeezed between smaller structures and narrow streets. After landing easily on the flat, grassy field with no people in sight, they alighted and secured the aircraft.

Unable to keep the excitement buried, he sprinted over the playing field to the sidewalk protected by an older building from much of the water. Carefully placing one foot onto the street, he could see that the water was only an inch deep and didn't cover the entire road. Looking over his shoulder, he called out, "Once we get in, we need to assess who we can carry out first. The hospital that will take them is only a few miles away, so if we work efficiently, we should be able to evacuate the remaining patients and staff."

When he turned toward the clinic again, his heart pounded at the thought of seeing Lori. *It hasn't even been seven weeks since I last saw her in Tennessee, yet it seems like yesterday and forever ago, all at the same time.*

Making their way around on the sidewalk to the front door, they entered the clinic and found themselves inside a reception area. The comfortable seats scattered about were empty, but a woman in nursing scrubs came from the back.

Just as it looked as though she were going to ask why they were there and who they were, the sound of his name shot straight through him.

"Hop!"

He jerked his head to the side, and his chest squeezed as his gaze landed on Lori for the first time in seven weeks. Her dark-blue scrubs did little to hide her figure, one he remembered well, although it appeared she'd lost weight. Her hair was pulled into a ponytail, tendrils falling around her face. And her eyes... her gorgeous eyes were lit as they stared back toward him.

The air rushed from him as she dashed around the reception desk, stopping at the corner. Not waiting, he stalked straight toward her, his arms spread wide. She rushed forward, slamming into his chest as his embrace encircled her. His mind was filled with the crashing of emotions all hitting him at once. The longing from having missed this woman who had come to mean so much to him. The fear of the danger she'd been in. The knowledge that she carried his child. As emotions threatened to overtake him, he buried his face in her hair, breathed her in, and squeezed his arms tighter.

She leaned back and looked up, her eyes moving back and forth over his face, and once again, his heart skipped a beat. She was beautiful as always, but signs of fatigue and stress were etched on her face, along with dark smudges under her eyes.

"Hey, babe," he said. The simple greeting instantly seemed inadequate, but it brought a smile to her face.

"Hey to you, too," she replied. "I wish we had longer to talk, but I've just gotten word that we need to finish evacuating as soon as possible."

"I wish we had more time, too, but we'll get this done and then be together. We've got a helicopter, and I can take three people out at a time. If you have women who can be strapped in holding their babies, then I can take two of them and a nurse. Or if someone needs more help, you've got to let me know what they need. It's not a medical helicopter, but it'll get somebody from here to the hospital in a few minutes."

Her hands had been wrapped around his waist, but now they slid forward and grasped both of his, holding them between their bodies. "This means everything, Hop. The ambulances have been running, plus some people have volunteered with Jeeps. We've discharged most of the moms who were ready, and we've sent the others who could travel this morning. A few had babies in the last few hours, and I want to get them to the hospital to be checked out further before being sent back home."

"The closest I could land the helicopter was at a school field about three blocks away." She grimaced, and he added, "We can carry the women if we need to." Turning to the others, he said, "Babe, let me introduce you to my fellow Keepers. This is Dolby and Adam."

She smiled as she reached her hand forward, greeting both of them. Looking back at Hop, she asked, "What about wheelchairs to get the patients to your helicopter?"

Dolby interjected, "Right now, we can make that

work, but I can't guarantee it'll be very comfortable. The roads are passable, so I wonder if we can get a vehicle to get us back and forth from here to the helicopter?" Turning, he looked toward Hop and said, "I'm gonna see what I can arrange."

Dolby darted back outside, and Hop had no doubt he'd find something. Looking back down at Lori, he asked, "How are you doing?"

She nodded. "I'm okay. Tired and feel a bit more stressed than I usually do with something like this. But I'm okay."

"What about the baby?"

She sucked in a quick breath and stared as though uncertain what to say. Her lips curved slightly as she nodded again and said, "Everything seems fine."

"Seems fine?" he asked, his voice sharper than he meant for it to be.

"I haven't had any spotting or pain." Then she admitted, "No one here knows. So yes, at this time, everything seems fine."

Air rushed from his lungs, and he nodded. "I'm sorry. I should know you'd know what's going on. It's just been so…"

"Surreal? Surprising? Unexpected?"

He chuckled, pulling her in close again and kissing the top of her head. "Yes to all of the above. But I'm anxiously waiting for when we can leave this place and spend some time together."

She held his gaze, but he couldn't read her expression, and that bothered him more than he imagined.

"Dr. Baker?"

They both turned to watch a nurse walk from the back, her gaze darting around to Hop and the other men before settling back on Lori.

"Elisa, these are friends of mine who have come from America to help. They have a helicopter and are looking to get a vehicle to help us finish the evacuation."

The dark-haired Ecuadorian nurse nodded, smiling slightly. "Welcome to Quito. Although I wish it were under better circumstances. We certainly appreciate everything you can do to help us."

Following Elisa, the group walked up the stairs to the second floor and over to the nurses' station.

"I know you've evacuated areas before," he acknowledged, "so you'll need to let me know your priorities and plans."

"We have two Red Cross nurses and three staff nurses left here. We have four women and babies who need to be flown out now, plus one more who is in late-stage labor. I'll send Marilyn, one of my Red Cross nurses, out with them. You're to take them to St. Mary's Hospital. I've been told they have a landing pad on the roof—"

"I already have that information. We're on it. LSI-WC is coordinating with the ICRC and IRC."

Her brow furrowed. "Shit, Hop, that's way too much alphabet soup for my brain right now."

Grinning, he shook his head. "International Rescue Committee. International Committee of the Red Cross. And Lighthouse Security Investigation West Coast."

Lori snorted before laughing. "Honest to God, that's not much better."

A deep chuckle erupted. "Let's just say that you worry about the women and babies, and I'll worry about getting them out of here."

"Sounds good to me!"

She turned and placed her hand on his arm, her warm gaze on his face. No words passed between them, but then he was struck silent by her beauty and the protective emotions that coursed through his veins. With a pat, she turned and began giving orders while hustling into one of the rooms. Standing back, he watched in admiration as she assisted the new mothers and gave instructions to the nurses.

"Hop?" she said, drawing him from his observing.

"Yeah, what do you need?"

"I don't want to take a chance on the elevator, so can you help us carry the patients?"

Adam had come up behind him, and with a nod, Hop said, "Absolutely. Have you got the babies?"

"Yes, no problem."

He walked over and gently lifted the new mother into his arms and carried her down the stairs with ease as one of the nurses walked behind with the newborn in her arms. Adam followed with another mother.

By the time they arrived in the reception area, Dolby was standing in the doorway, a grin on his face. "Got transportation to the bird."

Hop looked out the glass door and saw a massive SUV with heavy tires. He knew not to ask where Dolby purloined the vehicle—Hop didn't care. Dolby had pulled it up on the sidewalk as close to the doors as possible, but the rain had ceased.

Carefully settling the woman onto the seat, he made sure she was buckled before stepping back and giving the nurse room to place the baby in the mother's outstretched arms. Adam repeated the process on the other side. The nurse who assisted Adam said, "I'll accompany you on this trip."

Nodding, he turned and smiled at Lori standing just inside the door. Not caring who was around, he placed his hand on the back of her neck and gently drew her forward. Bending, he kissed her. It was a light kiss, not at all like the one he wanted to give. But for now, it would have to convey all that he hoped she understood about where his head was at with her and him and the baby.

Stepping back, he choked back a sigh. He'd just arrived and had to say goodbye again, even temporarily. "Be back as soon as I can. Adam will bring the SUV back here, then he and Dolby will help get the next two women down here and ready to load."

"Okay," she agreed, nodding her head in quick jerks. "Come back safe."

"Always." He grinned, then chucked her under the chin before hustling to the driver's side and climbing behind the wheel.

The three-block drive wasn't long, and so far, the streets were passable. Once on the field, he drove as close to the helicopter as possible. He, Adam, and Marilyn assisted the mothers and babies into the back seats, trying to keep the rain off them. They managed to keep the babies carefully swaddled, protected, and dry, but the mothers were damp by the time they were strapped in securely. As soon as Marilyn was also buckled, he waited until Adam drove away before starting the blades whirling. Swiping the rainwater from his face, he lifted off, following the coordinates to the hospital. He was cognizant of his passengers and kept the aircraft as level and steady as possible. Once there, he tossed up a prayer of thanks that the helicopter pad on top was vacant. As soon as he landed, hospital personnel rushed out, not heeding the rainfall. He climbed down, bending low to assist Marilyn out as the hospital nurses placed the mothers into wheelchairs. Others held umbrellas, and others carried the babies. He watched them hurry back through the sliding doors. Marilyn turned, blinked the water from her eyes, and grabbed his hand to shake it. "Thank you so much for this! I know you've got to fly back to get the others, but please be safe!"

With a nod, he waited until she disappeared through the doors, then climbed back into the helicopter, taking off once again. Flying back to the field, he radioed to Adam, then looked over toward the volcanic mountains nearby and observed as some of the dark sides were already giving the appearance of oozing downward. "Fuck," he murmured, knowing time was of the essence since the slide would only get worse and faster. Setting the aircraft down, he watched as Adam drove close again.

Keeping the helicopter running, he climbed out and, bending low, ran over to the SUV. Again, they carried two more new mothers while Elisa assisted with the two newborns. Repeating their actions of earlier, they secured the mothers, babies, and nurse, and then after Adam pulled away, he rose into the air again.

He had to wait this time for the helicopter pad to clear before he could land. As the mothers and babies were wheeled inside, Elisa turned to him. Her lips were pinched as she held his gaze.

"You don't have to worry about her," he assured, smiling at the petite nurse. "I'll make sure to get her out."

She offered a tight smile while nodding. Turning, she raced after the wheelchairs and disappeared into the hospital.

Lifting off again, he concentrated on the flight, trying to ignore the mudslide to the west. The last load would clear the clinic as soon as the next group of evacuees was taken to the hospital. Then he and Lori needed to find a safe place to hole up. She needed rest, and he wanted to take care of her. Her and their baby.

20

Lori finished the last delivery, and since the umbilical cord was wrapped around the baby's neck, she, along with Rosa and Jackie, performed an emergency C-section. She'd headed directly into surgery as soon as Hop had left the hospital with the first group. Dolby had disappeared, but Adam had reported that Hop had returned and was now taking the second group of patient evacuees.

She glanced at the clock on the wall, seeing that it was only an hour since she'd seen him, but had missed him immediately. Shifting her gaze over to Rosa and Jackie, she murmured softly, "We're going to need a stretcher, and only one of you can go with her, I think."

"I'll stay," Rosa volunteered, looking toward Jackie. "You'll be more skilled for her care in the helicopter, even if it's a short ride." While both were competent nurses, Rosa's specialty was in anesthesia, while Jackie's was not only maternity but also pediatric.

Not seeing a reason to disagree, Lori nodded, then

turned to the new mother clutching her baby. The woman was sutured and stable, although still anesthetized. The newborn had been examined, and Lori looked at Rosa, saying, "Tell her that we know it won't be easy, but it's a short helicopter ride, and our rescuers will make her as comfortable as possible. Then she'll be in the larger hospital, out of danger, and she and her baby will be taken care of."

Rosa relayed the message, and after Lori washed up, she headed out into the hall to find Adam and Dolby.

Dolby had what could only be described as a shit-eating grin on his face when she walked up. Cocking her head to the side, she wondered what he was smiling about.

He glanced around, then leaned forward to whisper, "I got into the doctor's computer. Already uploaded the info to my boss."

Her chin jerked back, brows lowering. "How... how did you do that?"

He gave a quick shake of his head as Rosa walked into the room, and as curious as Lori was, she had no time to focus on Dr. Rocha's computer when she needed to make sure the patient was safe for transport.

For the next ten minutes, they strapped the woman onto a stretcher, and with the gentlest of care, Adam and Dolby carried her down the stairs while Jackie carried the baby. Once on the first floor, they managed to transfer her on the stretcher to the back of the SUV. Jackie turned and grabbed Lori into a deep hug.

"Take care, and I'll see you soon," Jackie said, holding

her tight. "You're an amazing doctor, and it's an honor to serve with you."

"I feel the same about you, Jackie," Lori said. "You'll be at the hospital in a few minutes, and they can take care of her there, but I know you'll watch over her carefully until you arrive."

Adam assisted Jackie into the front of the SUV, where she cradled the baby as the mother rested in the back seat.

On this trip, Adam would drive, but Dolby would have to accompany them since they needed to make sure they could get the stretcher onto the helicopter.

"Be safe, and I'll see you soon," Lori called out.

"This leaves just you and Rosa here, but Adam will come for you as soon as Hop takes off with this group," Dolby said. "I've already sent the information I pulled from his computer to our boss, plus I'll take a look at it while Adam comes back for you and Rosa."

With a nod, she watched as he climbed into the very back of the SUV and waved as they pulled out onto the street, heading the few blocks to where she knew Hop's helicopter would be waiting.

There was little movement outside the clinic. The nearby shops were closed since residents had left for safer ground. Pressing her lips together, she turned and stared at the empty reception area, quiet for the first time since she arrived. No patients. No staff. No crying babies. No nervous dads. Finding it strangely eerie, she walked past the reception desk and down the hall, hurrying to the second floor.

Once there, she made a sweep of each room to

ensure that no one had been left behind. Unlike the usual empty hospital room where the staff would clean, change the linens, and prepare for the next patient, these rooms showed evidence of patients hastily discharged. Once she'd checked every room, including the surgery unit, she stopped at the nurses' station. Not seeing Rosa, she moved into the stairwell to go to the third floor.

She noticed it was still quiet as expected and hurried into the lounge, where she gathered her belongings. Deciding not to worry about her luggage, she crammed everything she could into a large backpack. Turning, she opened the small cabinet nearby and snagged a water bottle and several packages of cheese crackers. Uncertain when her next meal might be, she wanted to have a snack if necessary.

Looking around the room, seeing nothing else to take, she looped her crossbody purse over her shoulder. Heading back into the hall, she dug into her scrub pocket for her phone. She had no idea when Hop would return but wanted him to know she was ready. If it would make it easier for her and Rosa to meet him at the field, then that was where she wanted to go. Still not seeing Rosa, she called out for her. Hearing footsteps from around the corner where Dr. Rocha's office was, she looked up to see Rosa approaching.

"I've checked the whole clinic and packed what I need," Lori said, offering a tired smile. "Gather anything you want, and Adam will be back in a few minutes with the SUV to take us to the helicopter."

"I don't think that's what's going to happen," Rosa said, stepping closer to her, her words clipped.

Brows raised, she tilted her head to the side, then jolted as she heard more footsteps coming from around the corner. A gasp slipped out at the sight of Dr. Rocha walking forward, stopping next to Rosa. "What are you doing here?"

His eyes narrowed, and he leaned forward slightly from the waist, pinning her with a glare. "Have you forgotten that this is *my* clinic?"

Scoffing, she crossed her arms over her chest. "I think that question would be better answered by you, considering *you* haven't been here during the crisis."

"Oh, I assure you, while I've not been in the building, I've been close by, making sure the clinic's work was continuing."

She held his gaze, her suspicions now flying to the forefront of her mind. *For him to be confronting me now, he must wonder if I'm aware of his nefarious actions.* Lifting her chin slightly, she said, "The clinic was running during the crisis because of me and your dedicated staff."

His lips curved. "Oh yes, *my* dedicated staff made sure that the patients under my *special* care were taken care of."

"Your *special* patients?"

"I know you talked to one of them. I know you have your suspicions," he declared. "Don't insult my intelligence by pretending otherwise."

Swallowing audibly, she shifted her gaze to Rosa, finding the nurse's expression to be hard, her lips pinched and her posture rigid. Looking back at Dr. Rocha, she shook her head slowly. "I have concerns, but that's all."

He held her gaze for a moment, then huffed. "My personal staff made sure to see that the babies of special patients were taken to a place where they would be cared for."

Lori's lungs hurt with the effort of sucking air in so quickly. Her gaze darted between Alfonso and Rosa. "Oh God... what have you done?"

"Do not be so melodramatic, Dr. Baker. The babies are well cared for until their new adoptive parents can claim them."

"You're a monster," she breathed, her chest heaving. "You're buying and selling babies."

"No, I am a realist. There are those who do not want their babies and those who do. I am simply a mediator, ensuring medical care for all involved."

"You're circumventing the health care, social services, and adoption system. And what's more, you profit off selling babies!"

"Making a profit in life hardly makes me a monster," he retorted.

She dragged her gaze from his cold eyes over to Rosa. "Surely, you know this is wrong... criminal!"

Before Rosa had a chance to retort, a rumble began in the distance, and the three of them jerked their heads in unison toward the large window in the hall. As though the mountains in the distance were moving, the dark earth oozed downward toward the city, and in horror, she watched as it overtook trees and houses in its wake, pushing the mud and debris directly toward them.

"Go!"

Lori swung her head around at the shouted order from him, her eyes widening at the sight of a gun now in his hand. "Wh... What?"

"Go! Now!" he ordered, waving the barrel of the gun between her and the door to the pharmaceutical closet on the other side of the hall.

The dull roar in the distance was growing louder. "We're running out of time!" Rosa cried. "We have to get out of here!"

"She goes in the closet," Rocha ordered, sweat dripping down his face as he waved the gun closer to Lori.

Clutching the strap of her backpack and purse, she pinched her lips tightly together, not willing to take a chance on being shot. She walked forward, trying to think of a way out. Their footsteps stayed behind her, but just far enough back so that she had no chance to try to grab one of them. But then, not having any idea how to wrestle a gun away, she figured it was best to keep going. Her heart pounded as she tried to stay clear-minded.

He unlocked the door, then pushed Lori from behind. Stumbling through the door, she glanced behind to see Rosa moving behind Dr. Rocha as he lifted the gun.

"We've got to go!" Rosa shouted, her wide eyes now full of panic as she reached out for him.

"We have to take care of her first," he bit back, jerking his arm from her grip.

"Don't be stupid! Just go!"

"And if she lives?"

Rosa growled, "She has no proof of anything. Just go!"

Realizing they planned on leaving her there to be overtaken by the mudslide, Lori threw her hands up. "No!" she cried out as the door slammed shut. Racing over, she tried the knob, but it didn't turn. Banging against the door with her palms, she screamed, her chest heaving, but to no avail. All was silent as the building began to shake.

Lori jerked around in a circle, her gaze darting around as she searched for something, even though she had no idea what she was looking for. Her chest ached, but just as she thought of her phone, she felt the whole building shake harder. Without a window, she had no idea what was happening outside.

Her fingers shook as she hit the button to call Hop. It rang several times, and then the signal was lost. Trying again, she was plunged into darkness as the electricity cut out. Standing in the pitch black, the air expelled from her lungs, and she slid to the floor, her legs giving out. While she hoped the mud didn't get to her on the third floor, she knew she'd be crushed if the building toppled. *And no one will know where I am.*

21

Hop had assisted Adam and Dolby as they carefully maneuvered the stretcher into the helicopter's floor. They were in the process of strapping her down, and along with Elisa, who was holding the baby, was secure as well when a rumbling in the distance resounded throughout the valley. Looking upward, he could see the sides of the volcano that had appeared oozing earlier were now sliding downward with force, heading toward their area of the city. "Fuck!" he roared, climbing into the helicopter and starting the engine and blades. Barely glancing over his shoulder, he shouted, "Climb aboard! Now!"

Dolby and Adam had no choice but to clamber into the remaining seats. Without looking over his shoulder, he knew Adam in the back would keep his body as compact as possible so he didn't step on the woman lying on the stretcher at his feet. Just as the mudslide came toward them, he lifted the bird into the air, his heart in his throat as he let out a string of curses.

Unable to get to Lori, his chest squeezed, threatening to burst with anger at the idea that he was saving others but not her.

He swooped over the sliding earth, keeping the clinic in his sights. The mud filled the streets, pushing cars along as well as smaller structures crushed under the weight. His gaze darted from his controls to the clinic as the mud slammed into the back of the building. Heart in his throat, his mind battled what he needed to do and what his entire being called out for him to do, which was to get to her.

"Brother, the building is standing! It's strong!" Dolby shouted as they looked down.

So far, the mud piled against the back of the clinic, the rest of it rushing down the streets on either side.

"Get to the hospital, man," Adam ordered, his voice gentle but strong. "As soon as we do, we can get back here."

Agony filled every cell of his body as he roared another curse to the heavens. Knowing the woman and baby couldn't stand the jerking movements of the helicopter if he continued to dip and swoop around the clinic, he headed toward the hospital at the fastest speed he could safely manage. His mind was racing, barely aware of Adam and Dolby on their phones to the other Keepers.

"Abbie, we've got mudslides, and Lori is trapped. Get the real-time imagery…"

"Get Natalie on the logistics…"

"We need Lori's phone trace sent to us…"

"We need a vehicle that can make it over the debris…"

"Taking the last patient to the hospital. We need a new place to land the bird near the clinic…"

The air rushed from Hop's lips as his chest depressed, his body shaking with fear and adrenaline. He'd never felt such despair in his life. His gaze finally snagged on the hospital ahead. He managed to land just ahead of another incoming helicopter, feeling no guilt for snagging the landing pad first. As soon as they touched down, Jackie was unbuckled and, with Adam's help, was on the rooftop with the baby in her arms. She bent low and turned to him, agony written on her face. The noise wouldn't have allowed any words to be spoken, so she simply offered a nod and then raced toward the door as a gurney was rolled out.

Grateful for the hasty transfer of the new mother, he yelled for Adam and Dolby, who hopped back on board, and then lifted into the air as soon as the hospital personnel were clear.

"The mudslide is still active," Jeb radioed. "Abbie and Rick are looking for a site that will get you close but not be in the path."

Peering downward, all Hop could see was the gray, ashy mud that had swept trees, cars, and parts of houses as it rushed downward, burying everything in its path. "You've got to get me somewhere!" Hop shouted into the radio as he stared down at the muck that covered the streets and crushed smaller buildings.

"Hop, bro, you don't want to hear this, but you gotta

calm the fuck down," Dolby said. "We're going to get her."

"There's the clinic!" Adam shouted, pointing down. "Some damage, but it's still standing."

For a man used to quick decisions and who usually stayed positive, it was almost impossible for him to appreciate that the clinic was still standing when the surrounding roads and areas were impassable with the slush of mud and water and some damage already visible. Sucking in a deep breath, he stilled the racing thoughts in his head. *She's inside, and she's fine. I just need to get to her.*

He circled around the building, then expanded his path as he looked for a place he could safely land. The school's field was now covered in mud, and everywhere he looked, the area was unstable. It appeared to be slowing after fifteen minutes from when the slide began. The challenge was finding a clear area large enough for him to land, close enough to be able to get to her quickly, and not in the path of more mudslides that might be coming.

"There's a church nearby," Abbie reported, and she rattled off the coordinates. "It appears to be undamaged and not in the path. What's more, it's built in a square with a large courtyard in the middle. You could land in the courtyard and be protected from all four sides if the earth begins to shift again."

"Shit, that doesn't seem very close," he grumbled, but with the devastation all around, he could hardly complain.

Dolby radioed back. "I don't know how close we're

gonna be able to get on foot, but it'll probably be a hell of a lot easier than trying to get a vehicle that won't make it in this mud."

"Can you use the helicopter to get her in and out?"

"There's no place on her building to land."

"Just so you know," Rick radioed back, "I've been trying to call her phone, but she's not answering. She may have it turned off, or it might not be with her."

"She's alone in the clinic except for one other nurse, Rosa. What makes me nervous is that this is the nurse Lori suspected of working with Dr. Rocha."

Leo jumped in. "Chances are, the other nurse and Lori are doing nothing more than trying to figure out how to get out safely. I doubt the other nurse is worried about what Lori may or may not know at this point."

"I analyzed the doctor's computer data from what Dolby sent. The doc did keep records of what he called adoption sales," Jeb said. "I've compared it to his bank account, and there were deposits that coordinate with the adoptions, as well as payouts. Not our mission, but I thought you'd like to know so you can pass on to Lori that her suspicions were correct."

Carson added, "We've already started turning the evidence over to the Ecuadorian National Police. You don't need to look for more evidence. Just get your girl safely out of there."

Seeing the church below, Hop ascertained that he could safely land in the courtyard. "Okay, I'm going down to the church. It's only about six blocks from the clinic, and it looks like the easiest way to get to her."

With Adam and Dolby still talking to the others at

the Lighthouse compound, Hop expertly lowered his aircraft until the skids settled on the courtyard grass. He wondered if anyone would come out because the building appeared abandoned.

"Man, I hate to make things shittier," Jeb radioed, "but Abbie says the intel is that the volcanoes are still unstable. More might be coming your way."

"Are you fuckin' kidding me?" Hop groaned, shaking his head.

"Most people are out trying to help rescue efforts, but you've got to stay vigilant. We'll radio whatever we find out."

As soon as they landed, he turned to the others. "Adam, I want you to stay." Seeing Adam about to object, he pushed, "You're the only other one who can fly this bird if necessary." Adam had never flown helicopters in the service, but much like Hop, he'd learned from his uncle when he was still in high school on a ranch in Kansas. "I need you to do this," Hop pleaded.

"Absolutely," Adam gave in easily. "I know what you've got to do." He heaved a heavy sigh. "Let me know when you're close or what you need, and I'll get it done."

Looking toward the back, Hop called out to Dolby. "You ready?"

Giving the same answer as Adam, he shouted, "Absolutely!"

Lori shivered as her heart pounded loudly in the dark room. She shoved her hand into her pocket, her fingers closing around her phone. Tapping the screen, she waited as the illumination filled the space, instantly making her feel less alone. She tried to call Hop's phone, but no signal could be found. The building shook even more, and her breathing hitched at the idea that the walls could come tumbling down around her. "Oh, baby," she whispered aloud, "I swear, Mama's going to try to get us out of this!"

The floor's vibrating stopped, and for the moment, she was at least grateful the room she was in hadn't collapsed, although she'd heard the shifting of items all around her.

She knew if Hop could get to her, he would, but there was no way to discern what level of devastation might lie outside the door to her closet tomb. For all she knew, the entire first floor might now be filled with earth, or the upper floors might be ready to crumble.

The pitch black quickly became unnerving, and she occasionally turned on her phone to chase away the darkness, even momentarily. *I have water. I have some food. I can make it for a while until someone comes for me.* While those thoughts were comforting, the feeling of being trapped wormed its way into her mind.

She sucked in a ragged breath and felt the air rush from her lungs too quickly. Placing her hands on her belly, she forced the air in and out of her lungs, slowly and deeply, until steadiness replaced the panic. *Okay, baby, Mama's got this.*

Trying to call Hop again, she stared at the screen, hoping to see something, but all that greeted her was silence. She assumed that cell signals were also down along with the electricity. *Or maybe I'm buried under a ton of dirt, and no signal can get out.* Angry that those panicked thoughts crept in, she pushed to a stand. Flipping on her phone for light, she looked around the pharmaceutical room for anything that might help her escape. The room held cabinets with drugs. A metal shelving unit was on one wall, holding boxes and bottles of non-pharmacy medical supplies, some having toppled over and fallen to the floor. *Nothing I can use.*

As she looked up toward the top shelf, her gaze snagged on the drop ceiling tiles, and she sucked in a quick breath. A memory slammed into her of a water leak in the hospital she worked at in El Paso. The maintenance crew had to remove the ceiling tiles in several rooms, exposing the pipes that traveled between the large, open space above the tiles. *I could get out of this room!*

Setting her phone on the floor with the flashlight app shining upward, she moved to the shelves, tentatively placed her foot on the first shelf, and reached up, climbing it slowly like a ladder, careful to make sure it didn't shift or start to topple. When she was several feet off the ground, she lifted her hand and pressed her palm against the tile, lifting it off the rails. Shifting it, she managed to slide it to the side.

Dropping to the floor, she grabbed her phone and retraced her climb until she could peer into the space above the ceiling and shine the light around. Just like she remembered, the space was open, allowing her to escape the confines of the closet walls. Once again, she climbed back down to the floor. Securing her small crossbody bag, she then slid her arms through the straps of her backpack and hefted it onto her back.

Repeating the steps, she climbed to the top of the shelves, then looked around, orienting to where she was. The back of the room would be close to the outer wall, which would do her no good, especially since that might be compromised, considering it was the direction that the landslide was coming from.

Looking around more, she determined that if she could crawl toward the closet door, she would come to the hall, where she could escape down the stairwell.

Realizing the ceiling tiles would never hold her weight, she cast the light around again and spied the wooden beams that made up the various walls. Grabbing hold of one of them, she hauled her upper body onto the back wall, sneezing as dust billowed up around her. Her progress was measured in inches as her elbow knocked a tile loose and her knee poked through another one. A wrong move could have her crashing through the ceiling onto the floor below, which would get her out of the locked closet but could possibly harm her or the baby. Blowing out a heavy breath, she inched forward.

As she got to the end of the wooden beam that marked the corner of the closet, she pushed down against another tile, peeking below. The sight greeting her was frightening as she saw outside light coming through a crack in the concrete. Forcing down the panic, she re-oriented herself and decided to keep sliding along the wall that would lead her toward the hall. Once there, she could surely get down the stairs to the outside.

She blinked several times as her eyes burned and found it hard to breathe with the musty air. Inching along the wooden beam, she squeezed under some of the HVAC ducting, causing her knees and hands to bleed from the scrapes. Her progress was halted when her backpack caught on ductwork and pipes. She tried to maneuver it off her shoulders but felt trapped by the material. Shifting while balancing precariously, she managed to slide one shoulder strap onto her arm but was unable to remove the now-captured backpack. Swiping the sweat from her eyes, she knocked down another ceiling tile and leaned her head forward, gulping in cooler air as she spied the hall. *Keep going. A little bit farther.*

No one was visible, and she didn't want to waste energy trying to alert someone outside to her presence until she was sure they could hear her. With renewed vigor, she shifted backward to attempt to dislodge the pack still stuck on wires from the ductwork. Feeling for the end of the strap, she managed to slide it from the slider lock. With the strap now dangling, she was able to move farther, ready to drop into the hall.

She let her legs slide downward and held on with her fingers. Too tired and not strong enough to hold her weight with her hands, she dropped, free-falling to the floor. Landing hard, she rocked back, toppling onto her ass, barely ducking as her backpack landed on top of her. Shocked for a few seconds, she quickly pushed to her feet, ecstatic at having escaped the closet while immediately forcing her legs to balance her body as the floor sloped sharply. Pulling the pack on again, she steadied her body.

Looking toward the nearest window, she was aware that the world outside was at an angle... or rather, the building she was in was leaning. With a few vibrations still shaking her world, she dropped to her knees and crawled to the door leading to the staircase. The door was askew, and when she peered through, her heart dropped. The stairs leading to the second floor had crumbled.

Oh God... how will I get out? Her stomach clenched as desperation filled her. Knowing the building was now a death trap, she pressed her back against the wall as her gaze darted around the hall, seeking any idea of how to get outside. *The roof!* The thought hit her as her gaze landed on the door leading to the rooftop. She had no idea what she would find, but being outside and able to call out to someone on the street for help would surely be better than where she was now.

With a renewed sense of purpose, she crawled toward the door, her heart pounding as she pushed against the door and swung it open, exposing the concrete stairs that were still standing. Careful, terrified of going up and not knowing what awaited her when she got to the roof, she slowly crept upward.

She pushed at the door leading to the outside, afraid it might be stuck. Her chest heaved as relief poured from her when the door swung open with a loud groan, and daylight hit her face.

22

Hop and Dolby climbed from the helicopter, then as soon as his boots hit the ground, he raced through the church and out onto the sidewalk. The sight from the air had been shocking, but on the ground, it was infinitely more terrifying. His gaze darted all around as the sound of screaming met his ears, many people calling from the upper windows of buildings that were still standing while staring out at some of the less fortunate ones where the structures had collapsed, sliding into each other and becoming part of the landslide of mud, trees, and vehicles.

Coming to a street, they clambered in ankle-deep mud as they continued carefully toward the clinic. He climbed over debris, slipping several times as the mud was deeper in some places. Coming to a wide street where they had more visibility, he looked upward, observing the areas north where a sliver of the mountain volcano was missing. The avalanche of dirt, now covering the city street, piled high against the buildings still standing.

They managed to traverse three blocks when they had to stop to assist with several rescue efforts where a pedestrian was partially buried or stuck in a vehicle filled with mud. As much as he knew he couldn't walk away from someone in danger, he barely held on to his rage at the delay in getting to Lori. He knew she must be frightened and hoped she'd stayed at the clinic, knowing he'd come for her.

"The last signal from her phone had her still in the clinic, but there's no signal now," Jeb radioed.

"Dolby," Carson's voice called over the radio. "Abbie is getting imagery now. Sending to you."

Hop barely looked over his shoulder toward Dolby, who was looking at the screen on his watch. The expression on his friend's face caused his feet to stumble. "What?"

Dolby looked up at Hop, then shifted his gaze beyond him. "The landslide has hit the clinic, but while it's partially buried in the back, it's still standing... but... leaning."

"Fuck!" he roared as he tried to run, but the slippery terrain was deep, causing his pace to slow to a crawl. He was covered in mud, and each step was a slog through the thick terrain toward his goal.

Several times, he was forced to turn and grab Dolby. They assisted each other as they stumbled, sometimes the mud sucking their feet lower.

"Thank fuck the rain has stopped, and the fucking

mountain isn't fucking sliding anymore," Dolby shouted.

Hop agreed silently, but looking at the devastation all around and knowing it was keeping him from Lori, it was hard to be thankful for anything. Finally, making it around the corner of another building, the three-story clinic was in sight.

A huge crack had appeared in the back of the building, windows and walls partially crushed in, and the part of the building unburied was leaning at an angle. As they slogged closer, the only door he remembered seeing at the back of the building was now buried. The street to the side was impassable, with debris and vehicles piled like fallen dominoes. Climbing over the mud, they made their way around the other side, coming to the glass doors in front and seeing them crushed and filled with mud, as well.

Panic welled from deep inside, and a primal roar emitted from his lungs. He barely felt the clap of a hand on his shoulder and swung around to see Dolby holding him tightly.

"Hang in there, bro. We'll get to her."

A surge of adrenaline shot through his body as he lifted a muddy boot and kicked out the remaining glass of the front door, climbing carefully into what had been the reception area. Mud covered the floor, and he only prayed that she'd made it to an upper floor before the landslide hit. He began shouting her name as they slipped through the ankle-deep mud toward the back, finding exam rooms, a kitchenette, a nurses' station, and the janitorial closet... all empty. The very back of the clinic's first floor was filled with more mud, making it harder to discern what was underneath.

"Fuck! Hop!"

He twisted around, looking over his shoulder, his heart falling as he followed Dolby's line of sight. A naked foot was exposed from the mound of dirt and mud near the nurses' station. Racing back, he cried out as he dropped to his knees and began digging with his bare hands. With Dolby right beside him, they managed to uncover enough of the body to pull it from the mud. The woman's body was covered in gray muck, blurring her features. The air stuck in his throat as he forgot to breathe. With a gentle touch, he swiped his hand over the face, gasping at the sight. *Not Lori! Jesus Christ, it's not Lori!*

He fell back onto his ass, his hand covering his face as his chest expanded and tears streamed.

"I think it's the other nurse," Dolby hoarsely whispered, his chest heaving with the exertion of their dig. "The one working with Dr. Rocha."

Having no idea if the two women had been together when the avalanche hit, Hop jerked around in desperation as he called out Lori's name.

"Oh, fucking hell!" Dolby gasped.

Hop whirled around to see his fellow Keeper still staring at the nurse's body. "What?"

Dolby leaned forward, his hand gently swiping over the woman's chest, exposing a wound. "She's been shot."

Hop's mind struggled to catch up to Dolby's words. Kneeling again, he assisted Dolby with cleaning some more of the mud off, seeing the evidence in front of him. "She and Lori were the only ones here. They were the last two."

"Obviously not," Dolby replied, his voice harsh. Grabbing his phone, he called, "Find Alfonso Rocha. He may have been at the clinic with Lori. We just found the last nurse. Dead. Shot at close range."

Those words jolted Hop from his fearful stupor, and he leaped up, racing toward the rooms on the first floor, shouting for Lori as he ran. But each exam room, station, closet, and area was empty. Not stopping to dig through the mud that had seeped through the cracks in the very back, he hurried to the stairwell door. "Come on... let's keep looking upstairs."

Moving through the thick slime to the door leading to the upper floors, he found it pushed open. Once through, they were unable to race upward, with stairs crumbling on one side. Moving carefully, they managed to get onto the second floor, but looking upward in horror, the stairs to the third floor were mostly concrete pieces hanging from jagged steel bars. The mudslide had pushed the three-story building enough to cause deep cracks in the back, forcing it to lean forward and shatter the upper stairwell.

Stepping onto the second floor, he slipped on his ass as the angle of the clinic's leaning caused the still-standing floors to be sloped. There was no invasive mud here, but as the building vibrated again, he knew they were on precarious footing. A new prayer that the building wouldn't collapse formed on his lips.

The two Keepers began calling, racing, and slipping from room to room, but there was no sign of Lori.

While Dolby rechecked each room, Hop hurried back toward the stairwell to see if there was any possibility of getting to the third floor. "Fuck!" he growled, stepping back into the hall. "Was it Rocha? Did he kill Rosa and take Lori?" His lungs battled to breathe, fear for her and their unborn child rising to the surface.

With his hands on his hips and his entire body covered in mud and grime, he turned slowly in a circle, his gaze desperate to land on Lori. But all he saw was the empty clinic, void of sound.

Lori's chest heaved up and down, sucking in the fresh air as she looked toward the clouds above.

"Okay, baby, we made it this far," she whispered. "Now, if there was only a way to know where your daddy is." Still on her hands and knees, having crawled through the door to the rooftop, she could see that the building was leaning at almost thirty degrees. Not great, but then it was still standing and not crushed into a million pieces with her buried beneath the rubble.

Looking around, she spied the volcanic mountain behind that was now missing a large section, and her gaze followed the dark, freshly turned earth morphing into gray mud on its forced path toward the part of the city where the clinic had been built.

Needing to see what she was facing, she crawled to the wall surrounding the rooftop space. The closer she got to the edge, the more she could see the devastation of the nearby buildings. The ones behind were partially buried or completely annihilated. The shouts from others, the screams from survivors, and in the distance, the sounds of sirens began to fill the air.

Moving with careful stealth while filled with uncertainty, she reached out and gently pulled herself up, terrified of the concrete giving way underneath her hands. Once able to look over and down, she could see she wouldn't be able to get off the building from that side. Dropping back to all fours, she crawled toward the front, thinking that the sloped angle might make it easier for her to get to the street. Repeating her actions, she pulled herself carefully up until she could look over the wall but could still see that there was no way to safely get off the rooftop.

Wanting to cry with frustration, she crawled to the other side, almost filled with elation at the sight of dirt piled higher, making it possible for her to get off the roof from that direction. Seeing some people coming from nearby buildings that were still standing, she began to cry out while waving her hands. "Help! Up here! Help!"

Some looked up and shouted in return, but with the devastation all around, she had no doubt that her rescue might not come as quickly as she'd desired. She looked around the empty rooftop, finding nothing she could use. "Okay, baby, be patient. Surely, someone will help us eventually."

The building shifted slightly again, and she screamed, this time in genuine terror.

Shouts coming from outside penetrated Hop's frustration, and he knew nearby residents would be searching for their missing loved ones. "Christ," he moaned as Dolby approached. "Where the fuck can she be?"

"Do you think she was on the third floor when the avalanche hit?" Dolby asked, his brow furrowed as he pulled out his phone. "The last that Jeb sent was that her phone signal was from this site."

"Maybe she ran out and left her phone. Or shit, she may be on the third floor," Hop fretted, grabbing a paper towel from a nearby tray and swiping the sweat and mud from his face. "She would have no reason to leave knowing mudslides were coming. She'd stay here. Unless the other nurse was leaving and she was going, too? Then maybe she got out, and the other nurse got trapped in the lobby when the slide hit?"

"Maybe she saw something in the street? Someone injured and went to help? Shit, I'm just guessing, bro. I really can't imagine why she'd leave if she heard the avalanche," Dolby said, his brow still furrowed deeply.

Fear and rage built to a crescendo inside Hop, and he lashed out, his fist slamming into a nearby wall, shattering the drywall. Dolby stepped forward, but before he had a chance to speak, Hop jerked, looked around, then threw his hands up. "Did you hear that?"

"I heard something, man, but was it from outside?" Dolby's intense gaze darted around.

They remained quiet, barely breathing when the sound of a female's voice was barely heard again.

Heart leaping into his throat, Hop was startled as he

whirled around. "Lori? Lori!" he shouted. They ran to the stairwell again, curses erupting at the renewed realization that the way to the third floor was blocked.

"Outside," Dolby said, grabbing his arm. "Maybe we can find a way from the outside to get to her if she's up there."

With no other recourse, Hop raced down to the first floor, sliding once again on the mud. As soon as they made it to the street, they spied several Ecuadorians pointing upward. Lifting his gaze, he stared in awe at a face peering over the rooftop wall. *Lori!*

23

"Lori!" Hop cupped his hands around his mouth and shouted her name again. He could tell the instant she recognized who he was when her head jerked and eyes widened.

"Hop! Oh God, Hop! I can't get down!"

"I know, babe. I'm gonna get you!" he assured. Chest heaving, he turned to Dolby. "What do you think? Can we climb up the side to get close?"

"Maybe, but the mud is too unstable."

Pulling out his phone, he called Adam. "She's on the roof of the clinic. Get closer to picking us up. Then we'll go in from above." Gaining Adam's immediate agreement, he then called her number while looking up. Her head disappeared, but then he heard her voice.

"Hop? Is that you?"

Her voice sent shock waves throughout his body that rivaled the vibrations from the earlier avalanche. "Christ, babe. Jesus Christ," he groaned. Then hearing her voice hitch, he sucked in a deep breath and said, "We're gonna get you."

"They locked me in! They were going to kill me, but the mudslide came before they had a chance—"

"Who?" he growled.

"Rosa and Dr. Rocha. They waited until you left on the last flight and then pulled a gun on me. Hop, he admitted to selling babies! She was helping him!"

"What the fuck?" he roared, the beast inside reappearing.

"He was nearby. He said he was watching the clinic as Rosa took care of things. Some of the ones they discharged were part of his special group… the mothers he paid, I think. Then he pointed a gun at me, but we heard the roar, so they locked me in a closet. My death would look like it was because of the building collapsing."

Dolby ran over, interrupting. "Adam can get to the field where you were earlier. There's mud, but he can hover so we can jump on."

He hated to leave her but knew it was the only way to safely extract her from the collapsing building. "Lori, listen. I'm heading to the helicopter. As soon as I can, I'll be back and get you. Stay safe… both of you."

Her breath hitched again. "Okay. Hurry."

With a nod, he followed Dolby as they ran toward the school field where he had landed numerous times earlier in the day. Concentrating on not sliding in the slippery mud, he almost missed Dolby's question.

"Does the bird have any rope?"

"Shit. This is the most fucked-up mission—"

"Don't do that, man. We took what we could get. I'll look for something. Surely, we can get a rope from somewhere in the school."

As they rounded the corner and had the field in sight, it was heartening to see Adam expertly hover just over the mud. Ducking low, he raced to the opened door and shouted, "Dolby is going to try to find a rope—"

"Got one!" Adam called out, inclining his head toward the back floorboard. "Get in!"

Not wasting a moment, Hop climbed aboard, followed by Dolby, who shouted, "Where the hell did you get that?"

"I searched the church's groundskeeper's shed while waiting for you. Figured I might find something we needed. Got rope, a toolbox, an axe, a bottle of whiskey—"

"Fuck, Adam, you stole from a church?" Dolby asked, his eyes wide as he shook his head.

"Figured we might need it more than the priests."

"We'll make a donation when we get back," Carson radioed while listening in. "Now, Hop? You got your head on straight?"

"Just gonna get her out safely. I'm not thinking about that asshole Rocha for now. But when she's safe…"

"I see her!" Adam called out.

Hop looked down to see the clinic below, the devastation even starker from the view from above. The mud was pushed against the back of the building, having forced the lower floor to crumble and the upper part to lean forward. But perched on top was Lori, her upturned face showing wide eyes and an open mouth as she stared at the incoming helicopter.

He cleared his mind, sucking in a deep breath. Grabbing the rope from the floor, he inspected it, testing its strength. Looking back at Dolby, he said, "Adam can get us close. We don't have to use this for long. Just get me down to her and then pull her up. I'll go next, and we'll get outta here."

"Sounds good, brother."

He tied a butterfly knot near the end of the rope, once again checking it for strength, before repeating the knot about five feet higher. As Adam maneuvered the bird closer to the rooftop, he stuck one foot into the bottom loop and held on with his hand through the top loop. Sliding easily from the side of the open door, he swayed as Dolby lowered the rope. As soon as he was a few feet from the rooftop, he jumped down the rest of the way.

Grinning, he barely had time to prepare before Lori launched into his arms. He bent low as the winds whipping from the blades above nearly knocked them over. Her body was shaking, and he pulled her close. He knew she wasn't showing, yet he could swear he felt her stomach pressing in, allowing him to cradle their unborn baby in their embrace. Holding her was all he wanted to do, but he forced his hands onto her upper arms and gently pried her back. Bending, he searched her face, seeing exhaustion, as well as her resolute spirit, peering back. "We gotta get off this, babe."

She nodded, looking up in haste before holding his gaze. "What do you need me to do?"

In a fucked-up situation, he grinned. *Indomitable.* She was fuckin' indomitable.

Dolby had lowered the rope farther, and Hop held on to her as he showed her how to place her foot in the rope stirrup and wrap the upper loop around her wrist, grabbing it with both hands. "Just hang on for a few seconds, and he'll get you up."

She nodded in a jerky movement, then looked over her shoulder at him. Unable to resist, he kissed her hard and fast on the lips, causing her to blink and then grin. Using the momentary distraction, he motioned for Dolby, and she was lifted out of his arms.

His heart slammed against his rib cage as he watched her rise toward the helicopter's open door. He'd witnessed untold missions that included air rescues, as well as transport of his fellow service members and then Keepers. But nothing could have prepared him for the gut punch he felt as each second seemed to drag out. Finally, he could see that Dolby had her close enough that he could secure the rope and pull her through the door.

He let out a long, shaky breath, barely feeling the building shaking underneath his feet. As the rope dropped to him, he wasted no time grabbing it and sticking his boot into the loop. As his body lifted off the rooftop, he refused to look down, keeping his eyes on the woman waiting above. As soon as he could grasp onto the closest seat with one hand and felt Dolby's hand grab his arm, he swung up into the helicopter, giving Adam permission to get them away.

Dolby shut the door as Hop made sure Lori was

buckled in and then settled into the co-pilot seat. Adam radioed their status, and they headed to the hospital where they'd taken the other patients. Lori was quiet, and he kept looking into the back seat. Her face was pale, her hands were scraped, and she was almost as dirty as he was. When her gaze met his, she'd offer a slight smile, but he wasn't satisfied that she was all right.

Fifteen minutes later, they landed on the helicopter pad. As soon as they touched down, he unbuckled, and with Dolby hopping down to get out of the way, he moved to the back and assisted Lori. With his face near hers, he softly asked, "You okay, babe?"

She held his gaze for a moment and then nodded. "Yeah. But... what about Dr. Rocha? And Rosa?"

He steadied his expression and said, "Let's get you checked out, and then we'll worry about anything else. Once I know you and the baby are okay, I'll deal with the rest."

"Honey, I'm fine—"

"I need this, Lori. Please, let me have it."

She continued to hold his gaze and then nodded. He assisted her out, and she turned to wave to Adam and Dolby. As they bent low, they ran to the glass doors that opened, seeing Jackie standing just inside. At Lori's surprised exclamation, he said, "I called ahead."

She and Jackie embraced before the nurse led them to an examination room with a sonographer sitting next to the table. She blushed, then grinned as Jackie laughed.

"Hop sent word that he wanted you checked out,"

Jackie said, handing her a pair of clean scrubs. "I can't believe I didn't know you were pregnant!"

"I didn't want to tell anyone until I had a chance to talk to him, but then everything went crazy."

The sonographer smiled. "If you prefer, Dr. Baker, we can do a transvaginal ultrasound."

"Yes, thank you," she replied.

Hop eyed the equipment with a wide-eyed expression of concern.

"Um... do you want to stay? You don't have to—"

Turning his intense gaze back to her, he declared, "If you don't mind, I want to be here."

She nodded and moved behind a screen. A moment later, she came back with the clean scrub top on and a sheet around her waist. She moved to the table and lay back, sliding her feet into the stirrups. He blew out a breath, uncertain where he should stand or where his gaze should land. Nerves snaked through him, but her shy smile gave him strength. "Can I get closer?"

She chuckled and nodded as she reached out her hand. "Come over here so you can be right with me."

He tried to avoid looking at what the sonographer was doing, knowing that in the upcoming months, he'd see a whole lot more than just what was happening down there now. Blowing out another breath, he focused on her face and smiled as he reached out and took her hand in his. "I'm in, Lori. I'm all in." Her lips curved upward, and for the first time since he'd seen her again, the smile lit her eyes.

"Okay, Mom and Dad, here we go. How far along do you think you are?"

"Actually, forty-eight days, to be exact," Lori replied.

The clinician laughed. "Sounds like you can pinpoint the day."

He squeezed her hand and grinned. "Oh yeah. We can."

They turned their heads in unison and watched the screen, but all he saw was a vision of black-and-white squishy movements as the sonographer did her work. Then suddenly, the room was filled with the *whoosh-whoosh* sound that made his breath catch in his throat. Gasping, he turned his wide-eyed gaze to her smiling face. "Is that…?"

Her smile brightened her whole face, and she nodded. "Yes, that—" Suddenly, her smile dropped as her eyes widened, and she jerked around to look at the screen again.

His breath caught in his throat as he searched the screen for a clue as to what caused her reaction, but he still had no idea what he was looking at.

"It's early," the sonographer said, "but I'm sure as an OB/GYN, you're hearing what I'm hearing."

Lori gasped, and Hop felt like his lungs would burst from lack of oxygen. "What?" he rasped, tightening his grip on her hand. "What's wrong?"

She swung her gaze back to him, but her expression was unreadable. "It's… there's… two."

"T… Two? Two what?" he stammered.

"Two heartbeats. It's often hard to detect this early, but I'm hearing them."

"Them?" His brow furrowed as his fuzzy brain tried to piece together what she was saying.

"Hop, honey. There are two babies in there. Twins. We're pregnant with twins."

He looked from her to the screen and then back to her face again, now drowning in her beautiful smile, while the *whoosh-whoosh* continued in the background.

"Yeah, that's the babies' heartbeats."

Bending, he kissed her lightly, blinking away the threatening tears. "*Our* babies' heartbeats," he corrected, his own heart pounding out a rhythm he'd never heard before. The heartbeat of a dad.

24

Lori rubbed her head as she began to think that the fatigue settling in every cell in her body would be a permanent experience. After her examination, Hop hovered. And hovered. And hovered.

He'd finally walked her to the cafeteria, made sure she had a hot meal, and then surprised her by having Jackie and Marilyn sit with her. Then he'd kissed her and headed off with Dolby and Adam, telling her not to leave until he got back. Staring at his back as he left, she'd pressed her lips together, feeling sure that whatever he was doing had to do with Dr. Rocha and Rosa.

Between bites, she'd confided with the two nurses about her suspicions and then what had been confessed when she was held at gunpoint at the clinic.

"I can't believe it!" Jackie had fumed.

Marilyn's eyes widened at the news. "Do you think Elisa knew anything?"

"I don't know, but I don't think so. They didn't indicate it was anyone else but the two of them, but Hop told me to leave it to him."

The conversation turned to her pregnancy, but she kept the news about twins to herself. She'd barely digested the news and certainly needed time to process it and think about what she and Hop needed to discuss.

By the time she'd eaten, she looked up and smiled at the sight of Hop walking straight toward her, his lips curving as his gaze moved over her. As tired as she was, the desire slammed into her that she wanted to let him carry her off to a faraway island for weeks of private time for fun, talking, and sex. Lots of sex.

But that would have to wait because now she was sitting in a room with Hop, Dolby, Adam, Dr. Casta, and a variety of other men in suits. Considering the city's crisis of floods and mudslides, she was amazed that they'd gathered in such force.

Dolby had sent the information from Alfonso's computer to the head of the Ecuadorian National Police, and several investigators from their office sat at the table looking at the evidence. She'd given her statement, realizing that the records that Alfonso had kept gave her words more power. Dr. Casta and the other men from the Ministry of Health were horrified, both vowing to work with the local social services to verify the babies were safely placed.

Several people around the table glanced between her and the Keepers, and she wondered if they had more questions.

A hand on her shoulder drew her attention toward Hop, who leaned in close to whisper, "Let's go. We've turned the case over to the authorities, and I want to get you out of here now."

Nodding, she stood, but before she could reach the door, Dr. Casta reached out his hand and grasped hers. "I had no idea, Dr. Baker," he cried. "My heart aches that we placed a Red Cross doctor and nurses in that predicament."

She comforted him, shaking her head. "You had no idea. If it hadn't been for the one patient demanding to see him and wanting her money, I would have never suspected anything. You placed me where I was needed, and we delivered a number of healthy babies in the past three days. So please, focus on that."

Out in the hall, Hop drew her close, holding her tight for a moment before shifting her back enough to peer into her eyes. Now curious, she narrowed her eyes. "What's going on?"

"I asked them to let me tell you the part of the story you don't know yet."

Pressing her lips together, she waited.

"When we were in the clinic looking for you, we discovered a body in the mud—"

She gasped, her hand grabbing his biceps.

"I thought it was you," he said, his words hitching painfully and causing her fingers to dig into his skin. "But it was Rosa."

She gasped again. "Oh God, they didn't make it out." Her chest expanded as she sucked in the air, squeezing her eyes shut for a moment. Shaking her head, she heaved a heavy sigh. "The mudslide was coming, and we could see it from the window. He was going to kill me, but she rushed him out. He shoved me into the closet, and that's the last I saw of them." Startling, she said, "Was he with her?"

"Babe, I didn't see him, and there was no way to tell at the time. It will take a recovery effort to determine if he was there with her. I just wanted to find you, so we raced around the clinic. If I hadn't heard you, I would have thought you were buried also." His arms tightened as though holding her would chase the horror from his mind. Sighing, he said, "But there's more."

She jerked, leaning her head back, eyes now wide. "More?"

"Yeah... Rosa wasn't working with Alfonso. She was undercover, trying to gain enough evidence of what he was doing."

She gasped. "No!" Shaking her head, she couldn't reconcile his words with what she'd seen. "But she was talking to the patients. She worked closely with him. She was with him when he held a gun on me!"

"It seems the police had been tipped off from a mother who'd decided she didn't want to go through with the adoption, but he'd insisted, probably because he'd already taken the payment from whoever he sold the baby to. Rosa was brought into the investigation and managed to gain his trust over the past couple of months."

"I can't believe it. I feel as though I've landed in a nightmare and can't wake up." Still shaking her head, she added, "So the authorities know the whereabouts of the babies since she was working with him?"

"From what they said, the mothers and babies were

checked on by the Ecuadorian Social Services. It was handled carefully, I'm sure, so that Dr. Rocha wasn't tipped off. But, then, he's been doing this for a while…"

The implication of what Hop wasn't saying hit her, and she closed her eyes before dropping her forehead to his chest. Once more, she felt every fiber of her body filled with fatigue.

He sighed, pulling her close. "There's more, but I don't know how much more you can take." He waited until she lifted her face to his. "I didn't notice when I first found her body because she was covered in thick mud, and I was just crazy relieved it wasn't you, but Dolby discovered that she'd been shot."

Her knees threatened to buckle, but his strong arms kept her standing. "Rocha shot her and just left her to be buried."

"Oh God. He probably hoped no one would notice a bullet wound when they'd been buried in mud."

Dolby and Adam stepped from the room, having heard the last of his explanation. "They're going to start the recovery in that area," Dolby said. "They'll retrieve Rosa's body and search for his if it's there."

"It's still so unbelievable that she was undercover. She was trying to keep him from harming anyone while investigating him." She dropped her forehead onto Hop's chest again and sighed.

After a moment, he whispered, "Come on, babe. Let's get out of here."

Nodding, she said, "I'm ready, but I need to talk to my Red Cross supervisor."

"Okay, but I want you to leave with me. I want to get you out of here and get you back to the States."

"Hop, it's not that easy. I'm down here for a job—"

"Yeah, and that job nearly got you killed."

"It's a risk I take every time I come to an area that needs me."

A tic developed in his jaw, and she watched, fascinated, as he exhaled sharply, his warm breath puffing over her face. "There's still a lot to do," she continued to argue. "I was supposed to be here at least another couple of weeks."

"Yes, but there are others who can do it. You were brought in specifically to deal with the clinic that wasn't part of the hospital, right?"

"That was my assignment, but—"

"But now the clinic is gone, and the patients have been taken elsewhere."

"Yes, but I could still be moved to another clinic, work with those who had home births and now have no homes, or just where they need me in the hospital."

They stared, neither willing to look away first. He finally sighed, shaking his head. "You're stubborn. You know that?"

Her lips curved. "Yeah, I do."

"It's the quiet ones, you know."

She tilted her head to the side, waiting to hear his explanation. He didn't make her guess.

"The quiet ones have the most logical arguments. Not screaming their opinion but breaking you down with logic." He chuckled, tucking a strand of hair behind her ear.

She gave in to the desire to lean her face against his palm. Licking her lips, she said, "I know my time with the Red Cross missions is coming to an end. Or, at least, a pause. I can't just go everywhere when I'm further along in the pregnancy or when our children are young."

A sparkle lit behind his eyes, and he grinned. "Our children. I like hearing that."

Her heart leaped hearing his admission. She bit her bottom lip, fighting a grin of her own before admitting, "I like saying that."

"So where does that leave us now?"

Hefting her shoulders, she scrunched her nose. "I'm not sure, but I do know that I have to talk to my supervisor. I can't just leave."

He held her gaze, nodded, then looked over at Dolby and Adam. "You good to stay till we can see what she needs to do?"

"Hey, don't worry about us," Dolby said. "Thought I'd head to the cafeteria and grab a meal." He inclined his head toward Adam. "We'll hang there until you know when you want to leave."

She moved quickly before the two Keepers had a chance to walk away. Reaching out to grab Dolby's arm, he stopped, and she peered between his face and Adam's. "Thank you. Really, I... well, thank you."

Adam grinned. "No thanks needed, Lori."

Dolby patted her hand and laughed. "You had mostly saved yourself. I have no doubt that you'd have figured out a way to get off that building. But hell, woman, you gave us a great story to tell about the rooftop rescue in the middle of an avalanche."

A giggle slipped out as she shook her head. "Glad I could be of service to your mission legends."

He laughed, then offered a chin lift toward Hop before he and Adam turned and moved to the elevator.

Turning her attention back to Hop, she said, "Why don't you go with them? As soon as I talk to my supervisor, I'll come to the cafeteria."

He bent, and she lifted to meet his kiss. Settling her heels back to the floor, she watched as he moved to the elevator door. As the three stepped inside the elevator, she waved as the doors slid shut.

Turning, she pulled out her phone and found the contact for her Texas-based Red Cross supervisor. Before hitting the call button, she glanced around the hall and spied a small alcove next to one of the waiting areas to the side of the elevators. Desiring privacy lacking in the crowded hospital, she walked to the chair next to the window, grateful to sink into the cushions.

Pressing the call button, she let out a relieved breath when he picked up quickly. After she gave him the succinct version of events, he assured her that, under the circumstances, she could head home the next day since he had several other doctors on their way. Thanking him, she disconnected and shoved her phone back into her pocket. As she leaned back in the chair, her gaze drifted out the window. The clouds had parted, the sun was shining in the blue sky, and the mountains in the background appeared serene from the direction she was facing. Even when she dropped her gaze to the city streets below, the Quito cityscape appeared normal. But she knew that a short distance away, the city streets ran with mud, and many of the buildings had been destroyed, along with lives and livelihoods.

She sent a message to Jackie and Marilyn, letting them know she would leave the next day. Uncertain if Dr. Casta was still in a meeting, she sent him a message as well, not wanting to interrupt the investigation.

Thinking about the investigation brought back the news that Rosa had been working undercover. Squeezing her eyes shut, she remembered Elisa saying that Rosa and Alfonso had a close relationship, and she thought it might be sexual. *Jesus, she was trying to keep tabs on him while finding out what was happening.*

Glancing at the time, she wanted to make sure Hop and the others had an opportunity to eat without feeling rushed. She was desperate for a shower and a chance to sleep in a real bed, acutely aware that for many in the country, that would be a luxury they would not have for a long time. Looking down, she placed her hand on her belly and whispered, "I'll worry about those things another day, sweeties. For now, let's go find Daddy."

Pushing to a stand, she walked toward the elevator when a doctor standing in front of the doors snagged her attention because his shoes were the same ash gray as the mud outside. Slowing her pace, she stared, but then he turned and powered through the door to the stairwell. Just as the door slammed shut, she could see his profile and recognized him. Alfonso Rocha.

25

Not wanting to lose sight of him, she pulled out her phone and dialed Hop while racing toward the stairwell door. He'd barely answered on the first ring, and she cut off his greeting. "Dr. Rocha! I just saw him! He's here in the hospital!"

"Where are you?" he bit out.

"Still on the fifth floor. He was waiting on the elevator and then headed down the stairs. I'm going to follow—"

"Don't you dare! We're heading up and calling security!"

"I'll just see what floor he gets off on," she said. She lowered the phone from her ear but could hear Hop cursing. Opening the stairwell door carefully, she could hear Alfonso's footsteps going down. Gently shutting the door behind her with a tiny click, she tiptoed to the center rail and peered over, seeing the top of his head two floors below and then the sound of a door opening. Bringing the phone back to her mouth as she hastened down the stairs, she reported, "He got off on the third floor."

"Do not do anything," Hop ordered. "We're on our way, and Dolby's just alerted the Ecuadorian police."

She had no hero complex and didn't mind the police doing their job, but she wasn't about to let Rocha out of her sight.

Glad for soft shoes, she tiptoe-raced down the stairs, stopping at the door leading to the third floor. Uncertainty filled her as she tried to decide what to do. *Wait here until the police come? No, he could come back through, and we're all alone in the stairwell? Follow him? What if he's standing just outside the door? But then, what if I don't follow, and they can't find him?*

Her hand moved to the doorknob, and she started to turn it slowly. *What if he sees me? What if he's armed?* Then giving her head a shake, she knew she had to do something.

Pulling the door open slowly, she peered first in one direction and then the other. Not seeing him gave her the courage to slip out onto the third floor.

As she looked around, it quickly became evident that she was on the maternity floor. *Oh my God! He's still trying to make contact with the women he'd agreed to pay!*

With her phone still on the open call, she whispered to Hop, "The third floor is the maternity wing. He must be trying to talk to one of the women we sent from the clinic!"

"We're on our way, and so is security! Don't do anything!"

She headed straight to the nurses' station, knowing

her scrubs would allow her to blend in with the other medical professionals, just like Alfonso was doing. Looking up at the board behind the station where the patients' last names were listed, she recognized one of the last women evacuated. *That's got to be who he's talking to.*

Seeing the room number, she walked down and whispered, "Where are you?"

"Rounding the stairs to the third floor."

"He just went into room 325. I'm following." She wanted to see the look on his face when he realized she was alive. Adrenaline took over her body, sending tingles, emboldened with the knowledge that Hop was almost there. Peering around the doorframe, she watched as he bent over the hospital bed, talking to the young woman she recognized as the last C-section she'd performed at the clinic before Hop had flown her to this hospital. A nurse moved from the corner of the room toward them, and Lori swallowed a gasp as she recognized Elisa.

"No, no," the woman whispered with a desperate edge to her voice. The wrapped bundle in her arms moved, and the woman clutched it tighter. "My baby. I want my baby now."

"I've already got a buyer." His harsh words were whispered as he leaned in closer. "Do not back out on me now, or you'll regret it."

Lori had no trouble understanding their simple conversation but couldn't understand why Elisa was standing there as a silent witness.

"You will do as the doctor says," Elisa ordered,

reaching out to pull the baby from the woman's arms. "We've gone to a lot of trouble for you."

Lori blinked, her mind barely catching up to the new realization. *Elisa and Alfonso?* She could only imagine what pressure they'd put on the young woman to convince her she needed to give up her baby for money. With one hand on her stomach, her heart ached for the new mother now clutching the blanket covering her lap.

"No, no! I want my baby. I won't let you take her!" the young mother cried, her face contorted in fear and agony.

He stepped over to the hospital bed with something gripped in his hand. "Sleep. When you awake, you'll feel better knowing your baby has a good home."

Lori spied a hypodermic needle and gasped. Unable to wait one more second for anyone to come, she rushed into the room. "Stop!"

At the sound of her cry, Dr. Rocha's spine snapped to attention, and his head jerked around, his wide-eyed gaze pinned on her, the needle suspended in his hand. Elisa's response was to clutch the bundled baby closer to her chest as she side-stepped toward the bathroom door.

His mouth opened, but no words came forth for a few seconds. Finally, he gasped, "You. How can you have survived?"

"The same question could be asked of you."

Shock gave way to a sneer. "With Elisa already in the hospital keeping an eye on our latest patients, you locked in, and Rosa out of the way, it was easy for me to slip out, making it to a building just down the street where I could hide until the way was clear."

Lori shook her head, disgust filling her. "You killed her… Rosa."

"I couldn't trust her, and with the clinic about to be decimated, I needed to make sure there were no traces leading to me until we could rebuild our practice."

"The practice of buying and selling babies?"

She glanced toward the young mother in the bed, her eyes wide and brow furrowed, and Lori realized the woman wouldn't understand their conversation in English. "Uh… mantén a tu bebé." She hoped she correctly let the woman know she could keep her baby. Lori shifted her gaze between Alfonso and Elisa, her anger pouring forth as she growled, "You aren't going to get away with this."

Elisa's expression changed to one of fear as she moved deeper into the en suite bathroom, but he stepped closer to the patient again, and Lori shook her head. "You made an error. Rosa wasn't just a nurse. She was undercover, investigating you. The police are on their way and already have the evidence they need."

Elisa gasped, her gaze shooting toward Alfonso. He blinked, his head jerking. "No… you're lying." Looking around as though for an escape, he growled, "You'll be my way out." He pulled out a gun from his coat pocket.

She startled, and the woman in the bed screamed at the sight. He swung his weapon toward her, but she cried out more, now with the baby in Elisa's arms joining in the blood-curdling screaming.

"No, don't shoot!" Lori yelled, dividing his attention between her and the patient.

A shot rang out, the sound reverberating in Lori's head, and she bent over, her hands slamming against her ears. Alfonso jerked back, crying out in pain as the gun clattered to the floor and blood began pouring from his shoulder. The mother continued to scream, and Elisa disappeared from sight. Hop raced in, his weapon still on Alfonso even as he wrapped Lori in his free arm and pulled her behind him. The police swarmed into the room, taking over as Hop gently moved out of the way, his body protecting Lori's. She grasped the back of his shirt, shock mixed with fear shaking throughout her body.

As Hop maneuvered her into Dolby's arms, he stalked forward, his face full of fury. Not stopping until he was in Alfonso's face, he roared, "You aimed a gun at my woman? Left her to die the first time and then fucking did it again?" Ignoring the police in the room, he reared back and slammed his fist into Alfonso's face, the sound of his nose breaking resounding in the room.

Lori struggled against Dolby's gentle restraint. "Hold on, sweetheart," he whispered.

"No, I've got to get to the baby!" she cried, tearing out of his arms and dashing into the bathroom, expecting to see Elisa cowering in a corner. "Fuck!" Lori yelled, seeing that the bathroom led into the next hospital room, a wide-eyed mother lying in the bed and her door opened into the hall.

Unheeding any noise behind her, she darted out of the room, her head jerking from one side to the other as she searched for Elisa. At the end of the hall, she spied her pushing through a doorway and bolted after her.

"What's going on?" Hop asked, and she realized he was step for step right behind her.

"Elisa was in the room. She grabbed the baby and got away." It was hard to speak and run, but adrenaline coursed through her body, sending her speeding forward. Barely aware that Hop was talking or radioing or calling someone, she pushed open the stairwell door, and hearing retreating footsteps below, she raced unheedingly down the stairs in pursuit.

Hop tried to overtake her. Looking over his shoulder, he spied Dolby and Adam coming, as well. Holding out her hand when they got to the bottom, she cried, "No, let me... Elisa has the baby!"

They pushed through the final door, the sunshine hitting their faces, and she looked around at the parking lot but saw nothing but vehicles.

"There!" Hop whispered.

She followed his gaze and saw Elisa darting amongst the cars. Lori began running again. Elisa wasn't running fast, and Lori hoped it was because the nurse cared enough about the baby to not want to jiggle it too much. Catching up to her, she called out, "Elisa! Stop!"

Elisa halted and whirled around, indecision written on her agonized expression. She looked down at the bundle in her arms before lifting her gaze back to Lori.

Stepping closer, Lori tried to steady her pounding heartbeat and catch her breath. "Elisa... please... don't do this."

Elisa's chest heaved. "I... you wouldn't understand,"

Elisa bit out, her gaze now jerking around as the baby squirmed and began to cry.

Lori was aware that Hop was still behind her but saw Dolby and Adam moving around to the sides, ducking behind vehicles. Keeping her eyes on Elisa, she stepped forward slowly with her hands out. "Please, Elisa. Give me the baby."

Elisa's face contorted, indecision now morphing into despair, and she gently patted the baby's back as she held it to her chest.

"I know you don't want the baby harmed. I know you care too much about the baby," Lori whispered, keeping her voice steady and soft as she stepped closer.

"He… he promised me…" Elisa hiccupped.

"I know," Lori agreed although she had no idea what Elisa meant.

"He promised he would leave his wife. As soon as we had enough money, we were going to be together. Then Rosa found out what we were doing and started working with us, too. I didn't trust her. I told him she was not to be trusted." She looked down at the baby, a tear sliding from her eye. "He promised they were going to good homes. To parents who will love them."

"But he can't extort money to make that promise," Lori said, so close now that she could almost reach out to touch the still-crying baby. "Let me help you. Let me take the baby and make sure it's okay. You're a good nurse, Elisa. You don't want the baby to hurt."

There was no movement other than the squirming child. Elisa choked back a tear, and Lori stepped closer, her hands now gently pulling the baby from Elisa's arms. As soon as the baby was in her hands, a rush of activity swarmed them, and gentle hands pulled Lori back into Hop's chest.

She looked up to see the Ecuadorian police cuffing a sobbing Elisa, but her attention was pulled away as several hospital doctors and nurses moved toward her. She bent to kiss the tiny newborn on the head before handing him over to the waiting staff, who immediately whisked the child back into the hospital.

"Oh God," she groaned, the adrenaline spike leaving her now weak. "Elisa was working with him. Or for him." Shaking her head, she mumbled, "You shot him. You shot him and then hit him."

"Jesus, shit, babe," he whispered against her hair. "Christ Almighty. I didn't give a fuck that I was getting there at the same time as the police. I saw that gun pointed at you, and I was going to fuckin' take him down. You have to understand, Lori... I'd do anything to protect you and our babies—"

She leaned back to peer up into his face, her hands tightening on his arms. "Oh, Hop, I'm not upset with you. I'm thanking God that you got there in time!"

His arms spasmed around her, pulling her even closer as his head lowered, taking her lips. The kiss was filled with promise but short as others came to them. She recognized the head of the Ecuadorian police now talking to Dr. Casta before both men walked over to her and the Keepers. "It appears we'll need a new statement from you, Dr. Baker."

Still holding on to Hop, she nodded. "As long as it

means Dr. Rocha will be stopped, then I'll gladly give you what you need!"

Two hours later, she, Hop, Dolby, and Adam finally left the hospital and headed to the airport, catching a ride with the Red Cross driver who was picking up arriving volunteers. As she stared out the window, they passed neighborhoods that looked the same as when she arrived, as though nothing more than a heavy rain had occurred. But as she glanced to the side, she could see where the side of the volcanic mountain had slid down onto part of the city, decimating all in its path. Her chest depressed as the events of the past several days moved through her mind. Blowing out a breath, she had to admit it was the most adventurous Red Cross mission she'd ever been on.

At the airport, Hop walked around the small plane, and she stood to the side, watching as he interacted with Dolby and Adam. The three men worked seamlessly together, and suddenly, Lori was uncertain about her future. *They're doing their job, but my time as a Red Cross doctor who'll be a single mom of a baby... babies will be halted. He's got coworkers who are friends, but I'm more of a loner as I travel all the time. But I won't be traveling all the time.*

"Hey."

She looked up as the softly spoken word pulled her out of her thoughts. Staring into the face that was so familiar and still so new, she couldn't help but smile. "Hey."

Hop lifted his hand and cupped the back of her neck, his fingers gliding through her hair as his thumb swept over her cheek. "You're standing over here thinking too hard."

A tiny huff escaped her lips as she battled the urge to lean into his hand. There was so much to talk about. So much to figure out. So much to consider. And right now, the woman who usually had the answers had a blank mind. "Yeah." She nodded.

He applied gentle pressure and pulled her head forward so that her cheek rested on his chest. "Then stop."

"That easy, huh?"

Snorting, he tightened his arms around her. "No. Don't figure it is. But right now, you're exhausted. I want to get us back to the States so that I'll know you're safe. And then we have a lot to talk about."

She pressed her lips together, the urge to cry making her eyes sting. *A lot to talk about.* Swallowing deeply, she nodded. He was right— now was not the time to make any decisions. She didn't even know where he was taking her once they got to the States. Leaning back, she offered another nod, finding her lips curving at the sight of him staring down as he cradled her in his arms. His big, gorgeous arms held her so carefully. It might be temporary, but she'd take it. After all, his embrace felt like coming home.

26

Hop woke up, a smile on his face as he immediately felt the warm body in bed next to him. Lori had slept fitfully on the plane, barely waking for the time they took while he refueled, and they had a bathroom and food break. But the small plane was no place for a pregnant woman to sleep comfortably, and once they'd arrived in California, he assisted a bleary-eyed Lori to his SUV to drive her home.

Stepping to the side, he clasped hands with Dolby and Adam, knowing thanks weren't needed, but he wasn't the kind of man not to issue his gratitude anyway. "Couldn't have asked for better with me," he said, holding their gazes.

Adam shook his head. "Take care of her. Take care of both of you."

Dolby grinned, clapping Hop on the shoulder. "Always up for a mission, man, especially if there's a fuckin' happy ending."

"See you when we are back together," he said, offering a chin lift.

Dolby started to nod, then added, "Hell, it'll be at least a week for me. Carson informed me that our intrepid Rachel notified him that I was at leave-day-earning maximum. Gonna take time off and do a little hiking, camping, and enjoy some solitude."

"Solitude?" Adam lifted a brow in surprise.

Dolby rubbed his hands together. "Hell, yeah. Nothing like some time to myself and no distractions for a week."

"Then we'll see you on the flip side," Hop said, with a toss of his hand, eager to get Lori home. He climbed behind the wheel and pulled away, seeing her head already resting against the window and her eyes closed.

Once there, she'd barely looked around before he nudged her into the shower and then into bed. His bed. Where he hoped she'd stay. His thoughts strayed to what he would need to do in the oncoming months to ensure that would happen. First on the list would be to add another bedroom and bathroom to the house. The twins could share a nursery, but they'd eventually need their own space. Thinking of the floor plan, he already knew how that could be managed with little disruption to their lives.

Curling his body around hers, he pulled her in tightly, knowing in his mind that she was already staying. She stirred, shifting around, blinking her eyes open. He remained still as he watched the few seconds of confusion in her eyes morph into a smile curving her lips. Erasing the distance, he kissed her lightly, mumbling, "Good morning, sleeping beauty."

She laughed and then stretched, and he felt every inch of her curves as they pressed against the hard planes of his body.

"Good morning." She stretched again, this time wrapping her arm around his waist as they lay facing each other. "I can't believe I slept for so long. I don't even know what time it is."

He chuckled and asked, "Do you even know what day it is?"

Her brow crinkled then she shook her head, surprise in her voice. "Oh my gosh, no, I don't!"

"Don't worry, you didn't sleep for a week, although you probably felt like you could. We got home yesterday, and in case you forgot, I managed to get some food into you, and you took a shower before we crashed."

"Thank you. Thank you for everything." She lifted her hand and cupped his stubbled jaw. They held gazes for another moment before she continued. "Thank you for coming down just because you *thought* I needed you. And thank you for being there because I *did* need you."

"You don't have to thank me, Lori. I wanted to be there for you. For all three of you."

She captured her bottom lip with her teeth, worrying the soft skin until he leaned over and kissed her lightly. He knew they had a lot to talk about, but right then, all he wanted to do was hold her in his arms, know that she was safe, and make love to her.

He kissed her again, this time sweeping his tongue to the inside of her mouth. Her fingers clutched his waist before she pressed her front against his and slid her hand up his back.

Her movement startled him but gave him hope. He hadn't been sure that her desire reflected his, but the way she lifted a leg and pressed her core against his thigh left a little doubt that she wanted this as much as he did.

The kiss continued, her velvet tongue gliding over his, setting off sparks that threatened to combust both of them. His hand, splayed against her back, glided downward over her soft skin, squeezing the globes of her ass, then slipping underneath her panties and through her folds, finding her wet and ready.

She moaned, and he captured the sound with their kiss. He craved skin on skin and slid her panties over her hips. She pushed away, and his eyes flew open, uncertain if she had changed her mind. Or he read her signals wrong. But she rolled to the side and slipped her panties all the way off before grabbing the bottom of his T-shirt that she slept in and pulling it over her head. Now, displayed in all her beautiful, naked glory, his gaze roved over every inch as his smile widened.

"Christ, Lori, you're gorgeous."

She grinned, a twinkle in her eyes. "And you are overdressed."

"Then it's good that's a problem I can take care of."

She laughed as he sat up, jerking off his boxers. For a second, he started to grab a condom, then realized it wasn't needed for birth control. But wanting her comfortable, he hesitated.

"I haven't been with anybody since you," he said. "We

get tested for work, and I'm clean, but I'll wrap it up for you—"

"I trust you, and I haven't been with anyone either. And in case you're wondering, I'm ready."

Remembering how slick her folds were, he'd had evidence her words were true. With one forearm holding his upper weight off her, he held the back of her head, kissing her again. Slowly, his hand moved over her soft skin, circled her full breasts, then traveled down to her tummy. He knew it was too early to feel anything move, but he knew what lay underneath his palm. Their children. Unexpected but not unwanted. He'd said those words to her and hoped she remembered them. And he'd say them again and again if necessary to prove to her how much he wanted to be in their lives. "I want you. I want us."

Shifting between her thighs, he lined his eager cock up at her entrance, and she lifted her knees so that her feet could wrap around his back, pulling him closer. Moving gently at first, he entered her sex before slowly pushing into the hilt, memorizing the ecstasy that slashed across her face.

They moved together in unison, gazes never wavering, their bodies speaking what was in their hearts. He prayed that this was a sight that would greet him daily but was determined to memorize every nuance. The rasp of air as it left her lungs with each thrust. The feel of her short fingernails digging into his shoulders. The petal softness of her skin. The slight bounce of her breasts with each movement. The way her nipples pebbled, begging to be sucked, and as he acquiesced, the feel of the taut bud in his mouth. Her tight core as the friction built between them.

Just when he thought he had everything memorized, a new sensation could be felt. He finally lost himself as emotions threatened to overtake the current of electricity that filled the room, and he watched the blush rise from her breasts to her face as her muscles tightened and her orgasm gripped his cock.

The burning in his back increased, and suddenly, his own release hit at the same time as every muscle in his body tensed, and he filled her channel as his cock released every drop. Battling the urge to squeeze his eyes tightly shut, he kept them on her, noting she was doing the same.

No words were spoken as past and present, and the future swirled between them.

Rolling her toward him as he lowered his body, they lay with their hearts as entwined as their limbs. While their overheated bodies slowly cooled, he drew the sheet over them but kept his arms around her with no space between them.

Not willing to waste another moment, he said, "Lori, when you were in danger, I couldn't breathe. I've never felt for anyone what I feel toward you. I know there's a lot to figure out, but what I said earlier is true. I want you. I want us. I want us to be a family. If it's too soon, then we'll work toward it. If you have to stay in Texas, then I'll work at finding a job down there. And if your only objection is that you think this is just because of the babies, then think about where we were heading before we found out about the pregnancy. When we met in Tennessee, a lot of years had passed, but think about how quickly we got together. Think about the past we share. Think about how we just clicked as though all the years fell away."

She pressed her lips together as she blinked, a tear slipping from her eye and rolling down her cheek. A fissure started in his heart, threatening to crack it wide open. Then she lifted her hand and cupped his jaw.

"I fell for you when I was sixteen years old, sitting at your parents' kitchen table."

Her words were barely above a whisper, but they resounded throughout his body. Sucking in a hasty breath, he waited, a seed of hope planted. "What... What are you saying?"

Shaking her head slowly, she admitted, "I guess I'm not really sure. But like you, I want us."

The hope grew.

"And like you, I don't really know how to make it work. Or if we're crazy for trying."

"Great things can come from crazy ideas, Lori." His thumb swept over her cheek, tracing the trail of the tear.

"I don't know about my job—"

"Babe, we don't have to figure anything out right now," he hastened to say, not wanting her to start fretting.

She stilled his words with her fingers placed gently on his lips. "No, let me finish. You forget that I had time to ponder being a mom before I had a chance to tell you. I realized that my tiny apartment wouldn't be large enough. I have to move. I had already figured out that when I got further along in the pregnancy, I wouldn't be able to continue to drop everything and fly to a Red Cross emergency. And when the babies are young, same thing. I haven't had time to think it all through… but there's no reason for you to try to find a new job in El Paso." She hefted her shoulders and sighed. "The clinic there was never going to be my forever place."

The hope continued to bloom, but caution kept his stomach clenching. His fingertips pressed in as his hand drifted over her back. "So what are you saying?"

Licking her lips just before a smile slipped out, she laughed. "I guess… I'm saying that great things can come from crazy ideas."

27

SIX MONTHS LATER

Lori walked out of the house with both hands filled with platters. Her gaze sought his once she stepped onto the patio, and he immediately left the grill in the capable hands of Rick and Poole. Hustling to her side, he divested her of the dishes.

"I can carry plates, you know," she grumbled, waddling along beside him as they walked to the picnic tables set up in the backyard that had a magnificent view of the mountains and the ocean in the distance. A view she woke up to each morning since the owner's bedroom had a wall of windows offering a majestic panorama.

She and Hop had renovated to make room for their burgeoning family. Creating a separate laundry room from a large utility space, they were able to add another bedroom that shared a connecting bathroom with the previous guest room. For now, though, the babies would share one bedroom. And to her great delight, the nursery had a smaller window that faced the sunrise, and Hop had positioned a comfy rocking chair to take advantage of the vista.

He still had an office in another bedroom but said he'd gladly give it up if they had another child. Her brows had lifted at that proclamation, not sure she wanted to consider more children until she had a chance to see her feet for a while. Hop had turned a shed at the side of the patio into a small guesthouse with the same aged cedar siding so that when his parents visited, they had their own space.

Suddenly, her view was nothing but his face as he bent and planted a smacking kiss on her lips. A giggle slipped out, and her gaze followed as he turned to set the plates down.

"Married five months and still checking out his ass?" Natalie asked, sidling up next to her. "Granted, it's a great ass. Me? I prefer Leo's, but then I'm not dead, so I figure I can appreciate any guy's nice butt." Leaning closer, she added, "But don't tell my husband."

Another burst of laughter rang out, and she shook her head. It had been an easy decision to make their home in California, considering he loved working for Carson and the other Keepers. But she'd never realized how easy it would be to find new friends for herself. Jeannie, Rachel, Abbie, Natalie, and Stella were a tight-knit group, but they welcomed her into their fold. And Jeannie had been instrumental in helping her find a clinic to work with that offered assistance to lower-income and uninsured patients. She'd also taken a part-time administrative position with the local Red Cross, overseeing the OB/GYN needs in emergency situations.

Looping her arm through Natalie's, she agreed, "Yep, my husband has a great ass. But I've always loved his arms." And it was the truth. She loved his smile, his eyes, and his incredible body, but when his muscular biceps surrounded her in a hug or pressed her against the mattress as his hips thrust when they made love, she swore she could have climaxed just from the feel of being enveloped by him. She looked over as he talked to Carson, who was cuddling his two-month-old son. *Okay, maybe seeing big, gorgeous guys cooing over a baby is what makes me spontaneously orgasm!*

The past seven months had been a whirlwind of changing jobs, moving, and getting married. Hop was insistent that the babies would have his last name when they were born, but in truth, that was fine with her. Remembering their simple wedding where Hop's parents and sister, brother-in-law, nephew, and niece had flown to California, she smiled. She had been willing to return to Tennessee for the wedding, but Hop knew that without her parents there, her memories of their important event would be marred. In California, they were surrounded by his family and all their friends. Carson and Jeannie hosted the sunset ceremony at the lighthouse, and then they'd traveled to a nearby restaurant for the laid-back reception.

She had even been invited to participate in Leo and Natalie's wedding, also a simple affair since Natalie had no parents either. That was another way the two women had bonded. They both knew what was important in life.

She and Natalie walked over to the table, and she had to admit everything looked delicious.

"Hungry?" Stella asked, handing her a plate.

"Strangely, even though this is wonderful, I'm not very hungry."

Abbie's gaze looked at Lori's protruding stomach. "I'm not surprised, sweetie. You look like you could pop any second."

Crinkling her nose, she nodded. "You've got that right."

"Well, I've never seen Hop more content," Rachel added, walking up to give her a one-armed hug from the side. "He beams every time he talks about the upcoming births."

Jeannie munched on a carrot stick. "He's been drilling me with questions about the birth process."

Blinking, she jerked. "Why? I'm an obstetrician, for crying out loud!"

"Oh, honey, he's just scared but doesn't want you to know he's afraid." Jeannie patted her arm.

"Men." Natalie rolled her eyes. "They want to be all big and badass but inside are mush when it comes to the thought of a woman giving birth."

"I think it's because they can't control the events," Jeannie surmised. "I know Carson was like that."

Rachel smiled, drawing their attention. "Ladies, these men have been taught to be completely in charge. Plan, execute, evaluate. And when you add in feelings, emotions, and lack of control, they don't handle their human frailty very well."

Staring at Hop across the patio while absorbing

Rachel's wisdom, Lori nodded. As though he knew she was thinking of him, he handed the baby to Carson and walked over to her. Soon, they were seated around the picnic tables, enjoying the meal with enthusiasm.

Her meal was only half eaten when she rubbed her back, digging her fingers into her aching muscles. Her due date was only six weeks away, but she wasn't sure she would make it. Needing to relieve her bladder, she placed one hand on Hop's shoulder to push up to a stand, then immediately bent over as a sharp pain sliced through her.

She gasped, then began breathing through the contraction, surprised at how quickly they'd started. Barely aware of the others, she wasn't surprised when Hop shifted quickly, knocking his chair over, his hands grabbing her arms.

"Shit! Is it time?"

As the contraction eased, she nodded and looked into his face, seeing the terror in his eyes. "It's okay, honey. But I think we need to go now. They've been causing some discomfort all day but have decided they don't want to wait any longer."

The gathering of Keepers jumped into mission mode as many of them raced to make sure their vehicles weren't blocking Hop's SUV in the driveway. Carson and Leo made sure the grill was turned off and secured. Natalie and Stella hurried inside to get her bag while Abbie and Rick secured the house as soon as Hop had Lori in the back seat with Dolby behind the wheel. Once buckled, she leaned against Hop as they breathed through the contractions for the twenty-minute drive to the hospital.

The next morning's rising sun greeted the new family as she sat in the hospital bed with Hop sitting next to her and two sleeping babies filling their arms. She looked at both, then turned her gaze up to Hop. The look of adoration on his face as he stared at their babies was priceless, bringing tears to her eyes.

A knock on the door drew her attention away from the bundles in their arms. Jeannie popped her head in and grinned. "Are you up for a short visit from a bunch of us?"

Laughing, she nodded, then was shocked as the room filled with all the Keepers and their women. Glad they had a large room, she waited until everyone had entered before looking over at Hop. "You can do the honors."

"Everyone, I'd like you to meet my son, Carl Martin Hopkins, and my daughter, Grace Jennifer Hopkins. We named them after their grandparents." The pride in his voice was evident.

The oohs and aahs resounded around the room, and Lori sucked in a ragged breath, fighting the tears once again. It didn't take long for Carl to scrunch his nose, and she knew a wail wasn't far away, undoubtedly gaining the same from Grace. The others left after pictures, kisses, hugs, and handshakes, leaving the new family of four alone once again.

Swinging his gaze to her, he smiled as he leaned closer, kissing her lightly. "You're amazing, Lori girl. I love you. I love them."

Heart singing, she nodded and whispered, "I love us."

He lifted one arm and wrapped it around her back, bringing the four of them closer.

Dolby's story is next!
Click to pre-order now! Dolby

Join my Facebook reader group!
Maryann Jordan's Alpha Fans

Sign up for my Newsletter!
Maryann Jordan's Newsletter

ALSO BY MARYANN JORDAN

Don't miss other Maryann Jordan books!

Baytown Boys (small town, military romantic suspense)
Coming Home
Just One More Chance
Clues of the Heart
Finding Peace
Picking Up the Pieces
Sunset Flames
Waiting for Sunrise
Hear My Heart
Guarding Your Heart
Sweet Rose
Our Time
Count On Me
Shielding You
To Love Someone
Sea Glass Hearts
Protecting Her Heart
Sunset Kiss

Baytown Heroes - A Baytown Boys subseries
A Hero's Chance

Finding a Hero

A Hero for Her

For all of Miss Ethel's boys:

Heroes at Heart (Military Romance)

Zander

Rafe

Cael

Jaxon

Jayden

Asher

Zeke

Cas

Lighthouse Security Investigations

Mace

Rank

Walker

Drew

Blake

Tate

Levi

Clay

Cobb

Bray

Josh

Knox

Lighthouse Security Investigations West Coast

Carson

Leo

Rick

Hop

Dolby

Hope City (romantic suspense series co-developed with Kris Michaels

Brock book 1

Sean book 2

Carter book 3

Brody book 4

Kyle book 5

Ryker book 6

Rory book 7

Killian book 8

Torin book 9

Blayze book 10

Griffin book 11

Saints Protection & Investigations

(an elite group, assigned to the cases no one else wants…or can solve)

Serial Love

Healing Love

Revealing Love

Seeing Love

Honor Love

Sacrifice Love

Protecting Love

Remember Love

Discover Love

Surviving Love

Celebrating Love

Searching Love

Follow the exciting spin-off series:

Alvarez Security (military romantic suspense)

Gabe

Tony

Vinny

Jobe

SEALs

Thin Ice (Sleeper SEAL)

SEAL Together (Silver SEAL)

Undercover Groom (Hot SEAL)

Also for a Hope City Crossover Novel / Hot SEAL…

A Forever Dad

Long Road Home

Military Romantic Suspense

Home to Stay (a Lighthouse Security Investigation crossover novel)

Home Port (an LSI West Coast crossover novel)

Letters From Home (military romance)

Class of Love

Freedom of Love

Bond of Love

The Love's Series (detectives)

Love's Taming

Love's Tempting

Love's Trusting

The Fairfield Series (small town detectives)

Emma's Home

Laurie's Time

Carol's Image

Fireworks Over Fairfield

Please take the time to leave a review of this book. Feel free to contact me, especially if you enjoyed my book. I love to hear from readers!

Facebook

Email

Website

ABOUT THE AUTHOR

I am an avid reader of romance novels, often joking that I cut my teeth on the historical romances. I have been reading and reviewing for years. In 2013, I finally gave into the characters in my head, screaming for their story to be told. From these musings, my first novel, Emma's Home, The Fairfield Series was born.

I was a high school counselor having worked in education for thirty years. I live in Virginia, having also lived in four states and two foreign countries. I have been married to a wonderfully patient man for forty-one years. When writing, my dog or one of my four cats can generally be found in the same room if not on my lap.

Please take the time to leave a review of this book. Feel free to contact me, especially if you enjoyed my book. I love to hear from readers!

Facebook
Email
Website